Party Till You Die

Party Till You Die

DAVID CHARNEE

St. Martin's Press   New York

Production Editor: David Stanford Burr

Design by Judith A. Stagnitto

Library of Congress Cataloging-in-Publication Data

Charnee, David.
      Party till you die / David Charnee.
          p.   cm.
      "A Thomas Dunne book."
      ISBN 0-312-06439-X
      I. Title.
    PS3553.H3263P3   1991
    813'.54—dc20   91-21561
                                       CIP

First Edition: October 1991

10 9 8 7 6 5 4 3 2 1

I dedicate this book to Nonny. One of the world's truly special people, she is well read, well traveled, and well loved. She has seen more of life than anyone I know, and yet she never fails to be delighted by something new. Those few people who don't know her as Nonny call her Ruth. I call her my grandmother, and I love her very much.

Party Till You Die

Chapter

ONE

*T*he first things I packed were the machetes. Three of them, chrome-plated and razor-sharp. I had bought them the year before from an asthmatic old man on Fisherman's Wharf in San Francisco. He assured me that they were perfectly balanced. He was right. The first time I used them, I flipped one a little too fast and damn near took off my right ear. Next I threw in my fire stuff. Three torches and a full bottle of kerosene. Gary had said that I wouldn't be needing the fire that night, but I always try to be prepared for the unexpected when I go out on a job. There are a lot of jugglers looking for work in New York, and if there's one thing I learned in my three years touring with Ringling Brothers and Barnum & Bailey, it's that the gig goes to the clown who can do anything at a moment's notice. Gary wasn't the best guy to be working for, but he paid top dollar and, from what I'd heard, booked entertainment at some great places. That night we were performing at a party for the employees of MegaBank. I was one of a group of performers hired to add a special touch to the festivities. I packed balls, clubs, scarves, and three changes of costume. I glanced at my Terry the Clown wristwatch and saw that it was just about time to go, so I zipped up my bag, stood before the mirror, and checked myself out. It wasn't easy since the mirror had been fastened to the wall by some prior tenant who couldn't have been taller than five foot two, and I stood an inch over six foot. By stepping back and bending my knees slightly, I was able to take in the total picture. It hadn't changed much since the day before. I still had short, thick, blond hair, pale green eyes, a small, straight nose that people were always accusing me of having had fixed (but that my mother said came from her father's side of the family), and a mouth that, when I smiled, seemed to have a few too many teeth. It was a face that men didn't mind, and women seemed to like. Below my face was a body that, during my three years on the road, had lost anything that wasn't muscle or bone. I was clean, rested, and as presentable as I could possibly be. I straightened up, took a deep breath, and did the only impersonation I do: Roy Scheider in *All That Jazz.*

"It's show time!"

I headed out the door.

My name is Patrick Arnold, but everyone calls me Pat. Maybe you've seen me. In the Terry Town Restaurant commercial I'm the dancing chicken juggling eggs and singing about the Terry Town biscuit breakfast. I'm still living off the residuals from that spot. In a kind of roundabout way, this is the story of how I got that commercial.

I left my studio apartment on West Ninety-fifth Street in the fashionable but slightly seedy Upper West Side of Manhattan, and headed downtown. Gary had told me that one of the other performers, D. L. Blacker, lived in my neighborhood, and suggested that we share a taxi to the job. I had called Blacker and we had arranged to meet at his place and then go down together. As I walked to his building I thought for the third time in as many days that I had heard Blacker's name before, but just couldn't place where. It could be, as they say, that only a dozen people really work in show business, so you quickly get to know the other eleven. But that didn't stop the itch in the back of my mind. The doorman announced me and then gestured toward an apartment at the far end of the lobby. Blacker was waiting at his door.

"Pat Arnold? Hi, I'm D. L. Blacker." We shook hands and he ushered me through the door. He was a nice enough looking guy. About five foot ten, fleshy but not really fat, probably about ten years older than me. Judging by the laugh lines around his mouth and eyes, his face looked like it spent more time smiling than frowning. This impression was reinforced by hazel eyes which twinkled from behind rimless glasses. His dark wavy hair was starting to gray at the temples and thin at the front. Truth to tell, he looked more like a cheerful accountant than a serious clown.

"Make yourself comfortable, I'm running a little behind." He left me in the hallway and headed back into the apartment. I stepped in, closed the door, and then dropped my bags and wandered after him.

His apartment seemed huge, or maybe I was just comparing it to my one room. As the old joke goes, my place is so small you have to step out into the hall to change your mind.

My life as a struggling entertainer was not atypical. The friends I had made during my six months in New York barely managed to make ends meet. We all aspired to fame and the fortune that would come with it, but none of us had yet reached the style to which we hoped to become accustomed. So, I just wasn't ready for the apartment of D. L. Blacker. He had room enough for a small mime troupe to perform in and the ceilings were high enough to practice five-club juggling. I was impressed. But what really caught my attention was a large office in a room off the front hallway. A massive oak bookcase filled with sets of hardcover books (not paperbacks) stood impressively against one wall beside a set of ornately carved oak file cabinets. There was a beautiful walnut desk bigger than my bed and behind it a leather chair that looked like something you'd find cushioning the bottom of a multinational corporation's CEO. It was hard to picture someone sitting there who made his living in a red nose and top hat. D. L. came in behind me. As I turned, it suddenly struck me where I'd heard of him.

"You're the lawyer!" I blurted out.

"Maybe," he said, with just the hint of a smile.

"No, really, I read about you in the papers. Didn't you help the police solve some murder that took place at a circus last year?" Before he could answer I raced on. "Sure, I remember. It was a clown. Everyone thought he had just had a heart attack or something, but you told the police that something was wrong with his makeup and when they checked it they discovered that it contained some poison."

"Nitro-benzene. I noticed that the black makeup the clown had used stained his face. I remembered reading about a case from the turn of the century where a man died with black feet." Blacker went to the bookcase and pulled down a small, faded, red volume. "Here we are, '*Poison Mysteries in History, Romance, and Crime*,' a classic treatise on poisons, written over sixty years ago." He tenderly paged through the book and then, finding what he was looking for, began to read: " 'For some time the cause of death was a complete mystery, when a few days later a bottle of blacking was found in his room, with which it was discovered he had blacked his shoes on the evening of his death.' " Blacker looked up at me, perhaps checking to see if I was really interested. I nodded and he resumed reading.

" 'The coloring had penetrated his socks and stained his feet and ankles. On analysis the solvent in the blacking was found to consist of nitro-benzene, an extremely poisonous liquid.' " He closed the book and looked at me. "Normally," he said, "clown makeup won't stain your face, but apparently blacking in nitro-benzene does. I mentioned this to a friend in the D.A.'s office and they ordered an autopsy. I was right, it was murder. It got a lot of press." He carefully returned the book to its place on the shelf.

I had never met anyone like D. L. Blacker, and I told him so. His life didn't make sense to me.

"Why do you do it? Why do you perform at parties and stuff when you're a lawyer? I mean, it can't be for the money."

"Oh, I don't know, the money's not bad."

"Come on, really."

"Okay," Blacker said and smiled. "I guess I do it because I can. As a kid, in school, I enjoyed just about everything. But my parents, teachers, they all kept asking me what I was going to be when I grew up. I started equating growing up with only being able to do one thing. It didn't sound like a viable alternative to me, so I rejected it. Now I practice law, perform, write, teach. And you know, all those people were wrong. You *can* grow up and do more than one thing. Doing lots of things is actually easier than doing just one. Eastern philosophies refer to it as yin and yang, keeping life in a balance. The two sides don't pull you apart, rather they support you, keep you centered. Even performing and law help each other. Do you know how I got this job tonight?"

I said I didn't.

"Gary Johnson, the guy who booked us?"

I nodded.

"I'm his lawyer."

Before I could think of anything to say, D. L. Blacker looked at a large antique clock hanging on the wall and asked, "Shouldn't we be going?"

5

*   *   *

We got to the MegaBank building with plenty of time to spare. Blacker allowed me to pay for the cab, saying that he'd pay me back later. At that point I had no idea just how prophetic his statement was to be.

We weren't the first of the entertainers to get there. Pamela Lockheed, a psychic and palm reader, was in a corner of the dressing room, putting on her costume. I had worked parties with Pamela before. A tall, stunning blonde with showgirl legs that seemed to start at her neck, Pamela was a real distraction in the co-ed dressing rooms that we were always given. The other entertainers never seemed to pay attention, but I grew up in Texas, where we notice the differences between a boy and a girl. Pamela said, "Hi," to Blacker, and smiled at me as she smoothed her fishnet stockings. Then she came over, gave me a kiss on the lips, and said, "Hey, tiger, it's been awhile." I agreed that it had and then babbled on about absolutely nothing. She glanced at her wristwatch, kissed me again, said, "Mmmm, not bad, I'll remember that," grabbed a shoulder bag off the table beside her, and headed out of the room. "Going to go set up my crystal ball and cards and stuff. I'll be right back." She flashed me another smile as she closed the dressing room door behind her.

"God, I love this business!" I blurted out.

D. L. began to unpack his bag, placing his makeup on one of the tables. "There are those attractive fringe benefits you just don't get working in a law office."

I knew just what he meant. "I'm actually kind of surprised to see Pam on this job," I remarked as I began to hang up my costumes. "I mean, didn't she and Gary have a falling out?" I waited for D. L. to say something. Maybe he felt he shouldn't discuss his client, or maybe, since he had started to apply his makeup and his mouth was busy being covered with greasepaint, he just couldn't talk. Regardless, I prattled on. "I heard that they were quite an item for a while. What do you think happened?"

He finished outlining his mouth in red and looked up from the mirror. "Maybe his wife found out."

"Gary Johnson is married? I never knew that. Wow, who's he married to? But I always heard that he slept with just about. . . . Who would marry—" I never got a chance to finish my sentence, because just then the door opened and Gary entered, followed by the most beautiful woman I had ever seen. She was about five foot six, with a perfectly proportioned dancer's body, and fine, long hair that was too light to be called brown and too dark to be called blond. She wore no makeup. She didn't need it. She had high, broad Scandinavian cheekbones that framed her face and helped to direct attention to her eyes. Her eyes, pale blue, with a slight almost-oriental slant and long, dark, perfect lashes, seemed to leap from her face and demand attention. I couldn't look away.

D. L. got up, shook Gary's hand, and then took both hands of the goddess and kissed her on her cheek.

"Hi, Donna," he said.

Donna, her name was Donna. D. L. turned to me while he was still holding her hands. "Pat, meet Donna Johnson, Gary's wife."

I couldn't believe it. She was married to him?

I realize, as I read over these last few pages, that I haven't really expressed my feelings for Gary Johnson. There's a reason for this. Mrs. Avedon, my sixth-grade English teacher, taught me that when reporting on a factual occurrence it's best not to let your feelings get in the way of the facts. I've always tried to follow that rule. As a result, you may not understand why I was so shocked to be told that the most beautiful woman to ever walk the face of God's green earth should be married to that scuzz ball, Gary Johnson.

When I left the circus, my parents wanted me to move back to Dallas, get a master's degree to go with my bachelor's in education, and become a nice, respectable English teacher. But performing was in my blood, so I came to New York to be the next Richard Burton, or perhaps Danny Kaye.

Thousands of people like me come to New York every year looking to break into show biz. Most of them spend a few years tending bar or waiting on tables and then give up, never getting past the cattle call audition stage. I was one of the lucky ones. Within two weeks of my arrival in New York, I auditioned and, after several callbacks, was offered a role in a touring company of the Broadway musical *Barnum*. That was the good news. The bad news was, I didn't take it. Through a mutual friend I was introduced to Gary Johnson. Gary was a six-foot-five, charismatic, fast-talking promoter who ran a company called Johnson Entertainment. Although still in his twenties, too little hair and too much weight around the middle made Gary look at least ten years older. With hard work and an undeniable personal charm that he could turn on and off like a table lamp, Gary had carved a comfortable niche for himself, providing entertainment for corporate and private parties in the New York area. Parties in New York are a whole lot bigger than the barbecues and birthday bashes I knew from Texas. A New York corporation will think of nothing of dropping a hundred grand on a little get-together to celebrate some department's making its quota for the month. Proud fathers will spend more than that on their son's bar mitzvah. Johnson Entertainment catered to those kinds of people.

Gary convinced me that I shouldn't take the part in

Barnum. He said that he would keep me working steadily at private parties in New York. He pointed out that if I really wanted to make it as an actor, I needed to stay in New York where I could be seen by agents and casting directors. What he didn't mention was that agents and casting directors will talk to you only if you have solid acting credits. Like a national tour of *Barnum.* Performing at private parties doesn't get you to Broadway.

This doesn't mean that there's no reason to perform at parties. As a part-time job while you're waiting to be discovered, it beats tending bar or waiting tables. You only work a few hours and the pay per party is pretty good. Working at parties also gives you an opportunity to develop new material and fine-tune that *edge* you can get only by performing in front of real live people.

No, performing at parties won't get you to Broadway, but it's not a bad job and if you do enough private parties it might pay your rent. But Gary had lied about that too. In the six months that I had been in New York, he had hired me only twice. Luckily, other party planners hired me for other parties. I wasn't starving, but I wasn't living the rosy life Gary had painted for me. Was I bitter? You bet.

Gary and D. L. began talking about something that sounded like it had to do with contracts or business deals. By then, D. L. was in full whiteface. It was funny to see him made up as a clown and yet hear him talking like a lawyer. He was using words like *injunction* and *enforceable restrictive covenant,* trying to soothe Gary, who was clearly upset about something. I didn't really pay attention though, I was too busy gazing at Donna Johnson.

Donna had put on a Walkman stereo and was hanging

up costumes when she finally noticed that I was staring at her. She smiled, took off her headphones, and sat down beside me.

"Gary tells me you used to be a Ringling clown."

"Yep," I said and smiled back. "I was with the Blue unit for almost three years." I started to put on my makeup.

"Do you know Bill Cross, I think he was with the Red unit."

"We were at clown college together. Great acrobat. How do you know Bill?"

"I met him in Paris. We were both studying mime at Decroux's school."

"You studied with Decroux?"

"For two years."

"Two years with Etienne Decroux, you must be great." I looked up from my mirror and noticed that she was staring off into space. When she finally spoke, it was in a quiet, almost shy voice.

"I . . . used to perform quite a bit. I toured colleges and was invited to perform at the First International Mime Festival in Poland and at last year's North American Mime Festival."

"Really? I was there, I don't remember seeing you."

"I didn't go." At last, she looked at me. I wished she hadn't. There was real pain in her eyes. I had clearly touched on a bad memory. "Gary thought it best that I stop doing that kind of performing."

I nodded, as if I understood.

"I don't know how I got to talking like this," she said, a little more energy coming into her voice and a sparkle forming in her eyes. "You're just so easy to talk to. Maybe later we'll get a chance to try performing together. I once had a partner who juggled. He and I. . . ."

She became very quiet and once again stared at a spot behind me. This time though it seemed that she was looking at something, so I turned my head. I was right; she was looking at something or, rather, someone. Pamela Lockheed had returned.

It's funny how sometimes a person can enter a room and it feels as though the entire universe is holding its breath. That's what happened when Pamela stepped into the room. Donna seemed to shrink into herself. I could see in her eyes that she knew about Pam and her husband. I felt like a jerk for kidding about it with Blacker just a few minutes before. D. L. and Gary stopped talking. Pamela, surprised that by just walking through the door she had become the center of attention, looked around, said, "Hi," and walked back to her little corner of the dressing room.

Gary turned his back on D. L. and went over to Pam.

"I didn't think you'd show up. I put Donna on the job to replace you." Gary's angry voice filled the room. The rest of us had no choice but to listen.

"We have a contract, mister. You hired me to work. I'm here to work."

"I booked you on this job over a month ago. Last week, when we broke up, you said you never wanted to see me again."

"Do you really want to talk about this here, now, in front of your wife?"

They both looked at Donna.

Then Gary turned back to Pam and said, "This has nothing to do with her; it's between you and me."

Donna jerked her head to the side, as though she had received an electric shock. Our eyes met, but I couldn't think of anything to say. Neither could she. Her lips moved, but no words came out. She started to cry and then she ran from the room.

Pamela turned on Gary, her voice filled with a quiet fury. "You know, Johnson, you're a bigger shit then I ever realized. God, I must have been crazy to get involved with

11

you. I'm working this job because I need the money, but don't talk to me, don't touch me, don't even look at me. Get too close and I'll kill you. I mean it!"

Gary laughed and walked out the door.

I didn't want to, but I went out after him. I had brought several different costumes. On jobs like this we would often change costume two or three times in the course of an evening. Gary hadn't told me which one he wanted me to wear for my first set. He was walking quickly. At first, I thought he was going to look for Donna. I was wrong. She had probably gone to the women's room, but Gary walked past the rest rooms and into the hall where the party was to be. I caught up with him in the middle of the dance floor. As I reached him, Gary was talking to a man who bore him a striking resemblance. The man was dressed in blue work clothes, with the name "Bob" embroidered on the breast of his shirt. Bob did not seem happy.

"Look, Gary, I'm getting sick and tired of you poking your nose into things you know nothing about. You've been doing this since we were kids. I tell you the lighting and sets are perfect. If you think someone else can do better, get yourself another partner!" They glared at each other for a moment and then Bob stormed off.

I asked Gary about the costume but he just waved me away and told me it didn't matter. I figured he was a little shaken by everything that had just happened.

As I turned to go, a small, meek-looking man with wild, uncombed hair and deep-set eyes behind thick glasses walked up to Gary. I recognized him as Andy Costello, a disc jockey who spun records at the other party I'd worked for Gary. I remembered him as being fundamentally a happy-go-lucky, fun guy, and a very good disc jockey. I had been blown away that such a small and unassuming-looking person could have such an incredibly deep and resonant voice. He was clearly born to be on radio. We had talked briefly after the other job, and he quickly convinced me that he knew more about music than anyone I'd ever met. Name a band from the sixties, seventies, or eighties, he could tell you who was in it. Name an album and he could tell you every cut on the record. At that moment his mind didn't seem to be on music, though. He was holding a black cape and a mask like the one worn by Darth Vader, the villain from *Star Wars*, and he didn't look pleased.

"Johnson, what's the idea of the costume?"

"Andy baby, good to see you," said Gary. "What's the problem, you never bitched about wearing costumes before."

"You told me I was going to be inside a booth where no one would be able to see me, all night long."

"Come on, Andy, you've seen my Darth Vader booth. There are those sliding Plexiglas mirrors. You open them and people can see you; you close them and they can't see you. What's the big deal? You want privacy, lock them. But whenever you have them open I want you in costume."

Andy seemed to relax, but he still didn't look happy. "Okay, I can live with that."

"Then let's get going, party starts in twenty-five minutes."

Just then, a service door at the side of the room banged open and a freak of nature entered the room, lugging two huge speaker cabinets as though they were suitcases. The freak was a tall, gangling, anorexic-looking woman, standing six foot tall if she was an inch. Her hair, hacked short, was an unattractive shade of red that must have come from a bottle, because natural selection would have eliminated it from Mother Nature's palette generations ago. Her complexion suggested that she lived on a diet of fast food and chocolate, but she was so thin it was hard to imagine that she actually ate anything at all. Despite her apparent total lack of any muscle tone, she lugged the obviously heavy speaker cabinets around as though they weighed less than the ugly pair of cowboy boots she wore at the ends of her unsightly legs. She carted the speakers over to the disc jockey booth, set them down, and came over to Andy, Gary, and me.

As she approached, she extended her hand to me, smiled, and said, "Hi, I don't think we've met. I'm Debby Brill, Andy's girlfriend."

I shook her hand and said, "Hi." Her grip could have cracked walnuts. Then she turned to Gary, the smile disappearing as quickly as it had appeared.

"Gary, have you thought any more about that offer from WZBQ?"

"Look, Debby, I told Andy, and I told you. So long as Andy's signed to me, he's not going to work for anyone but me."

"But, Gary, you're his manager, you're supposed to help his career."

"His career is working parties. My parties."

"Johnson, you don't know what you're doing. You're wrecking his life, our life. I can't let you do that."

Andy, having listened to his girlfriend unsuccessfully argue his case, finally spoke up. "Gary, come on. You don't mean this. I'm going to take the job."

"You signed a contract, Costello. It says that you can't work for anyone without my say-so. Just try it and I'll lay an injunction on you so fast you won't know what hit you. Now come on, hop to it, we've got a party here." Gary slapped Andy on the back, flashed Debby a look filled with all the warmth and sunshine of a Texas monsoon, and walked away.

Andy sighed and watched Gary leave the room. So far, this was not a fun party.

Andy and his girlfriend went out the service door to get the rest of his equipment, and I wandered around the room. I always like to do this before a job; it gives me a feel for what I am going to do.

It was a large room, and Gary's people had done a good job creating a party atmosphere. The theme of the party was outer space. There were several theatrical flats set up around the room with scenes out of *Star Wars* painted on them. In a dark corner was a large moon with stairs leading up to a small round door in its center. A sign over the door read *Palm Reader*. I walked over to the moon, up the stairs, and opened the door. Inside were a table and two chairs. On the table was a small crystal ball and a deck of tarot cards. Everything that Pamela would need to foretell the future and amaze the masses—one at a time. As my eyes grew accustomed to the murky darkness inside the moon, I noticed a small door in the back. Pam was lucky. That extra door would allow her to slip out for breaks without having to walk past the people who were waiting in line for their psychic readings. This was necessary if she was going to avoid One More Syndrome. One More Syndrome is where you try to take a break and people keep asking you to do just *one more*.

I left the moon and continued on my tour of the room. A half-dozen well-stocked bars were strategically placed against the walls, and several long tables were set up in an area decorated as a spaceship's galley. The tables were already piled high with food. I was pleased to see lots of seafood. I admit it, I'm a sucker for shrimp, and one of the perks of working these parties is that during our breaks, we get to eat whatever is being served to the guests.

Two platforms, decorated to look like meteorites, were set up on opposite sides of the room. No doubt, I thought, I would be performing on one of them.—I jumped up on the nearest one and tested it for springiness. It was solid. That was good. If a stage gives too much, my juggling balls won't bounce back when I drop them. And I drop them much too often when I perform under the kind of strange, flashing lights Gary seemed to have installed for the party.

As I completed my circle of the room, I noticed that Andy and his girlfriend Debby had returned. She sat in a chair next to the booth as he set up his disc jockey equipment. The booth was impressive. It really did look like something off Darth Vader's Death Star: all chrome, black metal, and mirrored Plexiglas. It was located right next to the hallway leading to our dressing room, so I had to go by it to get back to the other performers. I stopped for a moment and watched Andy, lying on his back, connecting wires under the table, inside the booth. Debby came and stood next to me.

"Sorry you had to be a part of that little unpleasantness," she said. "But Andy doesn't usually stand up for himself, and I view us kind of like a team, you know?"

"I understand." I was saved from having to make further small talk with her by Andy standing up and coming out of the booth.

"Deb," he said, "could you go down to the van and get me the cable box?"

"Sure," she said, and skipped off to the service door.

We both watched her go, and then, searching my brain for something to say, I came up with "Quite a setup you've got here."

"Pat Arnold, isn't it? We met at that casino party a few months back, right?"

"Right. I'm still amazed that you knew the only song on *Tommy* not written by the Who."

"'Eyesight to the Blind,' written by Sonny Boy Williamson. In the rock opera there were also two songs written by John Entwistle and one song credited to Keith Moon. All the rest were written by Pete Townshend."

"Right." I stood there grinning and nodding like one of those dogs in the back window of a car. People who really know music have always impressed me, and when I'm impressed I tend to act like a jerk.

"Well," he said, after the kind of painful period of silence

16

that *always* seems to end with someone saying "Well." "I guess I'd better finish getting ready here."

I got the message. I waved goodbye and headed back to the dressing room.

When I got there Pamela, Donna, and D. L. Blacker were all ready to start. Pamela, dressed in a gypsy costume, had added antenna and rainbow glitter to her flowing blond hair to give it a space feel. She needn't have bothered. So long as she wore a tight skirt slit all the way up the front, no one was going to be looking at her hair. Donna had undergone a total transformation. She looked like one of those figurines you see on top of gift shop music boxes. Dressed in a black and silver satin Pierrot outfit, with a classic Pierrot whiteface, she looked as fragile and precious as a china doll. As she did her warm-up exercises, in time to whatever music she was listening to on her Walkman, I couldn't help but notice how perfectly she moved. Gary must have been either blind or crazy to not recognize how good this woman was. I was glad to see that Pamela's being there was not keeping Donna from performing.

Blacker caught me admiring Donna and smiled. He was quite a sight himself. His costume and makeup were a perfect blend of magician, clown, and spaceman; from his Mad Hatter top hat, down the length of his silver lamé cape, to the tips of his bright red clown shoes. He was practicing card fans with both hands, but it didn't seem to require much of his attention.

"Almost time to start, Pat," he said. "Better get ready."

I nodded and started pulling props from my bag. Scarves, clubs, balls, torches, and machetes. I lined them up neatly on a table in the dressing room. Then I went to the clothes rack, pulled down one of my costumes, a set of red and white striped overalls, and headed to the men's bathroom to change. As I said earlier, I'd always been self-conscious undressing in a co-ed dressing room.

As I left the room I ran into Andy, who was on his way in. He was wearing the black cape and carrying the Darth Vader helmet.

"Where's Debby?" I asked.

"She decided to go home. Why?"

"Just asking, no reason. I better go get dressed," I said and raced off.

I quickly got into my costume and went back to the dressing room. Gary was giving the usual pre-party pep talk to Pamela, D. L., Donna, and Andy, when he saw me. He stopped, stared at me for a moment, and then exploded.

"Just what the hell are you supposed to be?"

I didn't know what to say.

"I told you this was an outer space party, and you come in dressed like Mr. Green Jeans. Jesus Christ, Arnold, you bitch that I'm not getting you any work, and then when I do hire you, you prove yourself to be a total incompetent."

He went to the costume rack, pulled out my silver jumpsuit, and threw it at my feet.

"Get out of that hayseed outfit and put this on. You're not in Texas anymore. Jeez, this is what I get for hiring a frigging circus clown." He stormed from the room. "That's it, Arnold, after this party you're through, you're history."

With his leaving, an embarrassed silence filled the room. Finally Donna came over to me, bent down, and picked up the costume from the floor.

"He's been under a lot of pressure lately," she said as she handed me the jumpsuit.

All I could do was nod and walk out of the room.

Chapter

T W O

I went back to the bathroom. There's something comforting about a bathroom; a sense of security that seems to embrace me every time I enter one. Perhaps it comes from the enclosed womblike feel that all bathrooms seem to share, or maybe it's just the déjà-vu-like feeling that you've been there before. Despite the different styles, the different colors, even the different sizes, all bathrooms share certain unmistakable similarities; they all have toilets, sinks, water, most have tiles, mirrors, and some way to dry your hands. I guess I've always felt this way about bathrooms. I remember as a kid, when I'd get into a fight with my sister, I always used to go and lock myself in the family bathroom. It used to drive my parents nuts. We lived in a small house and had only the one john. My father, thinking he understood me, installed a dead bolt on my bedroom door, so I could lock myself away in my own room; but come the next fight with my sister, I headed back to the warmth and security of the bathroom. Maybe that's the real reason that I always change into my costumes in the bathroom rather than in the communal dressing room.

Maybe it has nothing to do with embarrassment over un-dressing before the female performers. And maybe if I won Lotto I could afford to go to a two-hundred-dollar-an-hour psychiatrist and discover the real reasons why I do all the things I do. But I doubt that knowing why would stop me from doing them, so maybe it doesn't really matter at all.

I was halfway into my silver jumpsuit when I heard the bathroom door open behind me. The bathroom was pretty big. Across from the door was a long counter with three sinks in it. I really wanted to be alone, so I kept my face to the sinks, my back to the door, and did my best to ignore whoever had joined me. I was doing a pretty good job of it too, until a hand, connected to a brightly costumed arm, placed a steaming cup of coffee onto the counter in front of me. I looked up and in the mirror I saw the smiling clown face of D. L. Blacker.

"I thought maybe you wanted some coffee," he said.

There were a lot of things I wanted at that moment in time; coffee wasn't high on the list. But, as I would learn when I got to know him better, D. L. viewed coffee as the universal cure-all. I mumbled a thank you, picked up the cup, and took a sip.

He leaned against the far wall and looked at me, as though deciding whether or not to talk. I was in no mood to en-courage him. I looked into the coffee cup, took another sip, and said, "I hate this," in a way that made it clear I wasn't talking about the coffee. Apparently it wasn't the best thing to say just then, because it started him talking.

"After my first year of law school," he slowly began, "I dropped out for a year. I took a job at one of those giant theme parks as a magician and roving clown. One day, a few weeks after I started, I poked some fun at one of the park's street sweepers. I mimicked him in front of a large group of tourists. The tourists all laughed at the man, he swore at me and left, and I thought that was the end of it.

I was wrong. The next week my props started disappearing. I would put something down, and when I turned back to get it, it was gone. Then little accidents started to happen. A stage unit that I performed on every day collapsed in the middle of my show. A flash pot that I used for a magic trick went off at the wrong time and almost blinded me. Stuff like that.

"Well, I was scared and I was upset and I was more than a little mad, but I remembered something one of my law professors had said to me. 'Ultimately,' he said, 'the best lawyer is the one who can keep his emotions from getting in the way of the job he has to do.' I remembered that and I looked at what was happening to me, objectively. I did a little investigating, figured out that it was the street sweeper that was causing my problems, talked to him, and discovered that he hated me in a big way. Another lesson learned. Some people hate big for little reasons.

"I think those are both good lessons for life. I've always tried to remember them. Don't let your emotions get in the way of the job you've got to do, and don't give someone a little reason to hate you, because he may hate you big. I've known Gary for a long time; I've performed for his company and I'm his lawyer. Sometimes he gives people little reasons to hate him. Maybe one of those people is going to end up hating him big. It's a problem, both for him and for the other person. Big hate can end up hurting the hater as much as the hatee."

I smiled and looked up at him. "The hatee?" I asked.

"What can I say?" He grinned. "I'm a lawyer, it's a legal term of art."

I grinned back. "Do you always talk like you're speaking to a jury?"

"I guess I do. You're not the first to mention it."

"Must be great on a first date."

"Look," he said, changing the subject, "when you're

ready, Gary said that you and I are supposed to take the first set. The party starts in"—he checked his watch—"about five minutes. You, Donna, and I will be rotating performances on the two platforms; so after twenty minutes Donna will come and take your place. Break for twenty minutes and then come and take my place, okay?"

I agreed, finished zipping up all the zippers on my costume, and followed him out the door of the bathroom. He went to the party room and I headed back to the dressing room. Someone had been messing with my props. I hate it when someone handles my props. I started to get mad all over again when I remembered D. L.'s story. I laughed to myself and shook my head. Quickly I loaded my balls and clubs into my performance bag. I straightened out my machetes, fire torches, and scarves, which were still laying on the table, and I headed out to the party.

The guests were starting to arrive. I climbed up on a platform, took out three clubs, and started tossing them into the air in a simple cascade. Across the room I could see D. L. in front of his platform, rolling a silver dollar across his knuckles. He looked at me and nodded. Over in the corner, I could see, through the moon's open door, that Pamela was already sitting behind the small table. She was slowly shuffling the deck of tarot cards as she waited for her first brave partygoer to climb the stairs and close the door. The only illumination within the little moon was provided by several lit candles on the table. The candles caused Pamela's crystal ball to glisten and glow with their reflected light. They cast upon her face slowly moving shadows that seemed to rob her of her youth but left a mysterious beauty that knew no age and no time. One could almost believe that she was some ageless goddess who truly could peer through the curtains of time and tell who would be successful and who would fail; who would live and who would die.

Pamela's head jerked up and she looked at the door to the kitchen. Gary came striding into the room, glanced quickly around, and then rushed over to the Darth Vader booth. He knocked on the closed windows and, when they opened, said something to Andy. The windows slid shut again and the disc jockey's deep voice came booming out over the loudspeakers.

"MegaBank and Johnson Entertainment welcome you to an evening of Star-Bank Wars. We invite you onto the dance floor, so get out there and celebrate."

The sounds of Kool and the Gang flooded the room, singing "Celebration." The party had begun.

Everything seemed to be going well. I finished my first twenty minutes and Donna came and took my place. I wanted to stay and watch her perform, but as I got down from the platform I saw Gary watching me from across the room. I didn't want any more grief from him, so I hightailed it back to the dressing room.

Being on break didn't really mean escaping the party. I could hear the sound system booming as loud as if it were in the dressing room with me. Andy was playing a medley of familiar Motown hits, talking about each of the recording artists as their songs began.

The music changed to Steve Winwood's "Higher Love," and Andy gave a quick history of Winwood's recording life from the Spencer Davis Group, through Traffic, Blind Faith, back to Traffic, and finally an up-and-down solo career.

As that record ended, I checked my watch and saw that it was time to get back to the party. I grabbed my juggling scarves from the table, stuffed them into my bag, and headed out.

D. L. had a large crowd around him. He was talking to a woman who was holding a billfold out in front of her.

"Lisa, we're agreed then. I will guess your card, the card that you selected at random from a deck of cards. You wrote your name on the card with my Magic Marker, and while all these nice people watched, you returned it to the deck that Craig over there is now holding. If I cannot guess your card, you will get all the money in my wallet that you are holding. Is that agreed?"

Lisa nodded her head and watched D. L. very carefully.

D. L. closed his eyes, held one hand up in the air, and then announced, "Your card . . . your card is the four of hearts. Is that right?"

Lisa started to laugh, and said, "No, my card was the nine of spades." The whole crowd around D. L. cracked up.

D. L. looked a little uncomfortable and said to Lisa, "Well, a deal's a deal. I promised you the contents of my wallet if I was wrong." He took the wallet from Lisa and opened it. "As you see, inside the wallet there is a zippered compartment. That's where I always keep the real valuable stuff." He pulled down the zipper, reached inside, and slid something out. "Valuable stuff like this card." He turned it over so the crowd could see it. It was the nine of spades, with the name "Lisa" written in big letters across the face. The crowd exploded in applause.

D. L. smiled, took a little bow, and said, "If you think that was good, just wait until you see the incredible juggling of my good friend Pat Arnold." Then he hopped off the stage, patted me on the back, and walked off toward the food tables.

As I started to perform I noticed Gary walk over to D. L. who, by that time, had just about finished loading a small plate with hors d'oeuvres. Gary looked like he had something on his mind. He spoke to D. L. for a few moments and they then went together to the dressing room. Neither of them was smiling.

By then the party was in full swing, and my mind quickly focused on my performing. The crowd at the party was terrific; they seemed to love everything I did. Occasionally I would catch a glimpse of Donna, performing on the other side of the room, and she also had a large and enthusiastic audience surrounding her. All the problems of the last few hours were lost in the glow I always get from entertaining a good crowd of people. Unfortunately the glow didn't last.

About twenty minutes into my set I finished one of my best comedy juggling pieces. I start by juggling three balls, and have an attractive woman stand beside me, holding two extra balls in front of her, at chest level. I pull them out of her hands as I'm juggling, finishing with some fancy five-ball juggling. It's very flashy and very funny. I always get big laughs because my attention seems to be focused on the balls in the air and the crowd expects my hands to grab more from my embarrassed assistant than just the juggling balls. As I finished and sent the woman back to her date, D. L. came onto the stage and told me that I was supposed to take a break.

"But I've only been on twenty minutes," I protested. "Aren't you supposed to break Donna?"

"Sorry, Pat, Gary wants to talk to you." He gestured toward the dressing room.

I looked and saw Gary standing just inside the hallway, next to the D. J.'s Darth Vader booth. He was looking right at me. I turned back to D. L. I was starting to get mad again.

"Look, Blacker, what's this all about? I'm doing my job; the people love me. Come on, give me a break. What does he want from me?"

"Pat, I'm a lawyer. We never answer people's questions. Sometimes we can't, sometimes we won't. Sometimes we pretend we are answering the question, but use words so big that no one understands what we're saying. All I can tell you is that Gary asked me to take your place and then send you over to him."

I couldn't tell what Blacker was trying to tell me with all of that. By then, I don't know if I cared. I muttered an obscenity, threw my juggling stuff back into my performance bag, and strode over to Gary. He watched me coming, but before I got to him, he turned and went into the dressing room.

I followed him there, threw down my bag, fell into a chair, and glared at him. He took a deep breath and started to talk.

"Pat, I think I owe you an apology."

I couldn't believe that I was hearing this.

"I was all set to fire you here and now, but I caught some of your last bit; it was real good. I guess I forgot that there was a reason I hired you in the first place. I have great instincts when it comes to discovering talent. I like to think that I discovered you. I think on Monday we should get together and talk about the possibility of my managing your career."

I didn't know what to say, so I just kept my mouth shut.

"I shouldn't have snapped at you before. I've been under a lot of pressure, the business, this party, my partner, some personal things." He stopped talking, and despite the sound of the music from the party, the room seemed unnaturally quiet.

"Anyway, I'm sorry. Okay? Now go on back out there. Why don't you take Donna's place? Tell her to take a break." He sat down, opened his briefcase, and began reading some papers that looked like contracts.

Apparently, I was dismissed. I went back out to the party. Donna had just started a new mime routine, so I joined the crowd around her and watched as she effortlessly and without a word created an entire love story. The crowd watched breathlessly as we saw the lovers meet, fall in love, lose each other, and then be reunited. If anything, it seemed too good, too much like art to be presented at this kind of party. I wondered if the crowd really appreciated what she was doing. I know I did.

Apparently, the crowd did too. When she finished, they cheered. A few of the guests wanted to talk to her, and it was several minutes before I was able to catch her eye and tell her that she could take a break.

She touched my arm as she stepped down off the stage and that little physical contact left me feeling like a teenager again. I found myself thinking of possibilities that I knew I shouldn't consider, so I forced my attention back to my juggling. A few minutes before, Andy had started a rap song where he talked in rhythm and rhyme over an instrumental jazz number with a syncopated rhythm track. I'd never heard him do that. I was never a big fan of rap, but I had to admit, he was good at it. Rap music has a strong beat and I decided to try juggling to the rhythm of the music. I pulled my juggling scarves from the bag, and silently cursed myself for not grabbing my machetes the last time I was in the dressing room. I had the feel of this crowd and I knew they would love the implied danger that juggling machetes always creates. Somehow, tossing six scarves into the air didn't have the same effect.

There is one neat thing about juggling scarves. Because they take so long to come down, juggling scarves makes everything seem to be happening in slow motion; not just the scarves and not just me, everything. I took advantage of this to watch Donna move slowly across the room to the food tables as I passed three of the scarves in a circular pattern before me. I added a fourth and fifth scarf as she piled a plate high with crab legs and shrimp. Between catching the red scarf and tossing up the blue one, I saw her ladle some cocktail sauce onto a corner of her plate. As I tossed the black scarf high over my head, I saw her stop at a bar and ask for a glass of orange juice. The bartender was busy and it took her awhile to get it. I added the sixth scarf and saw her leave the room, balancing her food and drink as expertly as I balance a spinning ball on my finger. It was probably all for the best that she left the room at that point, because keeping six of anything, even scarves, in the air, takes all my concentration. I began plucking them from the air faster and faster, going double-time to the music under Andy's rap song. I tossed the scarves higher and higher and began spinning myself around every time the scarves left my hands. I was just about to do my big finish when a scream tore through the room. I missed a beat and the scarves fluttered to the ground.

I had been concentrating on my juggling, so I didn't know where the scream came from. I looked around as Andy stopped the music and slid open the window to his booth. The scream came again, piercing the relative quiet that always seems to fill a room when loud music is abruptly turned off. The scream had come from our dressing room. People were rushing toward the room, and I jumped off the stage to join them. I pushed my way through the crowd and made it into the dressing room; but I stopped short just inside the door. Donna was standing in the middle of the room, looking at something behind the table and screaming. I rushed to her, took the plate of food that she still clutched in her hand, put it on the table, and led her to a chair. On the floor, in a slowly spreading pool of blood, lay her husband, Gary Johnson. One of my juggling machetes was planted several inches into the back of his head.

Chapter

THREE

"*E*veryone, out of the room.
Now!" I looked up and saw D. L. Blacker talking to the
people who seemed to keep pushing through the door.
"Don't touch anything in here, and no one leave the building." It was amazing the degree of authority he was able to
command, despite the makeup and costume. The crowd
started to leave the room and he turned to Donna and me.
He spoke slowly and carefully, as though he somehow knew
that I was hearing everything through a layer of cotton;
seeing everything from the end of a long dark tunnel. "Pat,
I'll need your help. Get Donna out of here, and then come
back right away, okay?"

He continued to look at me. I slowly realized that he was
waiting for a response, so I nodded my head and helped
Donna from her chair. She hesitated for a moment as if she
wanted to say something. I stopped and looked at her. "Is
it all right," she asked, "can I have my Walkman?" I grabbed
the player and her bag of tapes from the table, handed them
to her, and again took her arm. She shook her head, said,

"I'm all right," straightened herself up, and walked from the room without looking back.

I turned back to D. L. and found him hunched over the body, checking all of Gary's pockets. He didn't seem to be taking anything, but maybe he didn't find what he wanted. When he was done he stood up and saw me watching him. "I want you to guard the door. Make sure no one comes in here," he said, and went over and opened Gary's briefcase.

I felt like I should have stopped him. I mean, I've seen enough cop shows on TV to know that you're not supposed to disturb anything at the scene of a murder. But he seemed to know what he was doing, and the one thing I knew was that I didn't really know what to do, so all I said was "Should you be touching things?"

He looked through the papers in the briefcase, put them back, and closed the case. "No," he said, "but I wanted to check on something." For a brief moment I thought I saw him put something in his pocket, but I couldn't be sure. "Now guard the door. Make sure no one comes in while I'm gone. I'm going to go call the police." He started to leave but then stopped, snapped his fingers, and turned back to me. "Do you have a quarter for the phone?" he asked. I pulled one from my bag and handed it to him. He rolled it across his knuckles, gave me a thumbs-up sign, and walked out of the room. There were a lot of things that should have been playing across my mind just then, but the only thing I could think of was that calling the police to report a murder ought to be a free call.

It took about five minutes for the first of the police to arrive. Two officers in uniform, a man and a woman, came rushing in, yelled at me for being in the room, told me not to touch anything, and proceeded to touch all kinds of things themselves.

The male cop hustled me out and brought me to the main party room. Most of the people from the party were in there, milling around or sitting in small groups. He told all of us to stay put, and then headed back to the dressing room. More uniformed police showed up and pretty soon we had several of them watching over us.

I joined the rest of the entertainers, who had gathered in front of the D.J. booth. Donna was sitting on the floor, a glazed look on her face. She wasn't moving. She seemed to be barely breathing. She just sat there, listening to her Walkman and staring at the hallway to the dressing room. Andy and Pamela were leaning against the booth, talking quietly to each other. Andy had discarded his mask, but still wore the Darth Vader cape. D. L. Blacker seemed to be the most relaxed person in the room. He had taken off his top hat and sat on a chair, with his feet resting on another one. He sipped at a cup of coffee and watched the passing parade of police and now-subdued partygoers. When he saw me he smiled, put his feet down, and sat up on his chair. I walked over and took the chair beside him.

"You should get something to eat," he said. "It's probably going to be a long night."

"I don't have much of an appetite," I muttered. It seemed kind of insensitive to be talking about food just then, what with Gary Johnson lying dead in the next room.

D. L shrugged, reached down to a plate sitting on the floor beside his chair, and grabbed a large piece of fried chicken. He took a bite from the chicken, chewed it slowly, and washed it down with a healthy sip of coffee. "If I were you," he said, "I'd eat. You're going to be answering a lot of questions. Way I see it, you're the prime suspect in this thing."

It's a good thing that I was sitting, because at that moment had I been standing, I would have fallen down. "What do you mean? I didn't, I wouldn't." I realized I was stammering and stopped talking.

D. L. Blacker took another long sip of his coffee, swallowed, and regarded me intently. Perhaps he was waiting for me to say something more, but my mind was a total blank and I don't talk when I have nothing to say. He finally broke the silence. "Pretty soon the police are going to know everything that happened here tonight. If that isn't enough for them to catch the killer, they'll begin digging into everything that happened in our lives since the day we were born. They probably won't think that that's necessary. Not after they hear that you were the last person to see Gary alive. As I recall, I told you that Gary wanted to see you and you went back to the dressing room where he was waiting, still, presumably, alive. You came out a few minutes later and told Donna to take a break. When she went into the dressing room she found him there, dead. And it was your machete that was used to kill him.

"They're also going to hear about the way Gary laid into you before the party. How he said that you were never going to work for him again. How he embarrassed you in front of the rest of us. It doesn't look good, Pat. Besides, you're an entertainer, and people in the real world, people like police, prosecutors, judges, and juries, they don't think show people are all that stable to begin with." D. L. Blacker took several long swallows from his coffee, finally emptying the cup. He stood and looked down at me. "So if I were you, I'd have something to eat. You're in for a long, tough night." He crossed over to a large coffee urn on a table in the food area and refilled his cup. I watched as he added milk and a single cube of sugar, stirred, licked off the spoon, and came back to me. He sat down again and took a careful sip of his now steaming-hot coffee. "So, did you kill him?" he asked.

Before I could answer there was a commotion at the main entrance to the room and a large, heavyset, middle-aged man with long, thinning, blond hair came striding into the room. He looked around for a moment and one of the uniformed policemen, a short, fat cop with a large nose and no hair, rushed up to him. They talked quickly and the blond man started toward the dressing room. The bald cop with the beak walked with him a few steps, nodded at something he was told, and then came back to the center of the room and shouted out, "Who called the police?"

D. L. Blacker stood up, walked toward him, raised his hand, and said, "I did."

Blacker was right, I should have eaten. The next several hours were filled with questions and hostile accusations. By the time I realized that I was hungry and went looking for something to eat, all the food was gone.

The big blond guy, who quickly established that he was in control, turned out to be Lieutenant Jesse Longreen, NYPD, midtown Manhattan homicide. He found a small room off the main party hall to use as his command center and began interviewing people. Statements from the partygoers were being taken by several of the uniformed policemen. Longreen himself interviewed the entertainers. D. L. Blacker was first, I guess because he had called the police. I was next. I don't know what Blacker said to the lieutenant, but when I was brought into the room, Longreen was not in a good mood. I was to learn over time that Lieutenant Jesse Longreen was rarely in a good mood.

The room I was ushered into for my talk with Lieutenant Longreen was about eight feet by ten feet. There were several chairs, a table, and no window. It struck me as being perfect for a police interrogation. Except for the quality of the furniture, it could have been located in the subbasement of any police station in America. Longreen sat behind the table.

He studied me with intense gray eyes beneath almost non-existent eyebrows. His thin lips were pressed tightly together, like a child refusing to taste anything new. His bulbous nose, the only really prominent thing on his face, flared with distaste as I sat down across from him. Another man, with red hair and a red, neatly trimmed beard, dressed in an ill-fitting brown suit and a tie that my father might have worn when he went to college, leaned against one wall. He was taking careful notes with a Bic pen in a small black notebook. Longreen asked me about what had happened that night and I told him. I have a good memory, not photographic, but pretty close, so it took me quite a while to tell everything I remembered. I tried to talk slowly so the guy taking notes could write it all down. Just as I got to the part of finding Gary's body, the door opened. A small, well-dressed man with a neatly trimmed mustache entered, thanked the policewoman who had opened the door for him, and walked the two steps from the door to the table.

Longreen glared up at him. "Wyman, what are you doing here?"

The small man smiled, pulled a chair up to the table, sat down, and said, "I understand there's been a killing."

As the two of them talked I focused on the small man, the one Longreen had just referred to as Wyman. I felt sure that I had seen his face somewhere before. As I said, I have a pretty good memory, and I'm particularly good with faces. His was topped with a full head of brown hair carefully blow-dried and set with mousse or some such thing so each hair managed to stay perfectly in place at all times. His eyes were the shade of deep blue usually reserved for soap opera stars. His nose was as good as mine. I found myself wondering if *he* had had a nose job. His neatly trimmed mustache and slightly cleft chin completed the image of a face that cried out to be photographed. Finally it came to me. I *had* seen his picture. It was in the papers every now and then, and not just in the *New York Post*. He was Jim Wyman, an assistant D.A. The press said that he was the best prosecutor the city had. There were dozens of long-term residents on Riker's Island who had him to thank for their current address. I seemed to remember that the *Times* figured him for a career in politics, so I took another good look. He always seemed taller in the papers.

"Look, Wyman, I told you, there's nothing here for you yet." Longreen was trying to hold in his anger at having an assistant D.A. looking over his shoulder. "Why don't you leave me alone and let me do my job. I've just started interviewing the suspects. When I have something I'll turn it over to you, okay?"

Wyman lit up a cigarette. "Lieutenant, I'm not stopping you from doing your job, so don't try pulling attitude on me. I have a right to be here, and I'm staying. If you don't like me here, I'm sure I can quickly arrange for another lieutenant who will."

Longreen glared for a moment. "Sorry, Wyman, no offense meant." The tone of his voice carried a different message entirely. If Wyman heard it, he chose to ignore it.

"No offense taken, Lieutenant," Wyman said with the start of a smile. "Oh, one other thing; I understand you have an old law school friend of mine here. I think it's be helpful to have him join us."

Longreen turned to the red-haired cop leaning against the wall. "Sheski, go get Mr. Wyman's friend." He looked back at Wyman and asked, "Who is he?"

"Blacker, D. L. Blacker."

Lieutenant Longreen made a face that seemed to run rapidly through all the A emotions: amazement, anger, and finally amusement. He held the look for a brief moment and then snorted. He probably meant it as a laugh, but it came out more as a short series of snorts. "He's a friend of yours?" Longreen snorted again. "I just finished talking to him. He's made up like a clown and dressed like a Mardi Gras pretty boy. He must have been a real inspiration to his fellow law students. Sure, bring him in. The more the merrier. Sheski, go get Blacker." Sheski left the room. Longreen continued to snort. I decided I liked him better when he was in a bad mood. "Just wait till I tell the boys about your old law school chum."

Wyman didn't seem particularly upset by the ribbing he was getting. He carefully put out his cigarette and lit up another before he said anything. "Blacker graduated at the top of our class. He was editor of the law review and clerked for the chief justice of the United States Seventh Circuit Court of Appeals. Was he an inspiration to the rest of us? Yes, Lieutenant, he was. He showed that you could love the law, be a good lawyer, and still have other interests. He also added a welcome relief from the pressures of law school." Wyman seemed to be enjoying the memories; Longreen clearly wasn't. The frown that I had gotten used to was once again settling onto Longreen's face, but Wyman ignored the lieutenant's mood. He just looked up at the ceiling, blew a smoke ring, and continued. "Why, I remember once, we were taking a property class that met at night. Blacker showed up late for one of the classes. Seems he had been performing for a Knights of Pythias awards dinner. Anyway, he was dressed in full clown makeup and a tuxedo. He apologized for being late, and then twisted the professor a balloon animal, sat down at his regular place, and acted as if nothing was out of the ordinary. Lieutenant, I could tell you more stories about D. L. Blacker. . . ."

Just then the door opened and the red-haired cop, Sheski, led D. L. Blacker into the room. Assistant D.A. Wyman stood and shook Blacker's hand. D. L didn't seem surprised to see his old law school chum. "Jim," he said, "good to see you. Glad you could make it."

Wyman motioned him to a seat. "You always did give the best parties, D. L."

Blacker had somehow managed to remove his makeup and had left his cape outside. It was easier to imagine him in the company of lawyers now that he looked less like a clown. "Seriously, Jim, I'm sorry to have to call you, but I figured it might be a good idea to have a friendly face in on this from the start."

Lieutenant Longreen had been sitting quietly, glowering at the reunion, when suddenly he erupted at D. L. "You called him?" He turned on Wyman. "That's why you're here? Because you got a call from some clown?"

D. L. Blacker looked at Lieutenant Longreen. "He's here, Lieutenant, for the same reason you are. To represent the interests of the people of New York. To see that justice is done." I couldn't help but notice a small smile playing across Blacker's face.

The playful smile was mirrored by Wyman, but Longreen didn't seem to appreciate Blacker's subtle humor. He growled at Wyman. "Look, this has been going on long enough. I've got a room full of people to talk to and the night's not getting any younger. I talked to Blacker before, and his story was supported by what Arnold here just told me. Arnold says the deceased, Gary Johnson, was alive when he talked to Arnold in their dressing room. Arnold says he left the room and Blacker was in his sight, in the party room, continuously from then on, until he heard the scream. That's when the body was discovered by Donna Johnson, the deceased's wife. That seems to clear your buddy Blacker, so if you insist, he can stay, but I don't like it."

D. L. Blacker looked at me with a quizzical expression on his face that I couldn't quite read. Wyman said, "Your objection is noted, Lieutenant. Why don't you continue?"

Longreen growled again and turned to me. "Go ahead,

Mr. Arnold, you were telling me what happened when you first entered the dressing room, after you heard the scream."

I swallowed and cleared my throat to try to loosen the steel wool that had become lodged there. Slowly it allowed itself to move down into my gut, and I resumed the story. I told the lieutenant where Donna was standing when I entered the dressing room, what she was doing, and what she was holding. I told him how I had helped her to sit and described how I first saw Gary's body. I told the lieutenant of D. L. Blacker's entrance, his ordering the people to leave, and his request that I take Donna from the room and then come back and help him. I told him about Donna's request that she be given her tape player and how I handed it and the tapes to her before she left under her own power.

That seemed to get a reaction from them. Longreen's glare became even more unpleasant and he barked at me, "Don't you know you're not supposed to disturb anything at the scene of a murder? What's wrong with you?"

D. L. Blacker came to my defense. "Lighten up, Lieutenant, it's not like he touched the body or anything."

I stopped for a moment and looked at Blacker. Why did he say that? What game was he playing? He knew that I had seen *him* touching the body. He had gone through Gary's pockets and briefcase. Maybe he had even taken something. Supposedly Blacker was cleared in the killing, but what if he was part of a conspiracy? What if he had a partner who did the actual killing? Blacker was a brain. Maybe he had planned the whole thing out, signaled his partner when he should go in and do the deed and then, while I watched, lifted some important document that was the reason for the whole heinous crime. I knew I had to tell the lieutenant what I had seen. I had to.

I didn't.

Chapter

FOUR

I finished telling my story to Lieutenant Longreen, leaving out all reference to D. L. Blacker's *tampering* with the evidence. Maybe I was making a mistake, but looking at Blacker and looking at Longreen, I decided I liked Blacker a whole lot more. Longreen told me I could go, and as I got up to leave, he told the red-haired detective to go with me.

"Sheski, take Arnold out and bring back one of the others."

Sheski nodded and pushed off from the wall. "Sure, Lieutenant," he said and opened the door for me. "Come on, let's go."

I walked out of the room and over to the other entertainers. Sheski followed me, stopped, and then thumbed through his notebook. Donna had moved to a chair and I sat down beside her. Sheski looked up from his notes, fastened his eyes on Pamela who was still leaning against the D. J. booth, and asked, "Ms. Lockheed, Pamela Lockheed?"

Pamela raised her hand. "Still alive and kicking," she said, and then quickly looked at Donna and became very embarrassed. "Whoops, bad joke, I guess."

Sheski gave her a little smile. I suspected his smile was not in response to what Pamela had said, however. His eyes seemed to be focused several inches below her mouth. "If you'll come with me." He allowed her to pass and then followed her to the room where Longreen waited, along with Assistant D.A. Wyman and D. L. Blacker. Sheski was a conscientious cop. His eyes, still aiming a little low, didn't leave Pamela's back for a moment.

As soon as they closed the door Andy came and sat down beside me. "What happened?" he asked. "What did they ask, what did you tell them?" It occurred to me at that moment that this could turn into a never-ending circle. Initially, I had experienced certain things which I then told the lieutenant about. Now Andy wanted me to tell him about telling the lieutenant about things I had experienced. If I didn't stop it now, no doubt someone later on would ask me what I had told Andy. I would then have to tell him about telling Andy about telling the lieutenant about things I had experienced. I didn't really want to go through all this, so I didn't directly answer his question. "They'll be calling for you soon too. Then they'll probably search our stuff and let us go home." I sounded very knowledgeable for someone who didn't know the first thing about what was going on.

Andy nodded a couple of times and then stood up. Donna was changing the tapes in her Walkman and Andy turned to her. "You know what this party needs," he said, "is some music. Say, Donna, how about letting me put one of your jazz tapes on over the sound system?"

I thought it insensitive of him to ask that of Donna, just then. I mean, her husband had just been murdered. She seemed almost in shock. She seemed to have withdrawn into her own little world; probably her way of dealing with the shock. I was no psychiatrist, but this all seemed like a natural reaction, and one that should be allowed to run its course. It was clear to me that she wanted to be left alone, didn't want anyone to intrude on her private grief. I would have told Andy all of this too, except Donna seemed to brighten up a little when he spoke to her. So much for my amateur psychoanalysis. Donna nodded, managed a faint smile, took off her headphones, and handed Andy her bag of tapes. He took them into his booth and Donna turned to me with the same weak smile she had just given Gary. She didn't seem to be really focusing on me, but I took the smile as a good sign and smiled back. Now that I had seen that she reacted well to contact, I knew I should say something, but what do you say to a woman whose husband has just been found dead with your machete in his head? "I love you." I tried.

"What?" She shook her head as though loosening some invisible spiderwebs that held onto her, and then looked at me again, this time like she really saw me.

"Just testing," I said. I was saved from having to explain by the sound of vintage Gato Barbieri beginning to softly fill the room. Donna visibly relaxed as the music played.

Andy came out of the booth and handed Donna her tape bag. "I thought this might mellow out the crowd a bit. Good tape. Think I'll get a beer. Can I get you guys anything?" Donna and I both shook our heads, and Andy wandered over to the bar.

Since she appeared to be responding so well to social interaction, I decided to try to get Donna into a conversation. "You okay?" I asked her. Boy, was I smooth.

She nodded her head. For a moment I thought I would have to come up with another clever opening line if I was going to keep the conversation alive but she decided to talk. "Next week would have been out fifth anniversary," she said.

It seemed that she wanted to talk about Gary, so I asked, "How did you two meet?"

"It was in Paris, when I was studying with Decroux."

I nodded. She had mentioned this to me before.

"My parents paid my expenses the first three semesters, but then they said if I insisted on continuing to do that *mime thing*, I was on my own. So I had to find a way to support myself while I attended classes. There aren't a lot of things an American kid can do to make money in Paris, at least not a lot of honest things." She looked away as though she was embarrassed and didn't know if she should continue.

"I know," I said, just to say something, since she had stopped talking. "My parents *still* want me to be an English teacher."

This must have been the right thing for me to say, because she smiled and went on talking. "Through someone in my class, not your friend Bill"—she smiled at me again and kept talking—"I heard of a person who was looking for American kids to serve as international couriers. Supposedly the work was all done on weekends, so I wouldn't miss any classes. It seemed like easy work and I was told it paid very well.

"An introduction was arranged and one Saturday morning I met Wilhelm Broberg. I started working for him the next day, and living with him the next week. It was wonderful, at first. But then I found out what I was carrying in those courier briefcases. Willy was using us to transport heroin all over Europe. I was a kid from Highland Park, Illinois, and I was living with the biggest smack pusher in Western Europe."

I was surprised that I wasn't more surprised by what Donna was saying. I guess that being in show business I had already met enough people who used drugs: marijuana, cocaine, amphetamines, even heroin on occasion. So I didn't ask about the drugs, I asked about her. "Why did you stay with him?"

"I loved him," she said; like that simple statement answered any questions I might ask. "I did try to get him to stop dealing drugs. I even threatened to leave him. Maybe he believed me. He rewarded my efforts to reform him by hooking me on heroin. I guess he figured it was a way to make sure I stuck close to him. It worked. I was addicted to heroin and Willy was my only source."

"Donna," I interrupted her, "are you sure you want to tell me all this?"

She looked closely at me and nodded her head in a quick short jerk. "I think I have to talk about it. Gary never let me talk about it, but now he's. . . ." She stopped, pressed her lips together, closed her eyes, and took a deep breath.

When she opened her eyes, I said, "So what was life like with your pusher?"

"There wasn't anything I wouldn't do for him. He told me to drop out of Decroux's school; I dropped out. He thought it would be a good idea for me to get a job, waitressing at a small café. I became a waitress. He figured I could be a *message drop*."

"A message drop?" I asked. I had never heard that term.

"A place where his people could leave messages for him. That way if the police caught on, I'd be arrested and he could escape. Nice guy, huh? Anyway, it was while working at the restaurant that I met Gary. He was traveling across Europe after graduating from college. He came into the café and we started talking. I guess he liked me because he kept coming back."

Donna stopped for a moment, took another deep breath, and exhaled in a long sigh. I watched as she tightened her chin, perhaps squeezing off the urge to cry, and then continued with her story.

"I told Gary I was living with someone, but that didn't seem to discourage him. He started waiting around for me to finish work, asking me to join him for dinner. Finally I did. I was a little nervous, but I knew that Willy wouldn't worry if I came home late. Willy knew I'd always be coming home, if not for him, for my fix.

"I told Gary my whole story that night. Gary was a good listener, easy to talk to." She stopped and looked at me. "Just like you," she said. I met her eyes and what I saw made it difficult for me to breathe. The look in her eyes was deep, tender, intimate, and shot through with pain. It was the kind of look that curls your toes and leaves you shaking. I had to fight down the urge to tell her I loved her again.

"He took the story pretty well," she continued. "After dinner he walked me home, kissed me on the cheek, and walked away. I figured I had scared him off. I hadn't. The next day he was back at the café. He brought me a rose." She stopped for a moment and pressed her lips together.

"That's nice." I smiled at her and nodded a few times to encourage her to continue.

She smiled a weak smile at me. "I've always been a sucker for roses," she said. I made a mental note to remember that. At that moment, she looked like she could use a few dozen long-stemmed American Beauties.

She continued. "That night I went out with him again, and after dinner, we went back to his room. He had rented a small room with a bath in a not very good section of the Left Bank. He locked the door behind us, kissed me, and then threw the key out the window. He stayed with me as I went through cold turkey. It took me seven days."

"It takes a lot of guts to kick an addiction that way," I told her. "I don't think I could do it."

"I didn't have much choice," she said. "Gary wouldn't let me out of the room." She smiled, and I smiled back.

44

"When the hell part was over, he started to rebuild me. He fed me, bought me new clothes, and then arranged airplane tickets for us back to America. Luckily I always carried my passport with me and Gary had placed my purse out of harm's way before the worst of the withdrawal started."

"What about your friend," I asked, "the pusher?"

"I never saw Wilhelm Broberg again. Gary told me that Willy was furious and had issued a reward for my return. Imagine that, a reward for me. Like I was a valuable wristwatch that was stolen or a puppy that had wandered away. I think Gary took a certain pleasure in knowing he had upset Willy so much.

"Gary seemed to have two real talents, two real passions: organizing lives and pissing people off. I was never organized until I met Gary, and I've never experienced so much anger directed at one person since. And Gary always seemed to thrive on it. He said the anger showed that he was affecting people's lives; he didn't mind the anger, what he couldn't tolerate was indifference. Apparently he was always like that too. His brother, Bob, jokes that he's hated Gary since the day he was born." She tried a small attempt at a laugh and shook her head.

Gary has a brother named Bob? I thought. And then it struck me, something that had been nagging at the back of my head for a while.

"Donna," I asked, "does Gary's brother work with him? Was he here tonight? Dressed in work clothes, looks kind of like Gary?"

Donna nodded. "Sure, Gary and Bob are partners—were partners. Actually it was originally Bob's company. Gary joined him after we returned from Europe. Now Bob handles the technical side and Gary handles . . . handled, the talent and booking, why?"

45

I looked around. "Where is he? I saw him before the party, but not since the trouble began. Does he usually leave before the gig is over?"

"No," Donna said slowly. "He has to be here to strike and pack up everything when we're done."

"Well then," I asked her, "where is he? Where's Bob Johnson?"

Chapter

F I V E

Donna didn't know where Gary's brother Bob was any better than I did. But I figured thinking about that was better for her than thinking about a husband lying dead in the next room, or a past as a heroin addict. In truth, she didn't have much time to think about any of these things, because after a very few minutes the door to Lieutenant Longreen's interrogation room opened and all the inhabitants spilled out.

Pamela walked over to where the food had been, discovered that it was no longer there, and expressed her displeasure in a single appropriate obscenity. I mentioned earlier that Blacker had told me to eat, and that I would come to regret not having followed his advice. It finally happened when Pamela, by her appropriate use of a well-turned expletive, made me aware that all the food was gone. At that moment I realized that I too was hungry. Hunger may have been the least of my problems, but at that point in my life a chicken leg would have done an awful lot to lift my spirits.

Wyman and Sheski went to talk with one of the plain-clothes policemen who was interviewing the partygoers.

Longreen stopped at the door of his little room, looked around, and then stormed over to us. "Who turned on that music?" he demanded.

Andy Costello jumped up and tried to say something, but Longreen didn't let him get it out.

"Turn it off, right now," the lieutenant roared. "This is a murder investigation, not a party, for God's sake." He gave Andy a parting growl and stomped over to join Wyman, Sheski, and the plainclothes detective. Andy jumped into the booth and silence once again descended upon the room. He brought the cassette tape back to Donna and tossed it into her tape bag.

D. L. Blacker watched all of this from the door of the interrogation room. Then he sauntered to the coffee table, fixed himself a cup, drank some of it, and walked over to Donna and me. I stood up to meet him.

"Can I talk to you for a minute?" I asked.

"Sure," he answered, taking a sip from his coffee and leading me away from the others. "What's up?"

"You know Bob Johnson?"

"Sure," he said, his face giving away nothing.

"I was just talking with Donna, and we realized that he's not here. He was earlier, but he's not here now."

D. L. Blacker looked at me intently. "Why are you telling this to me?" he asked. "Why didn't you mention it earlier? Why not tell it to Longreen?"

I felt like he was accusing me, putting me on the defensive. I guess lawyers do that naturally, but it didn't seem fair of him to be doing it to *me*; not after he heard me with Longreen. He knew I didn't mention his messing with the body. He *should* know I was on his side. "I didn't mention Bob Johnson earlier," I said, "because I didn't know who he was or that he should still be here, until I talked with Donna

48

just now. And I told you and not the lieutenant because I trusted you and I don't trust him. Although now I'm not so sure." I realized that last part was kind of snotty, but the tension of the past few hours was starting to have an effect on me. Regardless, I didn't apologize. I just stopped talking and waited for him to say something.

I didn't have to wait long.

"Give me a dollar," he said, and took a sip from his coffee.

I reached into a pocket of my jumpsuit, pulled out my money, peeled off one of the few dollars I had left, and handed it to him. "Here you go," I said.

He took the dollar, pocketed it, and said, "Thanks, you've just retained yourself a lawyer. It's like I said before, you may be needing one." He finished off his cup of coffee and went back for another.

Before I could follow him to ask what he was talking about, the detective called Sheski came over to me. "The lieutenant wants to talk to you again. Will you come with me?"

Like moths to a flame we all went back into the little room: Longreen, Wyman, Sheski, me, and finally D. L. Blacker.

Longreen didn't even wait for me to get settled. "Why are you shielding Bob Johnson?"

"Huh?" was all I could think to say.

"You think you're a smart guy, don't you?" Longreen snarled. "You sat in here before with your long drawn-out story of everything you said you'd seen, everything you said had happened. You think we're not going to talk to anyone else? You think we're not going to learn what you intentionally left out?"

Longreen paused to take a breath and once again all I could think to say was "Huh?"

"This so-called psychic, Pamela Lockheed, tells me that the deceased had a partner, his brother Bob Johnson, and that he was here and might be able to tell us more about their business. I'm about to send Sheski to bring me this Bob Johnson when Blacker here chimes in and tells me that Bob Johnson is no longer here. 'Where is he?' I ask. He doesn't know, Blacker tells me. 'Why didn't you tell me this before?' I ask. 'You didn't ask,' he says."

I looked again at D. L. Blacker who sat smiling at me, ignoring Longreen's tirade against him. Blacker had known that Bob Johnson was no longer here, before I mentioned it to him. What else did he know? Was I right to be trusting him? My thoughts were interrupted by the lieutenant bellowing at me again.

"We have a witness who saw you in a three-way argument with Gary and Bob Johnson, shortly before the party began. But you didn't think to mention that, did you? With that great memory of yours, you didn't remember a little thing like that you and a guy who's conveniently disappeared were fighting with the deceased less than an hour before he's murdered? Murdered with your machete. A machete you conveniently left in the room where you knew the deceased would be. I'll tell you what I think, Arnold. I think you and this Bob Johnson are in on this together. I think the two of you killed him together. And I think the two of you are going to go to prison together. That's what I think."

All of the bad clichés from pulp novels and B movies started to play themselves out for me. I was having trouble breathing, the room began to swirl, and everything looked like I was seeing it through a fish-eye lens. I couldn't believe this was happening to me.

"Now come on, Arnold," Longreen said, suddenly all sweetness and light. "I'm not a bad guy. Tell me how it happened, tell me where we can find this Bob Johnson, and I'm sure Mr. Wyman here from the D.A.'s office will see that you've cooperated and he'll agree to a reduced sentence.

I bet Bob Johnson talked you into this murder, isn't that right?"

I'm not sure what I was going to say, but I never had the chance to find out. Before I could say anything, D. L. Blacker leapt to his feet and to my defense.

"I'm going to instruct my client not to say anything, Lieutenant," Blacker said, looking only at me.

"Your client?" roared Longreen. "What do you mean, your client?"

D. L. Blacker turned his forceful gaze to the lieutenant. "During the short break Mr. Arnold retained me to represent his interests in this matter. It has been, of course, perfectly proper for me to sit in during this interrogation, but now, as his lawyer I am directing him not to answer any further questions until we have an opportunity to confer."

Assistant D.A. Wyman stood up and joined the fracas.

"D. L.," he said, "you can't represent Arnold in this. The Code of Professional Responsibility expressly forbids a lawyer from representing a client on a matter in which he will be a witness. As the prosecuting attorney I can tell you that you're definitely going to be a witness in this. Hell, you're lucky you're not going to be a defendant."

"Jim, I assume you're referring to canon 5, ethical considerations 5 dash 9 and 5 dash 10, and disciplinary rule 5 dash 102. However, if you'll check the drafter's comments, you'll see they make it clear that refusal to accept a matter or withdrawal from a matter because of this potential witness-advocate conflict should not be done in such a way as to prejudice a client's case. Regardless, Jim, as was stated by the Iowa court in the landmark decision of Galarowicz v. Ward, where they interpreted this canon of legal professional responsibility, and I quote, 'It was not designed to permit a lawyer to call opposing counsel as a witness and thereby disqualify him as counsel.' Nice try, Jim, but it won't wash."

Wyman pulled out a small designer notebook and matching pen from the inside breast pocket of his perfectly tailored suit.

"Can you give me the citation for that case, D. L.?" he asked.

D. L. Blacker smiled again. "Sure," he said. "Two hundred thirty Pacific 2nd, 576. The section I quoted is on page 580."

"What the hell are you two talking about?" bellowed Lieutenant Longreen. "Look, Wyman, I want Blacker out of here and I want to finish this with Arnold. Sheski"— Longreen turned to his assistant—"get this joker out of here."

Sheski grabbed D. L. Blacker's arm, but Blacker pulled himself free and leaned across the desk toward Longreen. "I'm a lawyer and I represent Pat Arnold, and I have a constitutional right to be here if you intend to continue questioning him, unless. . . ." Blacker stopped, stood up straight, and seemed to relax, as though he had just had an idea that he really liked.

"Unless, of course, Lieutenant, this is a precharging interrogation. I don't specialize in criminal law, but as I understand recent rulings, a suspect doesn't necessarily have a right to a lawyer before he has been charged either with a crime or as a material witness. Are you charging Mr. Arnold?"

Longreen glared at D. L. Blacker and then sat back and smiled an almost serpentine smile. "No, Mr. Blacker, of course not. This is, as you say, a precharging interrogation."

Blacker took my arm and pulled me from the chair. "In that case, we'll be going. If you're not charging either of us you have no legal right to detain us. We've given our statements. If you think up any more questions, you've got our addresses, you know where to find us."

We walked out of the room and toward the door to the elevators.

"Is that all true?" I asked. "They can't hold us?"

"I don't know," Blacker whispered. "But we're about to find out."

Our path was blocked by a large uniformed policeman.

"Going somewhere?" he inquired. I didn't think we were, but D. L. Blacker, when he talked, expressed enough confidence for the both of us.

"Lieutenant Longreen and Assistant D.A. Wyman said we could go," Blacker told the cop.

I was feeling smaller and the cop was looking bigger with every loud beat of my heart. I knew it wasn't going to work, he wasn't even looking at us; he was looking behind us. I turned and saw Wyman walking over.

"It's okay, Officer," said Wyman, "they can go." He extended his hand to D. L. Blacker. Blacker took it and they shook. "That may have been a mistake D. L., Longreen is not happy."

Blacker laughed. "Is he ever?" Blacker turned to go, but then stopped and returned to Jim Wyman. "Oh, Jim, could you lend me a couple of bucks for a taxi? My wallet is now state's evidence, I left it in the dressing room."

Wyman chuckled, pulled out his wallet, and handed D. L. Blacker two ten-dollar bills. "How about lunch tomorrow?" Wyman asked.

D. L. Blacker said, "I'd love it," pocketed the money, and walked from the room, with me following close behind.

Chapter

S I X

The clock radio woke me at eight o'clock the next morning. The disc jockey on WZBQ mercifully disrupted a dream in which Donna Johnson and I were locked in passionate lovemaking when the bedroom door flew open and Gary, my machete still in his head, came running in, screaming at me that I would never work in this town again.

I quickly showered, shaved, drank some Kool-aid, and ate a bowl of corn flakes. Not much of a breakfast, but the best I could do in the so-called kitchenette of my one-room apartment. I piled the dirty dishes into the sink, along with those from the day before and the day before that, and headed out the door. D. L. Blacker had told me to be at his apartment by nine o'clock and I wasn't going to be late.

As I walked toward his apartment building, I rehashed the events of the previous evening. None of it seemed real. I was reminded that it was, by the headlines of the papers at the newsstand on the southwest corner of Ninety-fourth Street and Broadway. I picked up a *New York Post*. "Machete Massacre at MegaBank" screamed the headline in red, above a blurred picture of my machete embedded in Gary's head. Leave it to the *Post* to put everything in tasteful perspective. Hard to believe that it was a morning paper. When I grew up, a morning paper was the one you read while eating breakfast. Looking at the *Post*'s headline made me feel like I was going to lose what little breakfast I had eaten. I quickly read through the lead article and saw that I was mentioned by name several times. There's an old show-business saying, "It doesn't matter what the papers say about you, so long as they spell your name correctly." All things considered, I'd prefer that I hadn't been named. Blacker was also mentioned in the story, and they even included his picture; a flattering likeness, it made him look like he still had a full head of hair. I wondered when they had taken it. Then I remembered that Blacker had been written up in the papers before. They probably pulled his picture from their morgue. Pleasant thought.

I folded the paper, tucked it under my arm, and continued down Broadway, toward D. L. Blacker's apartment building.

The doorman who guarded the entrance to the lobby was different from the one who had ushered me through the day before. This man was a tall, young Hispanic with a ready smile and a thin mustache. When I told him who I was and that I was there to see Mr. Blacker, the smile seemed to change to a look of guarded suspicion. I wondered if I was becoming paranoid. Then I noticed that he had been reading the morning paper. Great, I thought. Yesterday I couldn't get any agent in New York to let me through his door, but today every doorman in the city knows my name.

The doorman continued to eye me as he spoke quietly into a telephone. He hung up and looked me over once again, from head to toe—perhaps checking to see if I had brought along another machete. "Mr. Arnold," the doorman said with a heavy Latin accent, "you're expected." It took me a moment to realize he was talking to me. I still think of *Mr. Arnold* as my father's name. Apparently, all you have to do to gain the respect of service people in New York to be named by a newspaper as a suspect in a flashy murder case.

I walked through the lobby to Blacker's door. He was waiting for me, dressed in a tie, jacket, and faded blue jeans, sipping on his ever-present cup of coffee. He shook my hand and led me in to his apartment. We walked in silence directly to his office. He sat down behind his massive desk, settled himself into his incredible leather chair, and gestured for me to sit in one of the client's chairs. After all, I was a client. I had paid him a dollar.

I dropped the newspaper on his desk and then sat down. I realized that my chair was several inches shorter than his. The result was that anyone sitting in the client's chair had to look up at D. L. Blacker. I didn't care. "Why are you helping me?" I asked him. "The papers already have me tried and convicted, the police seem sure that I'm guilty, why don't you?"

D. L. Blacker picked up the paper and paged through it while drinking his coffee. Perhaps he was reading, perhaps he was just organizing his thoughts. Finally he folded the paper, put down his coffee, and looked at me.

"Pat," he began, "you've done a couple of things that make me believe you didn't kill Gary Johnson. As your lawyer, though, I have to ask you the question: Did you kill him? You can tell me the truth. Any admission you make to me would be protected under attorney-client privilege."

"No," I protested, "I didn't kill him. Of course I didn't kill him." I stopped for a moment. When I began talking again it was slower, with more deliberation. "But you said you believe that I didn't do it. Why would you say that, unless you know who did?" Suddenly a lot of things fell together for me. "You knew Bob Johnson had left the party before I pointed it out to you. You went through Gary's pockets and briefcase. I think you took something. You were Gary's lawyer. Gary and Bob were partners. I bet you represented their business. Maybe you drafted some paper or document or something and screwed up, bad. Maybe Bob came to you, told you that Gary was going to sue you for legal malpractice because of your mistake. Bob has wanted his brother dead for a long time, so he convinced you to help. You planned the murder and maybe even signaled Bob when to go in and kill his brother. Then you had me keep people out of the room while you retrieved the paper you had drafted. And now you're claiming to help me so that I won't tell the police what I know about your taking that document from Gary's briefcase."

He could have reacted in several different ways. I was ready for denial, anger, even scorn. But D. L. Blacker laughed.

"I like you, Pat," he said. "We're going to get along just fine. Come on." He got up and left the office. I followed him down a hallway, until we finally reached his kitchen. He poured me a cup of coffee and filled his cup. While he poured, I looked around the room. It was as big as my whole apartment, filled with every kitchen gadget imaginable.

D. L. Blacker opened the refrigerator, took out a carton of milk, added some to his coffee, and offered it to me. I nodded and he poured some into my cup. He replaced the carton of milk and asked if I wanted sugar. I shook my head. He added a little to his cup, stirred it, and raised his cup in a little toast. I raised mine and took a sip. It was the best coffee I'd ever tasted. I told him so.

He smiled. "It's a special blend of Colombian Supremo and Jamaica Blue Mountain beans, flown in every week and prepared specially for me by an old Korean guy who runs a little shop on Christopher Street, down in the West Village. Glad you like it."

Blacker took another sip of his coffee and then walked

57

out of the kitchen. I followed and he led me back to his office.

When we got settled into our respective chairs he took another sip of his coffee and began talking. "Let me answer some of the questions you haven't asked. First, why do I trust you? Why do I believe that you didn't kill Gary? A couple of reasons. You provided me with an airtight alibi. Longreen said you told him I was in your sight from the last time you saw Gary alive until Donna screamed. If you had killed Gary, you wouldn't have provided an alibi for *me*. It would have been easy for you to say that you were concentrating on your own performance and hadn't noticed what I was doing or where I was. An intelligent killer—and you seem to be passably intelligent—would try to throw suspicion on everyone else. Which brings me to my second reason for trusting you. You didn't mention my looking through Gary's pockets. I assure you my reason was innocent enough, but you didn't know that. A guilty person would have told the police. Hell, most innocent people would have."

"I might, yet," I grumbled. He still hadn't told me one good reason to believe or trust him.

"But," he continued, choosing to ignore my comment, "my main reason for believing that you're innocent is that I watched you juggling six scarves."

A little of my coffee went down the wrong way. Through my coughs I told him that I didn't understand what he was saying.

"If I agree with the police version of what happened," he said in a condescending, talk-down-to-the-witness tone of lawyer voice that implied he didn't necessarily believe this, but I should know it anyway, "shortly after you drove a machete into Gary's head, you went up on stage and performed a complicated six-scarf juggling routine."

"So?" I asked.

"I've done a little juggling, and I know jugglers; one of my clients, Gene Smith, used to be president of the International Jugglers Association. Anyway, juggling six of anything takes a tremendous amount of concentration. More than I think you could maintain so soon after killing someone." He took another sip of coffee.

"Either that or else you're one hell of an actor. In which case I want to be your lawyer when you make it, and clearing you of a murder rap seems like the perfect way to get on your good side."

He was trying to be funny, but I wasn't ready to laugh. "What did you take from Gary's briefcase?" I demanded.

He opened a drawer in his desk and pulled something out. "I'm not saying I took anything from his briefcase, but if I did," he said, and dropped a pile of checks on his desk, "it would have been our paychecks from last night." He looked through the checks, pulled one out, and passed it over to me. It had my name on it. "Of course if anyone asks, Gary gave me the checks before the job and asked me to give them out to the performers after the party. I'd advise you to cash it soon. The bank account will probably be impounded by the probate court. I deposited mine in one of those automated tellers last night. Anyway, you'll be needing the money, my services don't come cheap. Off hand, I'd say the initial retainer is going to cost you about three hundred fifty dollars."

I looked at the check I was holding. It was for $350. D. L. Blacker didn't miss a trick. I was beginning to understand how he could afford the apartment. I took the pen he held out to me and endorsed the check over to him.

"Thanks," he said and placed the check in his desk drawer. He pulled another piece of paper from the same drawer and handed it to me. It was a receipt. "I prepared that before you came. I just made it out for 'legal services'; that way you can write it off on your taxes if you itemize."

I didn't have time to come up with a response. I don't know what my response would have been. Before I could open my mouth, one of the phones on his desk rang and D. L. Blacker picked it up.

"Yes, Roberto?" he said into the phone. "Yes, please, send him back." D. L. Blacker hung up the phone and stood up. "We have a visitor. But please, stay here. I think the two of you may want to talk. I'll be right back."

He left the room and I heard him walk to the front door and open it. After a moment the muffled sound of voices told me the visitor had reached the apartment. I heard the front door close and footsteps, as Blacker and his guest came slowly toward the office. Blacker walked around me to his desk and slid back into his chair.

I stood and turned to meet the visitor with whom Blacker thought I would want to talk. He was right. I had only seen him for a minute, but like I said before, I have a pretty good memory. This guy I was not likely to forget.

"The police seem to think you two know each other quite well," said Blacker. "Regardless, let me introduce you. Pat Arnold, meet Bob Johnson."

Chapter

SEVEN

Bob Johnson shook my hand. "Pat Arnold," he said, looking at me closely. "The police and the papers are saying that either you or I killed my brother. I didn't, did you?"

"No, no I didn't," I said. He looked awful. His dark brown hair was tangled, he hadn't shaved, and he had large, dark bags under bloodshot eyes. His wrists were raw, as though he'd been rubbing them for hours. He was still dressed in the work clothes he had been wearing the night before, but now they were stained and rumpled. He folded his tall, lanky frame into the other of the two clients' chairs, facing D. L. Blacker, rested his head on the back of the chair, and closed his eyes. I sat back down and continued to stare at him. Blacker looked at both of us, saying nothing, just sipping his coffee.

No one said anything for several minutes. Finally the silence got to me and I blurted out, "Does Lieutenant Longreen know where you are?"

"Probably," Blacker said, before Bob Johnson could respond. "You obviously were detained by the police and then

61

came directly here when they released you. No doubt you were followed."

Johnson opened his eyes and leaned toward Blacker, a questioning look in his eyes. I was a little more direct. "Huh?" I said.

Blacker finished his cup of coffee. "When you greeted Pat here, you said that the police think one of you killed Gary. That implied that you had talked with them. But even if you just read that fact in the newspapers, you have chafe marks on your wrists. The kind you would have if you had been wearing handcuffs. Therefore, I assume you were detained by the police."

"Fine," I said. "But how do you know he didn't go home. How do you know he was followed?"

"He's wearing the same clothes he wore last night, and from their condition and his appearance, it's clear that he didn't go home and clean himself up before coming here. That he was released indicates the police don't have enough to hold him, but according to the paper you brought with you, Bob's still a prime suspect in his brother's murder. It is therefore reasonable to assume that he was followed."

I was starting to hate the tone of voice Blacker took when he explained things. Or maybe I just hated that I needed to have the things explained. I had seen everything he had seen, but I hadn't made the same conclusions. It was clear to me that if I was going to play in Blacker's league I was going to have to work a whole lot harder. It was becoming more and more important to me that I play in his league.

"Yea," said Bob Johnson, "that's right. They picked me up as I was putting the key in my door at around four o'clock this morning. They grabbed me, slapped handcuffs on me, and drove me to some Gestapo building, downtown."

"You were questioned by Lieutenant Longreen." The way Blacker said it, it was more a statement than a question.

"Yeah, for several hours. When they let me go I figured I'd better see my lawyer. That's you."

"Good decision." Blacker went to take a sip of his coffee, realized the cup was empty, and stood up. "Can I get you some coffee?"

"Thanks, milk, no sugar."

"I'm fine," I said, and Blacker walked from the room.

Bob Johnson rubbed his eyes, sucked in some air, and let it out in a long sigh. We sat in silence for a while. Then he looked at me, I looked at him, and he began to talk. "How well did you know Gary?"

"Not well. I worked for him a few times."

"Gary was my younger brother. We never really hung out together when we were growing up. To be perfectly honest I always found him pushy and obnoxious, but I was always proud of him, of what he was doing."

First Donna and now Bob. It looked like I was destined to be the good listener to everyone connected with Gary's death. I settled back in my chair, nodded my head, and said what good listeners are supposed to say, "Uh huh." I don't know if he heard me, he wasn't looking at me. He had transferred his gaze to the picture of Gary on the front page of the paper that was laying on D. L. Blacker's desk.

"The business was originally mine, you know. I started it as a theatrical production company. Doing corporate industrial shows and stuff like that. When Gary joined me, it was his idea to go after big party work. He was a great salesman; he sold me and he sold our clients."

Something had been bothering me since Bob walked into the room, and I figured this was as good a time as any to ask him about it. Even if he didn't answer my question, he might stop unloading all these memories on me.

"Last night, you left the party. Where did you go? How did the police find you?"

He turned his head back to me, but he didn't say anything. He seemed to be hesitating.

"If you don't mind my asking," I urged.

"Huh, oh no, not at all. But I'm not real proud of what happened last night, of what I did. You see, last night, before the party, Gary and I had a fight. Nothing important. We'd argued over it hundreds of times before. My area of the business was the technical side, his was promotion, performers, and sales. Last night, before the party, he started complaining about what I had done wrong in setting up the party. I got mad."

"I know."

"Huh?"

"I overheard the end of your fight. Someone saw us, told the police I was part of it."

He nodded. "That's why the police think we may be in on this together?"

I nodded.

D. L. Blacker came back into the room and handed Bob a mug of coffee. "Here you go, Bob."

As he went to sit behind his desk, he noticed the newspaper and turned it over. I admit I felt better not having to look at that front-page picture of Gary and my machete.

Bob tried the coffee, put it down, and started to speak in a slow, deliberate voice. "I wanted to talk with you about a couple of things."

Blacker cut him off. "Before you begin, let me point out that although I'm a lawyer, Pat Arnold is not. Under the law, anything you say to me *in his presence* isn't protected under attorney-client privilege."

Bob started to say something, but Blacker cut him off again.

"I should also tell you that although I am your lawyer

64

with regard to your business, the terms of that retainer don't cover representation on criminal matters. Pat has retained me to represent his interests in the whole matter of your brother's untimely death. I would, of course, be more than happy to accept a similar retainer from you, but the lawyer's code of professional responsibility puts certain restraints on an attorney who is approached to represent two or more clients who may have dissimilar interests in a matter."

"That's not a problem," Bob cut in. "Arnold here says that he didn't kill Gary, and I know I didn't, so there's no conflict. We both have the same interest."

I noticed that Bob didn't identify just what that interest was, and I figured I'd do best not to ask. Blacker didn't seem bothered by this oversight either.

"Well," Blacker said, "in that case, I'd be happy to accept a retainer from you, say ten thousand dollars to start. That should be fair."

Bob nodded and pulled a checkbook from his pocket. I did my best not to react. I had just gotten over being upset at having to pay Blacker $350, and here he was taking $10,000 from Bob Johnson for basically the same job. Bob finished writing out the check, ripped it from the book, and handed it across the desk to Blacker. The lawyer's hazel eyes sparkled behind his glasses as he took the check, glanced at it, and set it down on the desk in front of him.

"Before I accept this, let me restate the terms of the retainer. You are giving me this ten thousand dollars as a nonrefundable advance, to represent your interests in regard to the murder of your brother Gary Johnson. You are retaining me with the full understanding that I have already accepted a similar retainer from Pat Arnold, and with the acceptance that if it should develop that your interests conflict, I will advise you to find other counsel. I will continue to hold Mr. Arnold's interests as my primary concern. You accept that?"

Bob nodded, and said, "Yeah, sure."

Blacker smiled, put the check in his desk drawer, got up, and walked over to a computer sitting on a table in the far corner of the room. He turned it on, tapped a few keys on the keyboard, and the printer began to spew out a letter. When it was done, Blacker read it over, returned to his desk, signed it, and passed it to Bob. "I took the liberty of preparing a retainer letter before you arrived. Just now, I filled in the amount and printed it out. If you'll read through the letter and then sign it at the bottom, I think you'll find it accurately spells out the terms I just discussed."

Bob took the letter and signed it. "I never called. How did you know I was coming?"

Blacker took back the signed letter and placed it in his drawer. "Lucky guess."

"It may be callous of me," Bob said, "but I came here to talk about some things besides Gary's murder."

D. L. Blacker nodded and sipped his coffee.

"Now, with Gary dead, I wanted to know the status of our business. You drew up our partnership papers, and I don't really know where I stand. Also, didn't you do Gary's will? I wanted to know the terms of the will. I was his brother, his only living relative—besides Donna, of course—I figure I have a right."

I raised my hand. "Just a second," I said to Bob, "before you get into all that. We were talking about something while Mr. Blacker was in the kitchen. You were about to tell me where you were last night. Before our fates are tied too closely together, I'd like that little bit of information."

Bob didn't seem too pleased with my interruption, but Blacker sat back, sipped at his coffee, and said, "By all means."

"Okay," Bob said. "I left right after the party started. Everything was set up, everything was going smoothly, so I left."

"Donna said normally you would stick around and truck everything out after the party. That that's part of your job."

"Yeah, that's true," he mumbled. "But Gary kept talking like he could do it all himself, so I decided to let him try."

Blacker slid a yellow legal pad from his desk onto his lap, picked up a pen, and leaned back in his chair. "Where did you go?"

"To a bar. Someplace on West Forty-seventh Street. Jimmy Ray's or one of those theatrical hangouts. There were a lot of actors."

"You don't remember where you went?" I asked, a tinge of disbelief in my voice.

"I didn't know I'd have to," he snapped back.

"Please," Blacker interrupted, as he finished jotting a note on his pad, "continue."

Bob slipped me another dark look and then turned to Blacker. "Anyway, I met some girl, we drank until the place closed, and then went back to her place. After a couple of hours I left, went home, and was picked up by the cops."

"What was the girl's name?" Blacker asked. "Have the police spoken to her yet?"

"No." Bob sighed. "I mean I don't know. I don't think so, I didn't tell them her name. I don't think she ever told it to me. It was Bonnie or Betty or something. Some B name."

This was getting too hard to believe. "You mean you don't remember her name either?" I demanded.

"Hey," he said, "I was drunk." His face seemed to brighten for a moment. "Wait, I do remember something."

"Yes?"

Bob's lips twisted into a whimsical smile. "She had incredible breasts."

"That should make her easy to find," I said. "You remember where she lived?"

"Midtown."

"That's it?"

"Look," he exploded, "I've already been over all this with the police. If you don't believe me, go work with them. I don't need to hear this at my own lawyer's. I was drunk, I was depressed over Gary's treatment of the business, and I didn't pay attention, okay? You've got no right to play all high and mighty. It was your machete that was used to kill him. If you hadn't brought it to the party, he'd still be alive right now. Maybe you're the one who used it on him. Maybe you killed my brother."

"If he did," Blacker said, looking at Bob Johnson, "the police will find out."

"If he did," Bob Johnson said, looking at me, "I'll kill him."

Chapter

The phone on Blacker's desk rang again, signaling that the doorman wanted to talk to him. Blacker picked it up, listened for a while, said, "Send him in," hung up the phone, and got to his feet.

"If you'll excuse me a minute," Blacker said and walked from the room.

I felt that I should talk with Bob Johnson, but after his crack about killing me, I didn't feel very loquacious. I got up and started wandering around the office. Blacker's shelves held an eclectic mix of law books, magic paraphernalia, expensive-looking first editions, books on illusions and card manipulation, and file folders jammed with official-looking papers. On a shelf near the desk, wedged between two large legal-looking books, I found a silver ball. About five inches in diameter, I recognized it as the type of sphere magicians use for a classic piece of magic called *Zombie*. It had always been one of my favorite illusions. Although I had seen it dozens of times, I still had no idea how the trick was done. In performing the Zombie, a magician takes a plain metallic ball, balances it on the top edge of a large silk scarf held taught between his hands, and then, as music plays, the ball seems to come alive. Traveling around the scarf and behind the magician's body, the ball moves as though it has a life of its own. I tossed Blacker's ball into the air and caught it. It had a nice, solid heft to it.

A few months back, I had started work on a new type of juggling. I had seen a juggler do it at a nightclub in Greenwich Village, and I was impressed with the beauty and fluidity of the performer's moves. That night, as I left the club, I decided to master this new area of juggling. After three solid months of practice, I was starting to feel comfortable with the technique. Using just one ball, like Blacker's, I would roll the ball across and around my body, balancing it here and there, but never letting it fall to the ground. When done properly, it looked like the ball was held to me by a blend of magnetism and magic.

I dropped Blacker's ball and caught it on the top of my foot. I hopped a few times, getting my balance and passing the ball back and forth from one foot to the other, and then I kicked with my foot, tossing the ball back up to balance on my forehead. I twisted my head to the side, letting the ball roll to my left ear, and then moved my head quickly and the ball rolled across my head and came to rest on my right ear. I centered quickly, staring at the ceiling, and the ball slid to the spot right between my eyes. Blacker's Zombie ball was perfect for this type of juggling, and I started thinking what a great stage routine it could be if Blacker and I performed together, him using the ball for a classic Zombie routine and then tossing it to me for some of this new-wave juggling.

My thoughts were interrupted by the reminder that I was not alone in the office. Bob Johnson cleared his throat and said, "Hey, Arnold, we've got company."

I turned slowly toward the office doorway, the ball balanced on my head. Before I could see who had entered the office, a hand reached over and plucked the ball from my brow. I turned smiling, expecting to see D. L. Blacker. My smile didn't last. The ball was held by a grim-looking Lieutenant Longreen.

Blacker reached around Longreen and took the ball from his oversized hand. "I'll take that, Lieutenant. You wouldn't want to drop it. It might break and release all the magic." Blacker strolled around to his chair, placing the ball back on the shelf as he passed. "Won't you sit down? Pat, you don't mind sitting over there, do you?" He waved a hand in the general direction of the chair by the computer. I walked over to it and sat down, keeping my eyes on Longreen. The lieutenant took the chair I had been using, and leaned in toward the lawyer.

"All right, Blacker," he said. "Get rid of these two, I need some information from you."

Blacker's hazel eyes went to me, to Bob Johnson, and then back to the lieutenant before he spoke. "These two men are my clients. You're sitting in my office, in my home. You came here uninvited, to discuss something of interest to both these men. They will stay."

"You're representing both of them?" Longreen bellowed. "What's with you, Blacker? First Wyman, then Arnold here, and now Johnson. Are you trying to tie up everyone connected with this case? You think this means I'm going to have to give you some special treatment. Or maybe you figure this way you can do some kind of cover-up."

I have to admit, the idea that Blacker was trying to engineer a giant cover-up had crossed *my* mind on more than one occasion.

Longreen let out with one of his low growls and ground his teeth together. "You think you're the belly button of the world just because you've got Wyman in your hip pocket. But I talked to a couple of other people at the D.A.'s office and you're walking on thin ice here, Blacker. You could be disbarred if you keep playing so fast and loose with your clients and the law."

Longreen turned his deep-set gray eyes on me. They seemed darker, more intense than I remembered from the night before. "As for you, Arnold"—he turned to Bob—"and you, Johnson, if either of you is guilty, I'm going to nail you and get enough evidence for a conviction, no matter who you've got for a lawyer. But if you're innocent, I've got some friendly advice for you. You should each get yourselves an attorney who isn't so likely to get you convicted and then end up in the next cell." Longreen stood up, threw Blacker a look that could wilt spinach, and started from the room.

Blacker didn't seem upset at this attack on his integrity. Maybe as a lawyer he was used to it. He watched Longreen cross the room and then used his voice, cold and deep as the bottom of the Hudson River, to stop the lieutenant at the door. "Before you go running off, Lieutenant, didn't you say you needed some information from me? You've got a real interesting way of asking for help."

Longreen slowly turned and I thought I saw the beginnings of a twitch at the corner of his left eye. By the time he faced Blacker he had collected his thoughts and calmed down a little. "The will," he said, "I came to get Gary Johnson's will."

First the brother and now the police; there was a lot of interest in that will. I looked at Bob Johnson, but he didn't say anything.

D. L. Blacker smiled at Lieutenant Longreen and said, "Sorry, Lieutenant, I'm afraid I can't help you."

Longreen lost his temper again. "That wasn't a request, Blacker. This is a murder investigation. You're holding evidence in a murder investigation and I'm telling you to give it to me."

"Lieutenant, please, sit down." Longreen remained standing, and after a moment, the lawyer shrugged and continued.

"We seem to be fighting all the time, and that's really not my intention. Obviously you want to know what's in the will because it may indicate a motive for Gary's murder. This doesn't entitle you to have the actual will. You need to know what's in the will. You don't really need the will itself. I do. As the estate's lawyer, I'll need to submit the signed original of the document to the probate court."

Longreen started to object. Blacker silenced him with a wave of his hand and continued talking. "Regardless, you seem to have a legitimate reason to want to read through the contents of the will. However, I can't show you the original will, because it's in a safety deposit box."

Longreen leaned over D. L. Blacker's desk and thrust his face at the lawyer. "Don't feed me that crock. I had a crew at Gary Johnson's bank first thing this morning with a court order. They opened his safety deposit box and there was no will—a lot of other papers, but no will."

"I didn't say it was in *his* box. I said in *a* box. It happens to be in mine. It's a service I provide for many of my clients. Look, Lieutenant, I'll say it again. I'm not trying to fight you on this. Clearly you have a right to know what's in that will. I'll tell you what. We'll be having a formal reading of the will to the heirs, tomorrow at one o'clock in the afternoon. Why don't you come then?"

Longreen straightened up but continued to glare at D. L. Blacker. The twitch in his left eye was now noticeable. "Don't think I won't," he growled, and stormed from the room. A few moments later I heard and felt the front door open and slam shut.

Bob Johnson exhaled and rubbed his hands over his bloodshot eyes. "God, I hate that man." He shook his head and looked at Blacker, who had picked up the phone and was dialing a number.

"Wyman, please," he said into the phone, and flashed Bob a sympathetic smile. "Jim, D. L. here. . . . Sure, we're still on for lunch, say one o'clock at that Mexican place with the great frozen margaritas. Maybe neither of us will go back to work. Jim, the reason I called, I hear that Longreen opened Gary's safe deposit box this morning. I'm going to be the executor of the estate. Can you get me a copy of the inventory from that box? I'll need it for the probate court. Thanks a lot. I'll see you at one. Lunch is on me. No, really, I'll just bill it to one of my clients. See you then." He hung up the phone and spoke to Bob. "Congratulations, you just offered to pay for an assistant D.A.'s lunch."

Bob Johnson didn't smile. "One o'clock tomorrow then, for the reading of Gary's will?"

D. L. Blacker chuckled, shook his head, and pulled open a drawer of his desk. "I suppose so. I mean I promised Longreen a will reading, so we'll have to have one. In the meantime, here's a copy if you want to look it over." He pulled an envelope from his desk and tossed it to Bob.

I didn't understand, and I said so. "You told the lieutenant that the will was in your safety deposit box."

"I said the *original* of the will was in the box. It is. This is a copy. This morning I went through my Gary Johnson file and pulled out the important papers. I always keep a copy of the will in a client's file."

"Should Bob be seeing it? Before the formal reading, I mean."

Blacker smiled and shook his head again. "I never understood why in the movies they always have a formal reading of the will at the lawyer's office. No law requires it and no one really likes waiting to hear what they're going to get. I've always called the heirs on the phone and told them what to expect. It's easier, quicker, and I don't have to deal with a lot of grieving relatives, here, in my home. Ah, well, when you're through with that, Bob, give it back, and tomorrow, act surprised when I tell you what you're getting."

Bob just nodded and continued to read through the will. It wasn't very long. He quickly finished it and looked up. "I don't understand, this leaves everything to Donna. I'm not mentioned at all."

Blacker looked at him and then reached into his desk for another paper. "When you and Gary went into partnership, you signed an agreement." He raised the new document and then set it down in front of him. "This partnership agreement contains a buy-out provision. If either party dies, the surviving partner has the right to take over the whole business. In other words, Donna has to sell you Gary's interest in the company. There's also a section indicating that you and Gary took out half a million dollars in mutual life insurance. There'll be some paperwork involved, and a small payment to Donna, but basically Gary's death has brought you half a million dollars and sole ownership of your company. Congratulations."

Bob Johnson started to stand up, and then plopped back down in his chair. He looked like he wasn't capable of putting words together into a coherent sentence, so I spoke to Blacker.

"Didn't he know about this stuff? He signed the agreement, didn't he?"

"Happens all the time," said Blacker. "Nobody really reads the things they sign, and those who do usually forget what was in them the moment they leave my office. My notes indicate that Gary came up with most of the provisions for the partnership agreement."

Bob Johnson slowly stood up, checking his balance on the arm of the chair. Finally he was erect. "I think I'll go over to Donna's now. She probably needs some help with the funeral arrangements, and whatever."

Blacker stood. "Good idea, Bob. Why don't you give me a call later." Blacker walked from behind his desk and led

Bob from the office. As he walked him toward the door I heard him say, "And don't forget to be here at one o'clock tomorrow."

The door opened and closed. Blacker was gone for a few minutes, and when he returned he had filled his ever-present coffee cup. "Okay, Pat, your turn. Get comfortable." I moved back to the plush high-backed client's chair I had previously occupied, and settled into it.

"I've noticed," he said, "that you have quite a remarkable memory. We're going to put it to the test. I have two hours until I have to leave for my lunch with the assistant D.A. During that time I want you to tell me everything that you've seen, everything you've heard, every contact you've had with everyone connected with this case. The way things are going, I think there's only one way I can protect all the innocent people connected with this—including myself."

I looked at him, but didn't speak.

"I'm going to have to tell Lieutenant Longreen who killed Gary Johnson."

Chapter

NINE

I felt my heart stop. "You know who killed Gary? Who? Why haven't you already told the police? Why—"

D. L. Blacker stopped my rush of words by holding up his hand. "No," he quietly said. "I don't know who killed him . . . yet. But I will. I'm going to catch Gary Johnson's killer and you're going to help me."

I looked at him and nodded my head several times. I felt like I had been hypnotized. "What can I do?"

Blacker took the yellow legal pad and a pen from his desk and leaned back in his chair. I heard it creak as he shifted around and found a comfortable position. "Just what I said. Tell me everything. I'll listen and take notes. Tell me everything about everyone even remotely connected with last night. Don't assume that anything is unimportant. I'll probably stop you and ask questions. Don't be offended if I ask you about something you've already told me. I may need clarification, okay?"

"Okay."

"Then let's begin."

And with that I began what was to become a regular practice. I reported to D. L. Blacker everything I did and saw, everyone I met and talked to that was connected with this case. I started way back with my first introduction to Gary Johnson. I talked about working other jobs with Pamela Lockheed, the psychic, and Andy Costello, the disc jockey. I told him about being hired for the job. I wasn't going to go over my meeting with him, but he asked me to. Maybe he was testing my recollections against his. I told him about everything that happened in the dressing room and in the main party room when I went out there before the party. I talked almost nonstop for the full two hours. When D. L. Blacker had to leave for his lunch, I was only up to the beginning of the MegaBank party, and from the looks of it, Blacker had already filled his entire legal pad with notes.

"We'll stop here," he said, "but I'll need the rest. Why don't you come back after dinner? Say, about eight o'clock tonight?" Blacker stood up and walked from the room. He didn't really wait to hear whether or not the time was convenient for me.

"Sure," I muttered to his back as I followed him into the hall. "Say," I said with an enthusiasm I didn't really feel, as he stopped at a mirror to straighten his tie and adjust his suit jacket, "is there anything I can do between now and tonight? Anything I can do to help?"

He turned to me and smiled. "Pat, I appreciate the offer, really, but the best thing you can do is just go home or to a movie or something. Your particular skills aren't really suited to what needs to be done, at this point."

I hated the way he said *your particular skills.* Like I was a secretary who wasn't getting the job because I couldn't take dictation. I was tired and frustrated and I wasn't going to be told to *just go home* by anyone. I realized that Blacker was an exceptional person who was trying to help me out of a bad situation, but I wasn't used to letting other people fight my battles. Sure, Blacker had more experience dealing with police and the law and even with murder, but there must have been something I could do to help, and I told him so, passionately.

His smile turned into a grin and he slapped me on the back. "You want to help? Dig around and see what you can find." He started toward the door.

"That's it? Dig around? See what I can find?"

He was at the front of the apartment. He opened the door and allowed me to pass. I stopped in the hallway and waited for an answer to my question. "I have a feeling you might be a good digger" was all he said.

I wanted more, and told him so. "What am I looking for?"

He smiled, said, "Evidence," and walked past me. I watched as he strode through the lobby and out of the building.

I found a chair in the lobby and sat down to think. I didn't think about whether I could trust Blacker. I'd spent too much time thinking about that in the last fifteen hours and I still didn't have an answer. I knew I liked him, but I still wasn't sure if I should trust him. I didn't think about going to Longreen. Him, I knew I didn't like. And while I may not have felt entirely secure with Blacker, he rated several points above the lieutenant on my personal trust scale. I didn't have any new information for the police anyway, and the only thing Longreen really wanted to hear from me was a confession. I didn't think about hiring another lawyer. I couldn't afford one. I'd just given my last $350, money that should have been used to pay this month's rent on my hellhole of an apartment, to Blacker.

There were lots of things I didn't think about. But, ultimately, when I got over my anger at Blacker for not giving me more direction, there was only one thing left in my mind. How could I help him. Where could I *dig around*, as he had said. I mulled it over for a while, and then reached in my pocket, pulled out a quarter, walked out of the building and over to a pay phone on the corner. I put in the quarter and dialed a number. I have a good memory for telephone numbers too. After three rings, she answered.

"Hello, Pamela Lockheed here." She sounded like she had just woken up.

"Hello," I said in my cheeriest and most likable voice. "Pat Arnold here. How're you doing, Pam?"

"What time is it?"

I looked at my watch. "Twelve thirty," I said.

"Day or night time?"

"Day."

"In that case I could be doing better. You left early last night, didn't you? They kept us there until four o'clock in the morning. I didn't get to bed until just a few hours ago. You want something, Pat?"

"I thought maybe you'd like to get together and compare notes on what happened last night. You know, kind of put our heads together."

"Pat, there is no one in the world I'd rather put my head together with than you. But, I assure you, the way I look right now you wouldn't want to be anywhere near my head."

Using all the charm and persuasive powers I could muster, I protested and disagreed, until finally she stopped me.

"Listen, tiger, if you want me that bad, I'm yours. Come on over. But give me half an hour to pull myself together, okay?"

"Sure," I said. "Where do you live?"

She gave me her address, on Hudson Street near Christopher in the Village, and I said that I'd see her soon. As I

80

went to hang up the phone I heard her call my name. I put the receiver back to my ear.

"Yes?" I asked.

"Stop on the corner and pick up some fresh-squeezed orange juice, okay?"

"Sure," I said.

"Thanks, you're a dear." And she hung up.

I cradled the receiver and reached into my pocket for another quarter. I had a few minutes to kill before I started for Pam's place, so I thought I could do a little more digging. I'd show Blacker that his feeling about me was right, that I did have a talent for rooting out useful information. I called information and asked for the number of Andy Costello. Luckily there was only one Andy Costello in Manhattan, and the mechanical operator's voice read off his number. I dropped my quarter into the slot and pushed the seven numbers.

After one ring an answering machine picked up. Music started playing, something with a heavy beat. After a few seconds the music got quieter and Andy's deep, mellifluous voice came on. "Hi, Andy Costello here. I didn't answer the phone because I already know why you called. You think I'm a great disc jockey, you wish you could listen to me all the time, wherever you go, and you want me to perform at your next affair or social function. Well, right now I'm off doing something more interesting and probably more fun than talking to you on the phone. But if you want to hire me, leave a message on this answering machine and I'll call you back." **BEEP**.

I never did like those cutesy messages. I always figured that if you have a stupid message on your machine, you deserve to get stupid messages left for you. So I disguised my voice and said, "This is Sergeant Sheski. We met last night. I think you're a great disc jockey. I even picked up a tape of your greatest hits and I carry it with me all the time, wherever I go. Anyway, I plan to win the lottery this week, and when I do, I want you to spin records at my retirement party. Why don't you give me a call?" Then I hung up.

I walked to the express IRT subway stop at Ninety-sixth Street and Broadway, and took the stairs down into the bowels of the earth. The number 2 downtown express train was pulling into the station as I reached the platform. I jumped in and sat down across from two very affectionate teenagers who seemed to be permanently joined at the lips. I found myself wondering if they would come up for air before the train reached the Fourteenth Street stop. They didn't.

I got out and checked my watch. I was still early. To get to Pamela's apartment, I could have either transferred at Fourteenth Street to a local train and taken it one stop, or just gone up to the street right there, and walked an extra few blocks. I decided to walk. On the way, I picked up the fresh-squeezed orange juice. It cost about seven times more than Tropicana and used up the rest of what little cash I had left. I got to Pamela's place right on time.

She lived in a medium-sized, art-deco building. She didn't have a doorman, but there was a complicated intercom system with two separate doors through which I had to be buzzed. An elevator whisked me to the top floor of the seven-story building, and she opened her door the moment I knocked.

I remembered what she had said about needing time to pull herself together, and smiled. She looked terrific. She was dressed in a short, red, silky kimono, knotted at the waist, but covering very little. It was partially open in the front, making it clear that she wore nothing underneath. Her long blond hair was piled on her head, strands hanging down to create a perfectly formed image of disarray. She smiled and asked me in. Her apartment was larger than mine, what New Yorkers' call an alcove studio. A large unmade bed filled the alcove off to one side. An overstuffed sofa was against one wall and a small writing desk against the other. The shades were drawn and what little light there was in the apartment came from two strategically placed table lamps. The bulbs in the lamps must have been colored a subtle shade of pink, because the entire room and everything in it seemed to share this common coloring. It reminded me of dubarry pink, the color of a special gel used in theatrical lighting. In a stagecraft course I took in college, I learned that actresses often insisted that their scenes be lit with dubarry pink because it hid any little blemishes and imperfections of the skin. I don't know if it was a good color for me, but it made Pamela look ever better. I suspect she knew this.

She closed the door and double-locked it, giving me a look packed with what might have been suggestive meanings; it was hard to tell in the low light of the room. She slinked over to me, took the orange juice, gave me a little push so I fell back onto the sofa, and said, "Get comfortable." I did.

She walked through a small arch into what I guessed to be the kitchen.

"You want coffee?" she asked from the other room. "I could put some on."

"No," I answered, "thanks."

She walked out through the arch with two glasses and the juice. I slid over on the couch, but she sat down right next to me. I was very aware of the entire length of her thigh pressed tight against mine. I think I mentioned it before; she has great legs. She poured juice into the glasses and handed me one.

Slowly, in one long continuous swallow, she drank down a full glass of juice. Then she smiled, ran her tongue slowly over her lips, and refilled her glass. "I don't drink coffee," she said, "but I know some people like it in the morning. I prefer fresh orange juice. There's something very sensual about fresh orange juice, don't you think? I love it first thing when I wake up, or right before I go back to bed." She locked her eyes with mine and drained her glass again.

"The O.J. is great," I said. "I feel like I've put down enough coffee lately to float a battleship."

Pamela laughed, a deep, full-throated laugh, and put her glass down on the coffee table in front of us. She stretched, causing her kimono to open a little farther and slide up her thighs a few inches more. When she brought her arms down, her left hand came to rest behind me and she started playing with the hair on the back of my head.

"That's right, you've been hanging around with Blacker, haven't you?" She laughed that great laugh again. "I admit, I find him fascinating. There was a time I would have welcomed the chance to make his morning coffee, but he wasn't interested. I guess he's still carrying a torch for his wife."

"He's married?"

"Well, he was. Not anymore. His wife's dead or something." She moved her hand from my hair to the back of my neck and started tracing little circles. I don't know how she knew to do that, but it always drives me nuts.

"Let's not talk about D. L. Blacker. It's depressing. Let me see your hands."

She took both my hands in hers and turned them over, so the palms were up. Without taking her eyes from mine she said,. "Left-handed or right?"

"Right," I said. "Why?"

"I'm going to tell your future."

She placed my left hand on her knee, and gave it a squeeze. Then she smiled at me and bent over my right hand, giving me an open view down the front of her kimono. I didn't know if she could tell me about the long term, but my immediate future was certainly looking brighter.

"I see upheaval in your life, major changes."

It didn't take a fortune teller to see that. Hell, anyone with forty cents for the morning paper knew my life was in turmoil.

"Including," she continued, "a change of address. Are you planning a move?"

She had my attention. In New York City, finding a cheap apartment—the only kind I could afford—was about as easy as finding a good agent. You knew there were a few of them out there, but if you ever found yourself with one, you weren't likely to go looking for a change. If I was going to move, I thought, it wasn't going to be my choice. So, if she was right, where was I going to move? The answer that rolled into my mind caused me to squeeze Pamela's knee. She viewed the squeeze as encouragement. It wasn't. It was panic. The only forced move I could envision was the one I never wanted to take—to jail. I said nothing, and Pam, no doubt encouraged by my hand clasped to her knee, continued.

"I see a beautiful woman coming into your life. Someone you want, someone you desire." She held my right hand in her right hand, her left hand having once again settled behind my neck. Her fingers, playing with my hair, traced little electric circles that vibrated down my spine. "I see the two of you in bed together, I see very passionate lovemaking."

She leaned closer and placed her lips by my ear. "But I can't tell who you're with. . . ." She kissed my ear. "Any ideas?" She kissed it again.

I know how in books and movies whenever a scene like this starts playing, they describe it as *steamy*, and the people doing it are always getting *hot*. For me, though, ever since I was thirteen and Susan Fields taught me how to French-kiss on a musty couch in her parents' basement, I've reacted differently. As long as I can remember, whenever I find myself alone with a beautiful woman (and, on occasion, some that were not so beautiful), if I think about sex with that woman, I get cold chills. Since it's difficult to have sex without first thinking about it, many of my sexual experiences have been preceded by a period of shivering and teeth chattering while trying hard to keep all of this hidden from the woman—with varying degrees of success.

I guess women find me attractive. Maybe it's because I've always *loved* the opposite sex. My happiest memories of growing up in Texas are filled with admiring the women around me. The way they looked, the way they smelled. I've always felt that women should be treated special because they *are* special. Maybe, subconsciously, I've always felt that women were to be admired from a respectful distance; to be looked at but not touched. That would explain my shivering. As I said, however, women seem to find me attractive, so I've often ended up close enough for my thoughts to turn to sex and my uncontrollable shivering to take over. The women rarely seemed to notice my chills, or at least they were kind enough not to mention them or aroused enough not to let them get in the way. Anyway, Pamela didn't seem to mind. Her tongue was in my ear and she was making little noises that seemed to start way back in her throat.

Somehow, I forced myself to remember that I was there to dig around and see what I could find out about Gary's murder, so I reluctantly pulled my ear away from her and pushed my newly disclosed future to the back of my mind. Then I put my glass down on the table, stopped the chattering of my teeth by thinking good, clean, businesslike thoughts, and turned to face her.

She was waiting for me. She pressed her body against me, draped one of her legs over mine, and gave me an open-mouth kiss that dissolved all of my good intentions and left me shivering clear down to my toes. I responded, returning her kiss, first slowly and then with more passion. I forgot about digging for information and stopped noticing whether I was shaking or not. I did notice that with a little help from my left hand, her robe had fallen completely open. I traced the line of her throat, first lightly with a finger and then more generously with my lips and tongue. I stopped here and there to leave a little kiss as I traveled downward toward the perfect V at the base of her throat. The little noises began again and she closed her eyes and leaned back on the sofa. My lips, moving slowly down her body, reached her breasts. I already held her right breast, stroking it lightly with the fingers of my left hand. I moved my mouth to it and began sucking slowly and rhythmically on the nipple, pulling it in and out between my slightly parted front teeth. She gasped and opened her eyes, placing her hands in my hair. She clutched me against her for a moment and then pulled me away and turned my head up to look into her eyes. "Come on," she whispered, and pulled me up from the couch.

As she stood, her silky kimono dropped to the floor and her body seemed enveloped in a warm glow, the low, pink lighting working a sensual magic across her slightly freckled skin. When I had seen her naked before, in dressing rooms, preparing for jobs, I had always tried to look away. I had worked hard at not appearing too interested. Now I had no such inhibition and I openly admired her. She really did have a great body. She molded herself against my side, slid her hand down the front of my pants, and smiled. "Come on," she said again, and pulled me toward the bed.

In traveling the ten feet that separated the couch and the bed, Pamela managed to remove my shirt, shoes, and pants.

I suspect I helped. We fell onto the bed with such force that I thought it might collapse. It didn't.

She pulled away for a moment to take a deep breath of air, let it out in a whoosh, and said, "How about losing the underwear?"

I yanked off my socks, threw them into the room, and pulled down my briefs. They became tangled on my feet, and I damn near dislocated one of my little toes before I managed to free myself from them. The exertion cooled me off enough to remember why I had come to Pamela's in the first place. I lay back on the bed.

Pam rolled over to me, slid one of her long legs over mine, placed one of her arms across my chest, and began nuzzling my neck with her face. "Mmmmm," she said.

I kissed the top of her head. "Pamela?"

"Mmmm hmmmm?"

"Last night, at the party, did you have a steady line of people waiting to have their fortunes told, or were there periods when you were just sitting alone in that little moon, waiting for someone to come in?"

She slowly undraped herself and pulled away from me on the bed. "There was plenty of time that I just sat there alone. Why?"

"When you were sitting there alone, was the door to the moon open or closed?"

"Why?"

"Well, if you were sitting in the moon alone, with the door closed, when Gary was being murdered, there isn't anyone from the party who can testify that you were there. Did you maybe slip off to the bathroom or something for a couple of minutes?"

She jerked upright on the bed, fried me with her eyes, and hissed out, "You bastard!"

"Huh?" I said, relying on my snappy comeback for all occasions.

Pamela wasn't impressed. "What the hell are you trying to do?" she yelled as she jumped out of the bed. "Is that why you came over here? To try to prove that I was involved in Gary's death? To get your own ass off the line? You shit!"

She must have realized that she was standing there naked, because she paused for a moment, pulled the sheet from the bed, and wrapped it quickly around herself. Unfortunately for me, the sheet had been my only covering. I found myself lying naked on her bed, while she towered over me, once again screaming at me. "You insensitive cocksucker. You motherfucking son of a bitch. Why do I always end up with assholes, why?"

I didn't think she really wanted me to answer her question. I scrambled out of her bed and grabbed for my clothes as she continued to spew insults at me. Any attempt I made to quiet her was met with a new stream of invective. Discretion got the better part of valor and I decided to cut short my visit. I pulled on my pants as I hopped past the sofa and got my last shoe on as she slammed the door behind me.

I stood in the quiet of the hallway and caught my breath. The hall was quiet, but not silent. I could still hear Pamela in her apartment, stomping around and occasionally throwing things. One of those things broke loudly against the apartment door and I decided that a further retreat was in order. I crossed over to the elevator and jabbed at the down button several times.

Maybe, I thought as I waited for the elevator to get there, I could have handled that a little better. Sure, I had come to Pamela's to try to get information from her. Things had taken an unexpected but pleasant detour, but I should have been a little more subtle in trying to get the conversation back on track; or perhaps just waited until later to broach the subject. What had I learned? Pamela may have had an opportunity to slip away and kill Gary. Anything else? Besides, of course, that Pamela Lockheed has a small mole on her left hip. No. Maybe Blacker hadn't been right, after all. Maybe I wasn't so good at digging. The elevator finally arrived, and I stepped inside. As the door closed and I started the slow descent toward the main floor, I found myself wondering if Blacker was having more luck with Wyman than I had had with Pamela. I laughed out loud. "I hope not," I said to no one as the door opened and I stepped into the lobby. I laughed again and walked from the building.

In the subway, heading uptown, I checked my watch. There were still several hours before I was due back at Blacker's apartment, so when I got out of the subway at Ninety-sixth Street and Broadway, I walked one block south, turned the corner, and went home.

As I opened the door to my apartment a depression hit me like a bowl of lime Jell-O. Perhaps, I thought, it was my body complaining that it hadn't been allowed to finish what had been so pleasantly and promisingly started. Or, perhaps it was just that all I'd put in my stomach that day was orange juice and coffee. Then again maybe it was the ongoing tension of being a prime suspect in a murder case.

I took a step into my apartment and looked around. Although it was the middle of the afternoon, my apartment, with its sole grimy window looking onto a small airshaft, was steeped in gloom. A writer for *Cosmopolitan* with whom I had enjoyed a short relationship had dubbed it "the land of eternal twilight." I flicked the wall switch for the overhead light. A flash exploded from the ceiling, followed by a loud pop, and then darkness returned. "Great," I mumbled to myself, "the light burned out, I don't have another bulb, and I've no money to buy one."

My stomach started to rumble so I groped my way over to the kitchenette, carefully opened the refrigerator, and was grateful to see that that light was still working. I took out a loaf of Wonder Bread that might have been celebrating its six-month anniversary in my apartment, but thanks to better eating through chemicals, it still felt as fresh as the day I bought it. There were no veggies in the vegetable bin, at least none that hadn't already completed the process of autodigestion, but there was a lump of mystery cheese. I managed to scrape off most of the mold, and what was left fit neatly between two slices of the bread. A dab of Miracle Whip and I had a meal fit for someone in my then-current state of mind. A depressing meal for a despondent individual. I replaced the bread and Miracle Whip. The way things were going for me, dinner the next day might have to be Miracle Whip sandwiches. I ate the sandwich, turned on the television, lay back on my bed, and did what wretched people have been doing for years. I fell asleep with the TV on.

I awoke with a terrible headache, a bad taste in my mouth, and Vanna White on the tube. I read my watch by the light of the TV. A quarter of eight, it said. How long had I slept? I used some of my newly developing deductive powers. The room was even darker than normal, and "Wheel of Fortune" didn't come on in the early morning; therefore, I reasoned, it was P.M., not A.M. Bully for me.

I remembered my appointment with D. L. Blacker and forced myself to sit up. My headache moved from the back to the front of my head, and I shuffled, ever so slowly, to the bathroom medicine cabinet for aspirin. I shook four into my hand, replaced the bottle, and turned on the water in the sink. I waited impatiently as it trickled from the faucet—first black, then red, and finally relatively clear. I filled my glass, threw back the aspirin, and sipped the water. Every time I drank the water in my bathroom, I was reminded of the study a few years back when they named New York City water the best in the world. Clearly they hadn't sampled it from my apartment. I looked again at my watch, and then looked at myself in the cracked mirror over the sink. I'd have to rush if I was going to arrive at Blacker's on time, but I clearly needed to clean up first. I turned on the shower, stripped off my clothes, stepped in, and soaped myself up. I was starting to feel better. Any bathroom, even that one, always made me feel better.

After the shower I dried myself off, stepped over my old clothes still lying on the bathroom floor, left the door to the john open, and by the light of the bathroom found clean clothes, dressed, and turned off the TV. Then I opened the front door, went back, turned off the bathroom light, and followed the light from the hallway out of my apartment.

The night was cool and I ran to Blacker's without working up a sweat. The doorman was standing outside, talking to the driver of a limo parked in front of the building. It was Roberto and I guess he recognized me; he just waved me through into the lobby, and I was soon knocking on Blacker's door.

After a short wait Blacker answered the door, smiled, said he was glad to see me, and that I should come in.

I followed him down the hall, into the office, and stopped. Donna Johnson was sitting in the chair I had filled earlier that day.

If it's possible for someone to look great and awful at the same time, Donna did. Her hair was mussed and had lost the sheen it radiated the night before. She was pale as death, and the little makeup she wore stood out in garish contrast. Her face seemed to have drawn in, with the result that as I looked at her, all I seemed able to focus on were her cheekbones and her eyes. The skin over her cheekbones seemed to be pulled taut, straining against some invisible tension. Her eyes looked enormous, pale blue, clear and filled with a pain and lost-puppy quality that made me want to put my arms gently around her and promise that everything was going to be all right. I didn't. I mumbled a greeting and sat in the other client chair.

Blacker sat down behind his desk, picked up some papers, glanced at them, set them down again, inhaled, and started talking. "Donna, I should go over those papers tonight. I think you should head on home, and then send the driver back up here with them, okay?"

"Okay, sure," she said without a great deal of enthusiasm. Then, apparently struck by an idea she liked more than Blacker's, she perked up a bit and, in an unsure voice, asked, "If you two don't have anything planned for right now, uh, Pat, do you think, maybe you could ride with me downtown, to my place, and then bring the papers back? I'd really appreciate it. I have a car outside."

I loved the idea, but what I said was "D. L.?"

"Of course," he said. "Certainly. When you get back, we can continue from where we left off this afternoon."

"Sure," I said. After all, what else could I say?

"Great." Blacker smiled a politician's smile as he stood up.

Donna looped the straps of her large bag over her shoulder and stood up too. I guessed it was time to leave.

We all walked to Blacker's door. He gave Donna a kiss on the cheek, shook my hand, told me to hurry back, and closed the door as we walked out.

We passed through the lobby in silence. I didn't know what to say, and Donna didn't seem to want to talk. As we approached the front of the lobby I held back and allowed Donna to exit before me. She stepped quickly to the limo.

The driver opened the back door and touched the brim of his hat as Donna stepped in and slid over on the plush seat. I followed her and the driver shut the door behind me.

"Nice car," I said, admiring the television, stereo, and full wet bar spread out between us and the tinted window that was silently rising, discreetly blocking off our view of the driver, and his view of us.

"Thank you," she said absently, and then seemed to blush and turned toward me. "Oh, it's not ours, or mine, rather. It's from one of those limousine services. D. L. says I can afford it and I just didn't want to have to deal with flagging down taxis and stuff for a couple of days."

She looked at me with eyes that still held all the pain and hurt, but also seemed to beg for understanding, and maybe even forgiveness.

"I understand," I said. And I did. Amazing, the power of the human mind when attached to the heart. There I was, feeling sorry for a woman who was driving around in a chauffeur-driven stretch limo, understanding that she didn't want to deal with flagging down taxis, and at home, I couldn't afford to change a lightbulb.

Donna brightened a little. Seeing this, so did I.

"The papers that you're coming to get," she began, talking slowly, as though she were carefully considering the use of each word, "are from the funeral home. They need to be signed before tomorrow's. . . . I thought they were okay, but D. L. said I shouldn't sign anything that he didn't. . . . I'm sorry to put you out. I could have just sent them back with the driver. I guess I've been feeling so alone. Not just since . . . but for a long time. And I feel so comfortable with you. It's like you're. . . ."

She seemed to be having a lot of trouble finishing sentences. "It's fine, really."

"Will you be coming to the funeral?"

I hadn't given it a thought. I didn't really like funerals. I hadn't really liked Gary Johnson. "Of course, I'll be there."

"Thank you." Donna rummaged around in her oversized shoulder bag and pulled out a cassette tape. "Is it okay if I put on some music?"

"Sure, of course."

She pushed the cassette into the car's tape player, and soft, gentle music flowed from speakers strategically hidden around us. After a few bars I recognized it as "Suite for Flute and Jazz Piano," the recording by Jean-Pierre Rampal and Claude Bolling.

Neither of us spoke for the rest of the trip. Donna sat, clutching her bag, staring out the window. I checked out the wet bar, found that it had everything you could want, so long as all you wanted was scotch and soda, and fixed myself a drink. Then I sat back and gazed at the back of her head.

Donna lived in a Soho loft. We pulled up in front of the building and the driver opened the back door. I got out, followed by Donna, who told the driver, "Please wait, Mr. Arnold will be going back uptown."

We went into the building and Donna led me up the stairs to the second floor.

"We have the whole floor," she said as she unlocked several locks. "It's pretty big. I'm not sure if I'll keep living here or not."

She slid the door open, stepped inside, and flicked a switch. As light flooded the large open space from industrial-style fixtures, high overhead, Donna gasped. The place looked like a tornado had plowed through it. Books had been pulled from the shelves, furniture was overturned, the contents of drawers were thrown about, and her stereo and cassette tapes were strewn all over the loft.

To tell the truth, it seemed a lot like my apartment, every day of the week. But judging from Donna's reaction, this was not how she expected her place to look. She started into the room and I reached out my hand, grabbed her arm, and whispered, "Wait, they may still be here."

She nodded and backed out the door. I began moving quickly around the apartment. There weren't many places to hide. It was basically one huge room, with an end closed off for a kitchen and a hall leading, I guessed, to a bathroom. I looked under the bed, nothing; in closets, empty; in the kitchen, all clear. I started quickly and quietly down the hallway to the bathroom, my eyes riveted to the closed door at the end of the hall. I stepped on glass and froze as the sound of splinters crunching and grinding under foot echoed in the hall, bouncing off the walls and announcing my approach to anyone hiding in the bathroom. I forced myself to breathe again, looked over and saw a broken window. That was how he or they got in and, I hoped, out again. Finally, I stood before the bathroom door. I took a deep breath, let it out, took another and flung open the door. No one.

I let the breath out and stepped into the bathroom. It was nice, lots of tile, a full wall of mirrors, a double sink, and a big old-fashioned tub/shower.

The curtain to the shower was drawn, and I figured I'd better open it to do a complete check, before I went back and told Donna it was safe to come into her apartment. I strode over to the tub, pushed back the curtain, and, for a brief moment, caught a glimpse of someone dressed all in black, with a ski mask over his face and a big flashlight raised high in the air. He brought the flashlight down on my head, hard. As I dropped to the floor he ran out past me. I thought about Donna having to face him. I thought that I should be out there to protect her, and then I thought of nothing for a long, long time.

Chapter

TEN

I heard voices and tried to open my eyes. The light that jabbed between my lashes cut like a knife through the back of my brain and a wave of nausea swept over me. I squeezed my eyes shut and considered whether vomiting would make me feel any better. The sound of Donna's voice talking quietly with someone convinced me not to find out. Some deep-seated macho sensibility buried at the bottom of my mind argued that it was better to avoid throwing up in front of someone as attractive as Donna Johnson.

Without opening my eyes, I transferred my focus from the pain that seemed to reside, in one form or another, in every nook and cranny of my body to my surroundings. I was lying on something soft, probably a bed, but not in a hospital. There was no smell of antiseptic. What felt like a wet towel was clinging to my forehead. My brain started to work again, so I used it to figure out that whoever Donna was talking to must have moved me to her bed. I admit that in the back of my mind I had hoped to end up in her bed someday, but not like this.

I tried opening my eyes again. The pain and nausea returned, but this time I was ready for them. I fought back and they retreated until it wasn't quite so bad. The effort caused me to groan, and Donna stopped talking. My eyes weren't quite focusing, but I could see that Donna and someone else had come over to the side of the bed.

"Are you awake?" Donna asked, concern and tender fear vibrating in those three words.

I croaked out a "yes," and she took the wet towel off my head and replaced it with another. This one felt cold and refreshing. It chased away some of the pain that had settled into the nooks and crannies of my brain.

My eyes finally focused and what I saw made me want to close them again and roll over. Standing next to Donna was Lieutenant Longreen. He seemed impatient.

"All right, Arnold, who was it?"

I started to smile, but the pain turned it into a grimace. "A little out of your line isn't it, Lieutenant? Aren't you homicide?"

Longreen growled.

"Or did you hear it was me that got clobbered and just hoped you'd be needed?"

"Can it, Arnold. You and Mrs. Johnson here are tied up in a murder investigation. This burglary, your getting hit, it could be a coincidence, but I don't believe in coincidences when I'm working on a murder case."

"Say, Lieutenant, do you always talk in clichés, or do I just bring out the best in you?"

He growled again. "This doesn't let you off the hook, Arnold. You're still my prime suspect, so don't get cute."

I nodded, and felt my brain slosh around inside my skull. I wish he hadn't said that about my being the prime suspect, at least not in front of Donna.

Longreen pulled a chair over to the side of the bed, sat

down, and took out a small notebook. "Now, describe the person who attacked you."

"Didn't Donna tell you?"

"I'm asking *you*."

"Right." I closed my eyes and instantly felt much better. I knew I couldn't keep the lieutenant closed out forever, and his gravelly voice soon cut through my self-imposed darkness. "Come on, Arnold, let's get on with it."

"Right," I said again and opened my eyes to light, pain, and Lieutenant Longreen. "The person who hit me was dressed all in black with a black ski mask. I don't know who it was."

"How tall was he?"

"I only saw him for an instant, when I pulled open the shower curtain. He was standing in the tub." I thought for a moment. "I didn't look down at him, so I guess he was at least my height. I'm an inch over six foot."

Longreen got up and walked to the bathroom. He was in it for a few minutes and then returned.

"He might have been shorter than you. The tub is raised off the ground." Longreen chewed on the tail end of his pencil; the eraser had long since been gnawed away. "Are you sure it was a man?"

"Well, sure," I started and then stopped. Longreen had a point. "I don't know," I admitted. "I thought it was a man, but only because he was dressed in man's clothing and seemed fairly tall. But you say he wasn't that tall. I guess it could have been a woman. Do you think it was a woman?"

Longreen grunted an unresponsive grunt and went back to chewing on his pencil.

"Anything else?" I asked.

"Not for now. I guess you can go." I got the distinct impression that it pained him to release me, but try as he may, he couldn't come up with justification to hold the innocent victim of an assault.

I sat up and little stars danced inside my head. I forced my eyes to focus and the stars slid away, leaving only a seven-and-five-eighths–size headache inside my seven-and-a-quarter–size head.

"A crew should be here in a little while to take pictures and fingerprints." He was talking to Donna, who had been standing by the other side of the bed. "If you don't mind, I'll stick around to make sure you don't disturb anything until after they're done."

"Of course, Lieutenant."

I carefully placed my legs over the bed, on Donna's side, and she helped me to stand.

"Are you sure you're all right?"

"No, but I never spend the night on a first date."

She smiled at me and we walked toward the door. After getting Longreen's permission to remove something from the *scene of the crime*, I took the papers Blacker had asked for, left the apartment, and walked slowly down the stairs. As I descended each step, the impact worked like an on button for a jackhammer that was chipping off pieces of my brain.

Finally, I reached the ground floor, and what I saw when I got to the street made me think, for a brief moment, that a little of my Texas-born luck hadn't abandoned me in the last twenty-four hours; the limousine was still waiting. I slid through the door held open for me by the driver, said, "Home, James," and shut my eyes.

New York is an amazing place. Among the multitude of wonders crammed within the borders of the busiest city in America are the world's largest potholes. A few weeks ago I heard about a company from Japan coming over to New York and making plaster casts of several New York potholes. I think it somehow appropriate that the two examples of

American life that have been transported to Japan are Disneyland and New York potholes.

On that limo ride uptown, it seemed like my driver managed to hit every one of the world's largest potholes in the world's greatest city. When he finally pulled to a stop and announced that we had arrived, my whole body felt like it had just gone ten rounds with a Cuisinart.

I opened my eyes and groaned. We weren't at my home. We were at Blacker's.

Blacker took Donna's papers from me and tossed them onto a small table in his foyer. Then he led me into his kitchen and offered me fresh-brewed decaf. "I never drink caffeinated coffee after nine o'clock at night," he said.

"To be perfectly honest, D. L.—and feeling the way I feel I don't want to be anything but honest—I'm getting pretty sick of coffee with or without caffeine. You wouldn't have any tea, would you?"

He chuckled a little, then opened a cabinet and offered me my choice from a less than dazzling selection of either Lipton or Red Zinger. I grumbled something about how no one could be truly civilized without some Earl Grey in their pantry.

"Sorry," he said, though I didn't believe he really was. "No Earl Grey."

"That's okay, forget it. I'll take the Zinger."

We moved to the office and I settled into a client's chair with my steaming mug of herbal tea. So far he hadn't mentioned Donna. I figured I would have to tell him about the burglary. I was wrong. He knew what had happened. He knew more than I did.

"Donna called me while you were unconscious," he said. "I told her to call Longreen."

"Thanks a lot," I grumbled into my tea. "The lieutenant

101

exhibited all the sympathy of a house plant. I was clobbered and he didn't even ask me how I felt."

"So"—Blacker smiled—"how do you feel?"

"Great, super, you got any aspirin?"

Blacker pulled a plastic bottle out of his desk. "Tylenol okay?"

"Sure, the way I feel, cyanide would be okay."

He tossed the bottle over to me. After three tries I was finally able to open the child-proof cap and pour out a couple of pills. I put two in my mouth and washed them down with Red Zinger. It was not my night. The tea was so hot I damn near burned out my throat all the way down to my stomach.

I handed the Tylenol bottle back to Blacker, and he asked, "How was Donna?"

"Fine, I guess." And then something in his tone of voice made me ask, "Why?"

He looked at me funny and the concern I had felt before I passed out came crashing back into my head. "Donna . . . the burglar!" I gasped out. "What happened?"

"You were there," he said, as though he were speaking to a child. The look on my face was enough to convince him that he wasn't, and he kept talking. "The burglar, after he slugged you, ran out into the loft, pushed past Donna, grabbed her handbag, and escaped down the stairs. She was shaken up, but he didn't hurt her. You didn't know about this?"

"No, she didn't say anything about it. Neither did Longreen."

"And you didn't think to ask?" he said with what seemed like a trace of disbelief or scorn in his voice. Or maybe I just imagined it. I certainly deserved it, I hadn't thought of anything or anyone but myself.

"No, but I'm asking now. Is Donna all right?"

"Yes, she was shaken up, but she's a survivor, she'll be fine."

"Thank God. Did the burglar get anything besides Donna's bag?"

"She doesn't think so. She'll know better after she can clean up."

Blacker clearly felt that enough had been said on the subject and it was time to move on. He pulled out the legal pad he had been using that morning and said, "If you feel up to it, I'd like to continue." He leafed through the pad, not looking up to see if I agreed. When he got to the end of his notes he saw that the pad was full. He took a fresh pad from a drawer, picked up a pen, leaned back in his chair, and said, "You were telling me about the start of the party. Why don't you continue from there."

And so I did.

At first, the effort to remember the details of what had happened made my head hurt all the more. But as the Tylenol clicked in, the headache receded, and giving Blacker what he wanted became easier. By one o'clock in the morning I had finished recounting the prior night's activities. By one thirty I'd also given him a quick synopsis of what happened that day, telling him only what I figured was important. My phone call to Pamela, my visit to her apartment, our small talk on the couch, and our brief conversation before she kicked me out. I left out some of the in-between details. He could tell.

"I asked you to tell me everything. What's the matter? Getting tired?"

"No . . . yes . . . maybe. I don't know. Look, D. L., sometimes things happen that a guy just doesn't want to talk about, okay?"

I think he understood; perhaps better than I did. I don't know if I was embarrassed over what happened, or over what, because of my bad timing, didn't happen.

Blacker looked at me funny and then closed his yellow pad, set it on his desk along with his pen, and stood up. "How about a drink?"

"How about several drinks?"

"Sounds good."

He walked from the office, but instead of turning right, toward the kitchen, he turned left. I followed. We walked into his living room and he waved me toward a couch. I sat down and he went to a large antique cabinet in the corner. He opened it. Inside was a well-stocked bar. As he worked at the bar I looked around the room. I had seen it the first day I came over (was it only yesterday?), but hadn't really noticed the furniture. It was clearly a man's room. A large oriental rug in shades of rust and green covered much of the floor. I don't really know rugs, but Blacker's was thick and rich and didn't look like something you'd pick up at a flea market, unless the market was in Marrakech. The room was furnished in what designers probably call an eclectic mix. There were two couches, both upholstered with glove-soft leather in a color that closely matched the brown of the rug. Opposite the couches an old barber's chair sat like a throne, its chrome gleaming and the patent leather of its seat shining like the first day someone sat in it for a six-bit shave and trim. An ornate crank Victrola stood open against one wall and a cabinet displaying an expensive-looking stereo system and large-screen television stretched across another. A garishly colored pinball-like machine stood on a small table beside a delicately painted oriental vase filled with several lush sprays of purple and white orchids.

Hanging on the walls was a combination of what seemed to be original impressionist paintings and well-preserved posters advertising performances by Houdini, Blackstone, and other great magicians from years past. They looked like originals too. I got up and went to one of the paintings, a well-done portrait of a woman with flowing wavy red hair. She was demurely dressed, with a lacy collar buttoned high up a throat that seemed long, slender, and unblemished white, and ruffles covering what were clearly world-class breasts. She looked out over the room through sea-green eyes that seemed to be laughing at everything she saw. I wished I could share whatever she knew that made life seem so free from care.

Blacker came up behind me. "That's a Tarbell."

"Huh?" I kept looking at the painting.

"Tarbell, an impressionist, American, painted in the twenties, up in Newcastle, New Hampshire, mostly portraits. I picked it up at an auction a few years ago. It was borrowed last year for an exhibit of his work at the Met. Here." He handed me a glass filled with something golden brown in color. It looked like clover honey but smelled like the stuff my friend Stu Alvarez stole from the pack of a migrant worker when we were both thirteen. We drank it in his basement, got so drunk we couldn't find the stairs to go back up, and agreed that we had become men. Kind of like a Texas bar mitzvah. Ever since then I've had a special place in my heart for tequila.

"Do you have salt and limes?" I asked.

He smiled, nodded, and walked back to the couch. On the Louis the Fourteenth coffee table he had set down a small cutting board with a lemon, a lime, and a knife. There was also a small beat-up salt shaker that looked like it had been stolen from a Stuckey's roadside restaurant. A three-quarters full bottle of golden tequila, without a label, completed this picture of anticipated insobriety.

D. L. Blacker sat down and began cutting the lemon into thick slices. "I've always preferred lemons, but help yourself." He put down the knife, licked the back of his hand, sprinkled some salt on the wet spot, sucked it off, threw back the tequila in his glass, and bit into one of the lemon slices. It was the first time I'd seen him drink anything besides coffee. It made him seem somehow more human. Suddenly, I liked him all over again.

I sat on the other couch, at a right angle to his, and reached for the salt.

After three or four rounds, not only was I feeling no pain, I was conveniently forgetting whatever pain I had felt. Blacker had stopped shooting down the tequila but continued to steadily sip at his glass. I had never done that with tequila, but I thought it might be a good idea so I refilled my glass and took a small taste. "This is really good."

"You sound surprised."

"Well, yeah," I admitted, "I am. I mean I guess I haven't really *tasted* tequila since I was thirteen. Ever since my first experience with the stuff, I've done it with the salt and lime, you know, to kill the taste."

Blacker picked up the bottle and looked at it. "You don't need to kill the taste of *this* tequila. A client gave me a case of it as a gift last Christmas. In my years of drinking, I've found that quality tequila has a smoothness and flavor as good as the best Irish whiskey. It's almost a crime to use the salt and lemon, but I do it too. I guess it's a holdover from my college days, a ceremony I still enjoy." He raised his glass to me. "Here's to meaningless ceremony."

We both drank, although I admit I'm not sure I understood the toast.

I promised myself once—after a college bender that left me in my underwear, under a tree, twenty-five miles from my home, with no memory of how I got there—that I would never again drink too much. For me, too much can be as little as two beers.

When I forget my promise and overindulge, the usual result is that I become wild, playful, uninhibited, and then, often at the most inopportune time, I quickly fall asleep. On more than one occasion this has led to some hard feelings on the part of the woman with whom I found myself exceeding my limit.

Blacker seemed to react differently to drink. If it was affecting him at all, it was making him friendlier, more talkative. I liked that.

"The way I see this," he said after draining his glass and filling it once again, "is that there are two ways to find out who killed Gary."

I perked up and tried to clear my head.

"There is Longreen's way—the police way—which is to use lots of men to look into everything. They dig out volumes of facts about everybody and everything connected with the case, and then sit back and wait for the answer to pop up, fully formed from that sea of information they brought in, and bite them on the nose.

"Then there's another way, what will have to be our way. We'll take our personal observations, interesting gossip, and whatever related prattle we can get. Then we'll use deductive reasoning and legal logic on that information to figure out where other key or relevant facts *should* be. We'll see if they exist, collect them if they do, and so on and so on until we've got enough support to build a case against one person as the guilty party. Ultimately the information that establishes that person's guilt will prove your innocence."

"In other words," I said, trying to follow what Blacker was saying through a filter of too little sleep and too much tequila, "if A plus B plus C would equal Gary's murderer, and we know A and B, we should go looking for C?"

"Exactly."

"Great, when do we start?"

"We already have. I've been collecting information. You've given me some, Wyman gave me some, some I observed on my own."

"And where do we go from here, what's the next piece of data we should be looking for? What have you deduced or legally logicked?" My English gets shot to hell when I drink.

"Let's put together some possible scenarios, based on what we've got."

"Okay." I was getting into this.

"Your job is to look for any flaws in my logic. Don't let me get away easy with this. Question everything."

He looked at me and I quickly nodded.

"I'm going to start with an assumption that the person who cracked you over the head at Donna's apartment was the same person who killed Gary."

"Why?" He asked for it, I wasn't going to let anything by.

"Couple of reasons. First, it seems like too much of a coincidence to be anything else."

"Longreen said that too."

"Then maybe it's not such a good reason." He smiled, so did I. "Seriously, there's more. From the way the apartment looked when you arrived, our burglar must have been there for a while, looking for something. He'd gone through drawers, tossed stuff around, and yet the only thing he ultimately took was Donna's bag. And that *appeared* to be taken as an afterthought as he ran from the loft. I might even go so far as to say that the bag was taken just to make it look like the person *was* a burglar. I imagine the bag will be found in the area, with nothing missing."

"But if he wants us to believe he's a burglar, wouldn't he take the money and credit cards from the bag?"

"Good point" Blacker smiled. It's the kind of thing a real burglar would steal. Easily fenced. Regardless, we must ask what he was doing in the apartment."

"If he wasn't there to steal something."

"Oh, I didn't say he wasn't there to steal, only that he wasn't an ordinary burglar."

"So," I asked, trying to understand, "he *was* there to steal something?"

"Maybe our thief went there looking for a *particular item*, and maybe he found it."

"What was he looking for? What did he steal?"

"Those are two things that we should try to find out. *If* he took something, and *if* we can find out what he took, it'll be very helpful to us." Blacker took a sip of his tequila and stared out into space. "Maybe we can deduce what he was looking for."

"Using legal logic?"

"And a little sleight of hand."

My head was swimming. I poured myself some more tequila and noticed that the bottle was almost empty.

"What the burglar was after will vary depending on who the burglar was."

"What do you mean?" I asked. Things were getting fuzzier and fuzzier.

"Let's start with Pamela Lockheed. You felt she was important enough to spend time with her this afternoon. Let's see if we should be looking more closely at Pam."

"Yes," I said, remembering the afternoon, "let's look at Pamela."

"I remember your mentioning that Pamela had just ended an affair with Gary. In the dressing room she shouted at him, said she must have been crazy to get involved with him, and threatened to kill him."

"She didn't mean it. She was just angry."

"Perhaps, but maybe not. When I went through Gary's pockets and briefcase it looked like someone had been there before me. Maybe Gary had something that Pamela didn't want him to have . . . something worth killing for."

"Like what?"

"Pictures? Maybe Gary took pornographic pictures of Pamela when they were involved and she became afraid he would show them to other people."

I couldn't stop a grin from plastering itself across my face. "I don't think Pamela would really care much if other people saw pictures of her in the buff."

Blacker raised his eyebrows in acknowledgment of my point and we both sat silently and sipped at our drinks.

I thought of Pam as I had last seen her—screaming at me as I ran from her apartment—and an idea popped fully formed into my tequila-soaked consciousness. "Maybe the burglary angle was just a cover for another reason, the real reason that she broke into Donna's apartment tonight."

"What's that?"

"Try this scenario. Pamela Lockheed is not a very stable woman. Hell, she makes her living as a psychic and palm reader; how stable can she be? She killed Gary because he had slept with her and then, in her words, proven to be a shit. People have killed for less. What with that door in the back of her moon she could easily have slipped away and done it. Now this is all conjecture, you understand, but during that period with Pam this afternoon that I didn't really tell you about, suppose we had fooled around, and then I did something to make her think *I* was a shit too. She *was* kind of mad at me when I left." I was getting into the concept. I leaned forward and the words came gushing out. "Maybe she went to Donna's loft because she was looking for me. Maybe she was waiting to bring that heavy flashlight down on my head just the way she brought my machete down on Gary's last night. Maybe Pamela Lockheed *is* our murderer."

Chapter

ELEVEN

I was exhausted. That little bit of deductive reasoning had put a near-unbearable strain on my beat-up and alcohol-sodden brain. I finished the tequila in my glass, leaned back on the couch, and closed my eyes. The roller-coaster ride through the blackness behind my eyelids convinced me to open them again. The swirling room convinced me that I had had enough to drink.

I looked over at Blacker. He was staring at me, waiting, no doubt, to compliment me on having figured out that Pamela was our murderer. Through a force of will that felt impossible until I did it, I pushed the dizziness from my mind and said, "Well?"

Blacker, apparently recognizing that he had as much of my attention as I was capable of giving, leaned forward and said, "I don't think so, Pat. I just don't see why Pam would be hunting you. And besides, if you're right, and she was at Donna's waiting for you, she would have had to know you were going to Donna's." He spoke slowly and carefully; as though he knew listening was even tougher for me than talking. "No one knew you were going to Donna's. Am I right?"

"*You* did."

"That's true." Blacker nodded. "But I didn't tell anyone. So that line of reasoning falls flat. Shall we try another?"

My mind screamed *no*, but for some reason my mouth said, "Yes."

"What if Gary's killer wasn't one of the people from our little circle? Anyone who was at that party could have slipped into the dressing room and picked up your machete."

"But then we have no chance of figuring out who did it. There were hundreds of people there."

"The police will look at all the guests at the party and try to figure out if any of them was the murderer. But let's you and I turn that around. Instead of looking at each of those people and trying to discover if they're guilty, let's try to find some good candidates for our murderer and then see if they were at the party."

"Okay." The booze and the late hour had caught up with me; I was having real trouble understanding where Blacker was going. Maybe it didn't matter. He seemed to be using me more as a sounding board than as a source of independent thought. So long as I could stay awake and make the appropriate sounds at the right times, I was probably helping him to prove my innocence.

"Donna said something to you that might be important."

At the mention of Donna's name a rush of adrenaline snapped my mind back to clarity and full attention. "What . . . what did she say?"

"This drug pusher in Paris, Wilhelm Broberg. I have to wonder why she mentioned him to you."

"I asked her how she and Gary met."

"Sure, but it's not a very pretty story. It's the kind of thing most people would try to forget, not tell to someone they hardly knew—no matter how clever an inquisitor that someone might be." Blacker delivered this unsolicited testimonial to my detective skills with a smile on his face.

I returned the smile, but I wasn't ready to let the subject go. He was accusing Donna of something, and like a knight errant, I was there to defend her. "What does all this have to do with Gary's murder? You've just said that the killer and the guy who slugged me are the same person, but Donna couldn't have hit me, so why are you talking about her?"

"Hold on." Blacker chuckled and held up his hands in a gesture of surrender. "I'm not accusing Donna of anything, but try this on for size. What if something happened earlier in the party to get Donna thinking of her old boyfriend? That would explain why she told you about him later on."

"Something happened, like what?"

"Like she saw him at the party?"

"But," I protested, "she would have told us . . . told me."

"If she consciously recognized him. But what if she only caught a glimpse of his face? Just enough for her subconscious to dredge up all the unhappy memories, but not enough to let her be sure. You know what it's like when we're performing. We look at our audience, but we don't really see any of them. If we did, it would get in the way of our concentration."

"Let me see if I'm following you. You're saying that this Willy guy was at the party, and *he* killed Gary?"

"It would fit. Try this scenario. Our Mr. Broberg, having made a bundle in the European drug trade, gets into some legitimate line of work, say international banking. He's in New York on business and gets invited to the MegaBank party where he sees Donna and Gary. We know from Donna that Wilhelm hated Gary, felt that, in seducing Donna, Gary had stolen his property. Might he not have slipped into the dressing room to confront Gary, spotted your machete, and used it?"

"But what about the burglary? What was in the apartment that Broberg would have wanted?"

Blacker must have been waiting for that question because he had his answer ready. "Why, Donna of course, he wanted Donna."

The tenuous grip that I had managed to maintain on my equilibrium began to slip away from me. The room began to slide from left to right and a swishing sound filled my head. "If that's true, then won't he be back? We've got to warn Donna, we've got to." I meant to shout, but it came out as a kind of slurred mumble.

I think Blacker said some things, and maybe I spoke too. I can't really remember what we talked about in those last few moments before I passed out. I don't think it was important.

I awoke with the sun streaming through a window, hitting me full in the face, and knew I was dead. Somehow, I had died in the night, that was clear. What would take some figuring out was whether I had made it to heaven or wound up in hell.

I felt like hell. My brain throbbed; the goose egg on my temple sent out regular reminders to the rest of my head that it had been seriously mistreated and was not amused. Beneath that misery a whole new level of pain lurked, like the stink of a girl's cheap perfume that you don't notice so long as you're kissing her in a cow pasture. I had a world-class hangover. As I lay there with my eyes closed tight against the abusive sunlight trying to ooze through whatever orifices it could find to get to my brain, I felt the morning-after demons finish chewing up the lining of my stomach and start working their way up my esophagus. On top of all this I had a pressing urge to go to the bathroom. If it's hell, I thought, there won't be any bathrooms. Slowly I opened my eyes to look.

The place looked like heaven. I was lying on a comfortable bed, my head cradled in what felt like goose-down pillows. After several months of waking up in the land of eternal twilight that was my apartment, the sunlight that filled this room gave it an otherworldly quality. To my left was a large, overstuffed easy chair, the kind that is comfortable no matter how you sit in it. Across from the chair was a portable Sony Trinitron color TV. In the corner of the room sat a small desk, a blue vase filled with daisies the only thing on it. Next to the desk was an open door through which I could see a bathroom, gleaming with black and white tiles. Hallelujah.

I slowly sat up in the bed, being careful to keep my head upright and to move it slowly. As I stood, the smell of bacon wafted into the room and the demons in my stomach went berserk. My reasons for needing a bathroom instantly changed. I barely made it in time.

Forty-five minutes later I was beginning to feel like I had reentered the land of the living. There had been aspirin and Alka-Seltzer in the medicine cabinet. The water that had flowed from the bathroom faucet was cold and clear and tasted as good when I drank my fifth glass as when I gagged down my first. The shower had had one of those massagers in it, so I had used the pulsating water to beat the pain out of my body; first hot, then cold, then hot again, I had changed the temperature to shock myself awake. Only then did I start to wonder, where was I?

My clothes were on the chair, folded neatly by person or persons unknown. I threw them on, opened the door, and stepped into Blacker's kitchen.

I tried not to look surprised. The lawyer/magician sat at a breakfast table by the window, the remains of bacon, eggs, and toast on a plate in front of him. He sipped at his ever-present cup of coffee and seemed engrossed by the *New York Times*.

"Morning," I said.

"Good morning; want breakfast?" He put down the paper and looked at me with a trace of amusement in his eyes.

"Coffee, juice, maybe some toast," I mumbled and sat at the table as he got up and went to the refrigerator. I checked the front page to see if we were still headline news.

The *Times* doesn't go in for the type of sensationalism they feature in the *Post*. There was nothing about Gary's murder, nothing about the attempted burglary at Donna's. The only real crime headline on the first page read "Off-Duty Police Sergeant Killed in Queens." Everything else dealt with politics, the economy, and assorted government scandals—the usual stuff.

I started paging through the first section, but stopped when Blacker brought over a large glass of orange juice and a cup of coffee. I put the paper down, drank the juice, and watched as Blacker went to the stove and started frying bacon.

"How do you like your eggs?" Blacker asked.

Once again the smell of bacon started my gut talking, but this time it was only telling me that my stomach was empty and didn't want to stay that way. I smiled weakly and said, "Scrambled firm, thanks."

He made the eggs, brought them, and sat down at the table. The eggs were perfect; the bacon, sliced thick and prepared crisp, like I love it, was to die for. Between bites, I asked questions.

"Why do you have a bedroom off your kitchen?"

"This building was constructed around the turn of the

116

century when people had live-in domestic help. That would have been the maid's quarters. It has its own bathroom, its own entrance. Now it's a guest bedroom; though you're the first one who's used it in years."

"It's great. If you ever decide to take in a boarder, put me at the top of the list."

"I'll do that."

"Last night, did we figure out who killed Gary?"

"No, but we did come up with some questions that need to be answered, and you expressed some concern for Donna's safety."

Suddenly the image of Wilhelm Broberg stalking Donna flashed into my mind and I remembered some of what Blacker had said the night before. I jumped up. "The dealer . . . Donna . . . we've got to warn her."

"We already did. I called her last night and advised her to move out of her apartment for a while. I didn't mention her old boyfriend, just that I was concerned because of the break-in. I also called Jim Wyman, and he's already faxed me a copy of the guest list from the party. There was no Broberg listed, but there was a group of European investment bankers. I've contacted an investigator I use in London, and he's doing background checks on all of them for me. We should get the information sometime tomorrow."

He'd been busy. "So where's Donna staying?" I asked, trying to sound as nonchalant as possible.

"You can ask her yourself, this afternoon."

"Huh?" I sat back down.

"The funeral." He checked his watch. "You'd better get moving. You just have time to go home, change clothes, and get there. Riverside Funeral Parlor, at Seventy-sixth and Amsterdam. It starts in about an hour."

I stood up, took the dirty dishes to the sink, and started for the door. Blacker called out to me.

117

"Oh, and Pat, figure on coming here afterward."

"A wake?" I asked.

"Sort of," he said enigmatically, and then turned his back on me and started washing the dishes.

Chapter

T W E L V E

I ran home, changed clothes, and rushed to the funeral parlor. A sign by the door said the service for Johnson would be in the East Chapel, so I followed the arrows and found Donna in a small room off to the side. We talked for a little while but she was so concerned about me after the *accident* at her apartment that I barely had the chance to say all those things you're supposed to say at funerals. Other people kept coming in to talk to her so I excused myself and went to get a seat.

By then the place was almost full, but I managed to find a chair near the front. I looked around before I sat down. There were several people from the MegaBank party/murder of two nights before.

Andy Costello sat over to one side, talking to his girlfriend Debby Brill. She was wearing a black minidress, but didn't have the legs for it. As I watched, Andy slid his arm around the back of her chair and leaned his head in to tell her something. They both burst out laughing and then Andy, perhaps realizing that laughter was inappropriate, nervously looked around to see if anyone had noticed. His eyes caught mine and he nodded before turning back to Debby.

Lieutenant Longreen leaned against a wall at the back of the room, surveying the crowd. Occasionally he whispered to a tall, solidly built black man with a thick mustache who stood beside him and bent over to hear what Longreen had to say. The tall man would then make notes in a small notebook.

Near the front of the room, beside the closed casket that held the mortal remains of Gary Johnson, stood D. L. Blacker in a conservative, gray, pinstripe suit, talking quietly with Bob Johnson. As I watched, they shook hands and Bob walked into the small room to join Donna.

I glanced at my watch; the service was scheduled to begin in two minutes. A rustling behind me signaled the arrival of a last-minute mourner. I turned and saw Pamela walking into the room. She took off her sunglasses, looked around, saw me, smiled, then stopped herself and turned away. Apparently she was still holding a grudge. As I watched her walking around the room, looking for an empty seat, I marveled at my own drunken foolishness of the night before—that I could have been so sure, if only for a moment, that Pamela was Gary's killer. I transferred my gaze to D. L. Blacker and wondered if his ability to figure this whole thing out would be any better than mine. I sincerely hoped so.

My rumination was interrupted by Bob and Donna coming out of the side room and taking seats that had been reserved for them in the front row. D. L. Blacker moved to the podium, and those of us who were still standing sat down.

"I have been asked," Blacker began after the room became absolutely quiet, "to talk about Gary Johnson. This is not an easy thing to do. Both because of who and what he was, and because this eulogy should not need to have been given for many, many years. Gary was a man who, judging by the size of this assembly, inspired strong feelings in many people. But judging by his all too untimely demise, the strong feeling inspired by Gary was, for at least one person, not a good one. What is there about a man that makes him special, sets him apart? What was there about Gary that allowed him to affect the lives of so many of us? Gary Johnson was a motivator. Many people cared for Gary, some did not. But everyone had to acknowledge that he was a man who got things done. He moved people to action. He inspired performers to perform, writers to write, and unfortunately, in the end, he motivated a murderer to lash out and take a life. Perhaps that person is here with us today. The police seem to think so."

Blacker looked directly at Longreen. Longreen scowled as everyone squirmed in their seats, looking left and right at the potential murderers sitting beside them.

"But we aren't here today to talk of the man . . . or woman . . . who brought Gary's life to an end. No, we are here to pay our respects to the memory of Gary Johnson."

He went on like that for another ten minutes, then Gary's earthly remains were carried from the room to be cremated. Everyone got up and milled around for a while before the room started to clear out.

Blacker appeared beside me and reminded me to go back to his place. "There'll be food," he said, having deduced one of my prime motivating factors in life. I watched him move rapidly around the room and talk to several of the others before I lost sight of him in the crowd.

I exchanged meaningless platitudes with several entertainers I knew, and then looked for Donna, to say goodbye. I couldn't find her anywhere. The room was starting to empty, and I didn't want to be the last person left in a funeral home, so I finally gave up, stepped out into the bright October sunshine, and began walking uptown.

* * *

When Blacker finally indicated that all the invited guests had arrived, there were seven of us seated around the large coffee table in his living room. Blacker was settled in his barber's chair, I was on a comfortable rocker brought from another room, and sitting on the couches were Donna, Bob, Pamela, Andy, and Debby.

Blacker opened his bar and everyone helped themselves. My head and stomach, still a little queasy from the night before, advised me to stick to seltzer and I listened to its suggestion. I may not have felt much like drinking, but I was happy to eat. The large coffee table was piled high with food from Zabar's.

Zabar's, a food emporium on Manhattan's Upper West Side, is to deli food what Rolls-Royce is to automobiles; they make the best, everyone knows it. I can't really afford to shop in Zabar's, but one of my favorite activities those first few months in New York had been to walk slowly through Zabar's and just breathe. The smells alone made it worth the walk down to Eightieth Street and Broadway. The miserable events of those last few days had led to at least one good thing: there I was, seated in Blacker's living room, in front of a mountain of Zabar's appetizers. I tried to stay cool, but every time I rocked forward to reach for something, my chair creaked. I was very conscious of the noise.

At one point while we were eating, I tried to cover up the all-to-often heard noise of my chair by thanking Blacker for providing so much food.

"You should really thank Bob here," Blacker said. "I ordered all the food, but when we went to pick it up, I'd forgotten my wallet. He paid for it."

"No problem, enjoy," mumbled Bob.

We continued to eat. The only sounds in the room were

those of people chewing, and an occasional comment on the food.

Finally Blacker set down his plate, cleared his throat, and looked around our little circle. "I hope nobody objects if I talk while you all eat." Nobody did, so he continued. "This get-together serves several purposes. First, because it's right after the funeral service, this is an opportunity for all of us to eat, drink, and hopefully relax. Second, if Lieutenant Longreen makes his threatened appearance, this is also a meeting for the formal reading of the will. I promised him it would happen today, and so, Donna and Bob, we can do that too."

"You know," Andy said into a pile of cold cuts he was assembling on a slice of fresh rye bread, "it feels kind of bizarre to be sitting here like this . . . with all of you."

"I know what you mean," Pamela chimed in. "We were all there . . . at the MegaBank job. I mean, one of us could have seen the murderer."

"Pamela." Blacker drew the attention back to him. "I believe one of us *may be* the murderer."

Blacker stopped talking and allowed the impact of his words to sink in. His statement silently echoed among us until the quiet was shattered by Debby Brill giggling.

"I'm sorry, really," she said between gasps of breath as she tried to remove the smirk from her face. "But it's all so theatrical. You"—she pointed a long skinny arm at Blacker—"sitting there in that chair, raised above the rest of us, telling us there's a murderer in the room. It's like bad summer stock." She turned to Andy. "Like that production I did last summer of *Ten Little Indians* at the Barn Playhouse, remember?"

Andy nodded. "They did the play with only six actors."

Debby turned back to the rest of us. "It was great, I got to do two death scenes."

Bob Johnson turned his attention back to Blacker. "What's the point to this, D. L.? What do you want from us?"

"Information." Blacker walked to the bar and poured himself a drink. I couldn't believe that he could touch anything alcoholic after last night. "I thought that if we all got together we might be able to work some things out among ourselves."

"Great," Bob said, "where do we start?"

"How about with you?" Blacker returned to his throne and leaned over toward Bob. "The police feel that you had a motive."

"What?" Donna asked Blacker but looked at her brother-in-law, sitting beside her.

"With Gary dead, he gets full control of their company. Also there was a lifetime of resentment built up between them."

Donna continued to look at Bob. "But he couldn't have done it," she said.

"Good." Blacker smiled. "He's my client, I'm glad to hear that. Why not?"

"He says he has an alibi," I said. I wanted to help Donna.

"That's right." Donna brightened. "He left the party early and went to a bar on Broadway. He told me."

"He told us the same thing," I said. "Except he said the bar was on West Forty-seventh Street."

Blacker leaned back in the barber's chair and said, "He also mentioned Jimmy Ray's, but that's on Eighth Avenue, between Forty-fifth and Forty-sixth."

"Stop talking about me like I'm not here," Bob exploded. "And stop trying to make it sound like I was lying. I told you, I left before the party started and I went to a bar. I'm not sure which bar I went to."

"Apparently not." Blacker turned to the whole group.

"Anybody know anything to either support or contradict Bob's story?"

Donna started to raise her hand, then put it back in her lap and quietly started to talk. "Before the party, you may remember, Gary and I had kind of a fight. When I left the dressing room, I went to the bathroom for a while. Anyway, when I came out, I bumped into Bob. Remember?" she asked him.

"Sure," he answered enthusiastically. "And I told you I was leaving, right?"

"You did, I remember." Suddenly her mood darkened. "You also said some pretty nasty things about Gary."

"But I told you I was *leaving*. That's the important thing; you saw me leave."

"Bob, I didn't *see* you leave the party. You could have been going anywhere."

"I left." Bob sounded like he was starting to lose control. "I left the party."

"I don't know if I should say anything." Andy cut off Bob's tirade. "But from what I gather, it seems that Gary must have been killed around the time that I was doing my rap number."

"I remember that," I said, "it was really good. I'd never heard you do rap."

Andy brightened at my compliment. "I'd never done it before. It just seemed right at the time and I thought I'd give it a try."

Debby squeezed Gary's arm. "Isn't he incredible? He's the most talented guy I've ever met. The first time I met him and heard that voice . . . well, I just got all squooshy and weird inside. I feel so lucky to have him. I'd do *anything* for him."

Bob exploded again. "Is there a point to all this?"

"Andy?" Blacker asked.

"Well, sure." Andy smiled a kind of uncomfortable smile. "During the rap number I was watching the people in the party closely. You know, to kind of see how they were reacting. Anyway, someone dressed in blue work clothes walked by my booth, heading toward the dressing room. It sure looked like Bob."

Bob jumped up. "That's a lie!"

"Hold it, Bob," Blacker shot out, "no one is saying it *was* you."

Blacker had succeeded in stopping the shouting, but nothing could relieve the icy silence that took its place. We all looked at each other, trying to come up with something totally inoffensive to say. Finally Debby poked Andy's arm, and in a whisper that cut across the room like a buzz saw through the middle of a magician's assistant, she said, "Andy, didn't you want to ask D. L. something?"

"Huh?" Andy said. "Oh, right. D. L., could I talk to you for a second, about some business?"

"Of course. Pat, could you take them to my office?"

"Sure," I said, and then had to rush to keep up with them as Debby led Andy into the hallway.

We walked in silence to Blacker's office. Andy and Debby planted themselves in the two client's chairs. I turned on the lights and then sat in the chair by the computer. Blacker arrived quickly and took his place behind the massive desk.

"Sorry about that, Andy, Debby. Now, what can I do for you?"

As I listened, it occurred to me that maybe I shouldn't have stayed, but no one had asked me to leave and I was curious.

"Andy has a few legal-type questions," Debby said. "He was hoping you could answer them for him."

"I'll be happy to try," Blacker said in his best lawyer voice. "Go ahead."

Andy took over. "It may be insensitive to be raising this

today, but time is of the essence here. The management contract I signed with Gary. Now that he's dead, the contract is over, right?"

"I'd have to look at it, but as I recall, you didn't sign a contract with Gary, you signed with his corporation. Gary may be dead, but the corporation still exists. So offhand, I'd say no."

"What?" Debby rasped out, the color draining from her face.

Andy said nothing. He just gripped the arms of his chair and looked back and forth from D. L. to his girlfriend.

"One of the first things every law student learns is that a corporation is designed to go on and on, regardless of whether the people who own that corporation die, leave the business, or whatever."

"But," Andy said, "I thought *Gary* was my manager. That's what he was always telling me."

"Let me check." Blacker went over to an oak file cabinet, pulled out a drawer, riffled through the files, and finally pulled one out. He took it back to his desk, flipped pages for a while, and then carefully read over one sheet.

"Well, Andy, the contract *is* with the corporation. However, there's something in here that I think you'll view as good news."

"Yes?" Andy was literally sitting on the edge of his seat.

"A key man provision."

"What's that?" Debby snapped.

"It means," Blacker said, smiling at her, "that the contract is tied to the participation of an individual; if the key man leaves, the contract is canceled. Here, it meant that Andy was managed by the corporation only so long as Gary worked for it."

"So, this means he's free?"

"Probably. I'll have to do a little research to see if death of the key man affects the terms. Also I should talk to Bob.

After all, it's his company now. But I'd say you're probably clear."

"Great." Andy beamed. "In that case I'd like to hire you." He took out his checkbook. "I got a job offer from WZBQ. How much do you want to negotiate the deal for me?"

"I think five thousand dollars should do it," Blacker said. "I'll let you know ahead of time if it looks like it's going to be more than that."

Andy quickly filled out the check, ripped it out of the book, and handed it to Blacker.

"Before I cash this," the lawyer said as he placed the check under an ornate paperweight on the right side of his desk, "let me make sure about your management agreement. I still represent Bob's corporation, and if there's any problem with that we should resolve it before I take on any work for you."

"Okay." Andy got up. "When will you know?"

"Let's talk tomorrow," Blacker said, and he stood too.

We all walked to the front door of the apartment and shook hands. Debby kissed me on the cheek, and then she and Andy left.

"Well," I said, "thanks for the party. I guess I'll be going too."

"Not yet," Blacker said as he headed back into the apartment. "We still have company, and you have some very important work to do."

When we got back to the living room, Bob, Pamela, and Donna were gathered around the pinball-like machine Blacker had on the small table in the corner, opposite the bar. Bob was playing. I could hear the sound of a ball bouncing around, and then a bell rang and more balls gushed into a tray set into the bottom of the machine. We walked over to them.

"Say, D. L.," Pamela said, reaching out a hand to squeeze the lawyer's arm just above his elbow, "what is this thing?"

"That," said Blacker, "is a Pachinko machine."

"I've heard of them," Bob Johnson said, leaving the game. "It's Chinese, right?"

"Japanese, actually." Blacker slid away from Pamela and went back to his barber's chair. "Although it's been played all over the Orient since the late forties. Just after World War II it was used as part of a subsidy program for Japanese war refugees. They played it for prizes of food, clothes, and other necessities of life."

"Like a cross between food stamps and slot machines?" I asked.

"Exactly. Except with Pachinko the Japanese felt they were earning the supplies, not accepting charity, which has always been frowned upon by Japanese society. Getting the food through their Pachinko winnings, the Japanese felt they had personally earned it."

"Do they still play it over there?" Donna asked, moving over to sit back down on the couch.

"Sure. Back in the early sixties people played for money prizes. The Pachinko parlors became gambling casinos, with organized crime connections. By the early seventies the government stepped in and prohibited the cash prizes. Now the parlors are like video arcades or bowling alleys. You find them all over Japan, filled with kids and adults. They'll play it for hours."

"This is all fascinating stuff," Pamela said in a voice that said she couldn't care less, "but I really must be going. That is, of course, unless *you'd* like me to stay, D. L.?" She took a step toward him, smiled, and made an offer with her eyes. He didn't see it, or else chose not to.

"No, Pam, that's fine," Blacker said, sounding just a little bit flustered. Apparently he had received Pamela's message. "I appreciate your coming, really."

Pamela flashed me a saccharine smile, said goodbye to Donna and Bob, and bounced from the room. "Don't bother to get up. I know the way out." A few moments later I heard the front door open and close.

"Pat, come sit." Donna slid over on the couch, making room for me next to her. I went over and sat down. Bob continued to stand by the Pachinko machine.

"Are you sure you're okay?" Donna said, putting her hand gently on my cheek. "A doctor friend of mine said you might have had a concussion. Have you seen a doctor? You look a little flushed."

How could I tell her I was flushed because of her? She took her hand away but her scent lingered, kind of squeaky-clean exotic, like a cross between jasmine and Ivory soap.

Bob broke the tense silence that, I suspect, only I was aware of.

"So, D. L., what now?"

"Well, I see two concerns. First, we have to resolve the details of Gary's estate. Second, we have to clear you of suspicion in Gary's murder. The two probably aren't related, but the police are going to think that the details of Gary's will and of your partnership agreement created a powerful motive for either you or for Donna to have killed Gary."

I glanced over at Donna. She had her lips pressed together and looked like she might cry. "Would you like some Kleenex?" I asked.

She just shook her head.

"So," Bob asked, with just a trace of annoyance in his voice, "what can we do?"

"Well, as your lawyer, I'll be filing the estate papers with the probate court. I'll also draw up the contracts for you to buy Donna's stock and assume sole control of the business. The police are investigating the murder. Pat and I are doing a little looking into it too. I guess all you should do is work at keeping your company going."

"Yeah," Bob said, "it's going to be tough without Gary. I don't really relate very well to the entertainers." Suddenly he brightened. "Say, Donna. You still own a piece of the company, and you know the performers. Why don't you work with me? It'll be good for you."

Donna thought about it, but quickly said, "No, Bob. I don't think so. Right now I just need some time."

"Sure," he grumbled, "I understand." He brightened again. "How about you, D. L.? You know the people, you have a background in business. You'd be great."

Blacker smiled and shook his head. "Thanks, Bob, no. I learned years ago that I can't really work *for* anyone and I'm terrible with a partner."

Bob's eyes came to rest on me. I smiled at him. He didn't smile back. "How about you, Arnold? Want a job?"

"I don't know." This was all moving too fast for me. "What would I have to do? What does it pay?"

Bob took a pen and a small pad from his pocket, scribbled something, ripped off the top piece of paper, and handed it to me. "Here's my phone number and address. Let's get together tomorrow and talk about it."

"Okay, great," I said and pocketed the scrap of paper.

"Good." He put the pen and pad back in his pocket. "I guess I'll be going then. . . ."

He was cut off by the sound of a doorbell.

"Either," Blacker said, getting down from his barber's chair, "Roberto is sleeping and someone snuck by him, or else Longreen has arrived."

Blacker was right, and Roberto wasn't sleeping. It was Longreen, together with Assistant D.A. Wyman and the tall, black, mustached cop who had been with the lieutenant at the funeral. Blacker brought them into the room.

"As I was telling you, Lieutenant," Blacker said, "you're a little late. The party's over. Ms. Johnson and Mr. Johnson were both about to leave."

Donna got the message and stood up. "Thanks for everything, D. L."

Bob joined her. "Yeah," he mumbled, "thanks." The two of them started to walk from the room.

"You can go too, Arnold," the lieutenant snarled.

I looked at Blacker who shook his head.

"Thanks," I said with a big smile, "but I'll stick around. I haven't finished my lunch." I spooned some tortellini in pesto sauce onto my plate and held the serving bowl out to Longreen. He just growled, so I put it down, leaned back on the couch, and started to eat.

Blacker followed Donna and Bob from the room, but before I could finish the pile of pasta on my plate, he came back and resumed his place on the barber's chair. "I don't think we've been introduced," Blacker said to the tall cop who had folded himself into the rocking chair.

"Sergeant Koslow. Good to meet you."

"Please." Blacker waved his hand at the food. "Help yourself, Sergeant, Jim, Lieutenant."

The sergeant started to lean forward and the rocker made its distinctive creak.

"We're not here to eat," Longreen said, and Koslow rocked back again.

"Is that Zabar's caviar cream cheese spread?" Wyman asked.

Blacker grinned and nodded. The assistant D.A. smiled back, then he spread a generous dab on a slice of bread and bit off a mouthful.

"Sorry to hear about Sergeant Sheski, Lieutenant," Blacker said. "He seemed like a good man."

"What do you know about Sheski?" Longreen roared.

"Ease up, Lieutenant. I only know as much as the million other New Yorkers who read about it in today's paper."

I remembered the morning headline, "Off-Duty Cop

Killed in Queens," and silently cursed myself for not reading the story.

"He was a jerk," Longreen spat out. "His wife said he got a call last night, went out without telling her where he was going, and never returned. Some kids found his body a few hours later in the doorway of a bank on Roosevelt Avenue. A bullet in his stomach, another one in his head."

"The papers said there were no leads."

"Screw the papers. Sheski used to work narcotics. We figure one of his old stoolies called him with something that sounded hot. He went to meet the guy, but it was a setup. He should have called in for backup. Anyway, it's being handled out of Queens. Not my problem. You are. Where's the will?"

"In my office. Just a second, I'll get it for you." And Blacker left the room.

Time passed. Wyman helped himself to more food, his deep blue eyes twinkling with obvious pleasure at Longreen's impatience. Koslow took out his notebook and flipped through it. Longreen glared at me.

Finally D. L. Blacker returned. He was carrying a large file folder crammed with papers. He climbed back up onto his barber's chair, opened the file on his lap, and began sorting through the documents. "Here you go, a copy of the will." He pulled it out and offered it to Longreen. The policeman took it, glanced through it, and then handed it to the assistant D.A.

"What's it say?" Longreen asked Wyman.

Wyman read through it for several minutes and then looked up at Blacker. "This is *very* well drafted."

"Thank you, Jim," Blacker said.

Longreen blew up. "Enough with the admiration society. What does it say?"

The assistant D.A. ignored the question and continued to talk to Blacker. "There should be a shareholders' agreement, financial statements, and insurance policies."

Blacker pulled several other papers from the file and handed them over. "Here you go." Wyman took them and resumed his examination. "Those are originals, Jim. I can make you copies if you want to take them with you."

"I'd appreciate it."

"No problem."

"Wyman!" Lieutenant Longreen was beginning to turn an unpleasant shade of purple. It contrasted sharply with his long, thin, blond hair.

"Hmmm." The assistant D.A. looked up and smiled. "This is interesting stuff. Correct me if I'm wrong, D. L., but as I read it, the will leaves everything to the deceased's wife, including the proceeds of a million-dollar life insurance policy, right?"

"Right so far."

Longreen's thin lips twisted into an unpleasant smile. "Sounds like a motive for murder to me."

Koslow flipped quickly through his notebook, finally stopping at a page near the front. "It would fit," he said. "We know she fought with her husband before the party began, and we only have her word for it that he was dead when she walked into the dressing room."

Longreen nodded. "Sure, she went into the dressing room, spotted the machete, and then when her husband turned his back on her . . . wham!"

Koslow had been flipping through his notebook as his superior talked. He found another page, read from it, and then looked up and said, "When she was sure he was dead, she could have screamed as though she just found him, and no one was the wiser."

"It *couldn't* have happened that way," I protested.

"Why not?" Longreen turned his cold eyes on me with a look that longed to violate all my constitutional rights.

I didn't back down. "There wasn't enough time," I insisted. "It couldn't have been more than two minutes between when I saw her leave the room and when I heard her scream."

"You were looking at your watch?" Koslow asked.

"No," I had to admit.

"You shouldn't be fighting this," Longreen growled at me. "It gets you off the hook as my prime suspect."

"If you're looking for suspects," Wyman said, holding up the papers, "there's another one here."

"What do you have?" Longreen looked like a kid in a candy store.

"As I read these insurance policies, besides the million-dollar policy that goes to the wife, there's a half-million-dollar policy, with the money going to the business. That right, D. L.?"

"That's right." Blacker nodded.

Longreen listened to this with a look on his face of someone trying to understand something just slightly beyond his mental grasp.

"You said *other* suspects," he said slowly. "But if the half million goes to his business and she gets everything that was his, doesn't she get the business *and* the half million too?"

"That's the beauty of this setup," Wyman said. "The agreement between the two Johnson brothers has a provision that deals with the death of either brother. Under that provision, Gary Johnson's estate has to sell his share of the company to Bob Johnson at half the value of the company's assets, *as reflected in the last financial statement*. According to the financial statement here"—he held up one of the papers—"the company is only worth about fifty thousand dollars."

135

Suddenly Longreen saw the light. "So with his brother's death, Bob Johnson will pay twenty-five thousand dollars and get one hundred percent of half a million."

"Exactly," Wyman said. "Not to mention getting rid of a brother with whom he fought incessantly, and gaining total control of a company that, although only holding assets of fifty thousand dollars, last year did close to two million dollars worth of business."

Koslow looked up from his notebook. "We still haven't found anyone who saw him at the bar. Also, no leads on this girl he claims he spent the night with. He hasn't given us much of a description to go on."

"He wouldn't," Longreen said, grabbing a handful of black olives and popping them gleefully into his mouth. "Not if there was no girl. And there wouldn't be any girl, not if he stayed at the party. Not if he killed his brother."

Chapter

THIRTEEN

After Wyman, Longreen, and Sergeant Koslow left the apartment, Blacker and I spent some time cleaning up the living room, not talking about much. We brought the dirty dishes into the kitchen; he rinsed, I put them into the dishwasher.

The phone rang just as he handed me the last wet plate. He patted his hands on a dish towel and reached for the phone. "Blacker here."

I wedged the plate into the last available space in the dishwasher, and then tried not to listen as he said, "Uh huh," a couple of times, followed by "No, sorry, I'm not available, but just a second, I may have someone for you."

He put his hand over the phone's mouthpiece and turned to me. "You free tomorrow?"

"Sure, why?"

"How much do you want for four hours of mime on the street, passing out leaflets for a new bagel health-food shop in Midtown?"

I wasn't really a mime, and I told him so.

"You wear whiteface, you don't talk, you're a mime. How much?"

"Sixty dollars an hour?"

He uncovered the phone and put it back to his ear. "You're in luck. I've got someone here who's terrific. He used to be with Ringling Brothers, Barnum and Bailey, he has extensive experience passing out leaflets for bagel shops, *and* because another job he had for tomorrow just fell through, he'll do it for you for only a hundred dollars an hour. Okay? Great, I'll tell him. Right, sure, bye now." And he hung up the phone.

"You're working tomorrow," he said to me.

"This is great! A hundred dollars an hour?"

"Actually, you'll keep seventy-five and give me twenty-five. That's still fifteen an hour more than you asked for, and I get my commission. They'll pay you when you're done, in cash, okay?"

"Uh, sure, fine." I was bothered that he was going to take 25 percent, but I needed the money and in a way he was right. I was going to get more than I asked for. So instead of complaining I asked, "How come you're not taking the gig yourself?"

He smiled. "I've got a great job for tomorrow afternoon. I'm doing a magic show for the three sons of a Saudi Arabian princess." He continued to look at me and smile. Then we both broke out laughing. I was going to pass out leaflets for a bagel and bean-sprout joint; he was going to do a show for three pint-sized princes. It's a weird way to make a living, but it sure beats working, and somebody's got to do it.

He gave me the information for my job and I went home. The light was still burned out. Just as well, that way I didn't have to look at my room. I found my bed by the Braille method, undressed the same way, and stretched out on top of the covers. The next day I would have some cash. I'd be able to buy a lightbulb. Things were improving. I fell asleep with a smile on my lips but without brushing my teeth. My mother would not have approved.

The first hour on the street was easy. I had followed Blacker's instructions and gone to the restaurant at noon. I met the owner who let me change in his office. I put on my makeup and the red-and-white striped overalls that Gary had hated. Artie the bagel baron loved them. He gave me a box of leaflets and sent me out to the street.

I did a kind of robot mime: Keeping my back straight, I bent over at the waist and moved in short, jerky motions. I hoped I looked better than I thought I looked. I don't really consider myself a mime. Especially after seeing Donna perform, I felt guilty even calling what I did mime. But I was getting paid to be a mime, so that day I *was* a mime.

People seemed to enjoy what I was doing. Occasionally they would stop and watch. Lots of people tried to get me to talk. One woman commented that I was so good she *had* to take a leaflet. The first hour passed quickly.

The second hour I began to feel like I was earning my money. The job was becoming boring and the pain had started. First in my lower back, then in my arms. Try standing for two hours bent to a forty-five degree angle at the waist with your arms out, and you'll see what I mean. At one point a mother rolled her baby's stroller over my foot and then picked the kid up and held him right in front of me. He got a good look at my expressionless white face and started screaming. She kept saying to him, "Look, Jeremy, a clown, you *love* clowns." The kid was smarter than his mother; he knew the difference between a clown and a mime and apparently he *hated* mimes.

By the third hour I found myself in serious pain, silently cursing Blacker for getting me the job. When the final hour was over I had a healthy respect for real mimes and a firm resolve never to do that type of work again. A resolution that evaporated the moment Artie handed over four hundred dollars in cash. I wiped off my makeup, packed my costume and stuff into my shoulder bag, accepted the sack of bagels Artie urged on me, and left the smiling bagel baron behind.

Walking down the street, chewing on a cinnamon raisin bagel, feeling prosperous and well fed, I stopped at a pay phone. I dug out the note Bob Johnson had given me and dialed his number. The line was busy. Figuring I could kill some time and then try again, I looked around and realized I was just a few blocks from Jimmy Ray's. Bob had said he spent part of that fateful night at Jimmy Ray's. The police didn't seem to believe him. Was it because they hadn't tried to find out, or because there was nothing *to* find out? I decided to go to the bar and see if I could, as Blacker had put it, "dig around." I hefted my bag back up to my shoulder and headed west. I was feeling good. Maybe, I thought, I'd even buy myself a beer.

I walked through the door into the cool semidarkness of Jimmy Ray's and slid into an open seat at the bar. The place was starting to fill up even though it was still a good thirty minutes shy of five o'clock. The regulars at Jimmy Ray's are theatre people and they don't keep nine-to-five hours.

I ordered a beer, a New Amsterdam. One of the best local beers brewed in America, New Amsterdam is just one more reason why I love New York. I paid for the beer, left a good tip on the bar, and swung around in my seat to look over the early crowd. At a booth near the back of the barroom sat two of the city's beautiful people. He was tanned, tall, and terribly good looking. She had striking Nordic good looks, with long, straight blond hair and a big, natural smile, showing teeth as white as clouds. They were throwing back something straight up and clear, either vodka or gin. She

140

caught me staring, laughed a little, and then playfully stuck out her tongue at me. I took this as encouragement, so I raised my glass in a silent toast. She acknowledged the salute with a tip of her head and a perfect smile, and then turned back to her drinking companion.

I sipped my beer and looked over the rest of the room. At the end of the bar near the door was an older man who looked like he had been sent over from central casting to be the bar's resident drunk. I didn't stare at him for long, because it seemed like he was gazing at me; at least he was looking in my direction. Judging by his general appearance, it was questionable whether his eyes were able to focus on me, or anyone for that matter. I turned away and signaled to the bartender for another beer. He brought it to me.

"Thanks," I said. "Can I ask you something?"

"Sure." He smiled, showing off a set of teeth too perfect to be real.

"Any chance you were working here three nights ago?"

A suspicious look came into his eye and he seemed to hesitate before answering. "Wednesday night? Maybe, why?"

"A friend of mine says he was drinking here or someplace in the neighborhood, but he had a few too many and can't remember exactly where he was. Maybe you remember him: tall, dark hair, dressed in work clothes with *Bob* embroidered on the front?"

"You don't look like a cop," the bartender said, the smile now gone from his lips. "You a reporter?"

"No, why?"

"Look, fella, in three days I've had four cops asking me questions about that night. I'm going to tell you the same thing I told them. I don't remember any of our patrons. When you walk out that door, I won't remember you, okay?"

"But I'm not a cop and I'm not a reporter," I protested.

"Uh huh." He smirked. "And like every other guy who

serves drinks or waits on tables in New York, I'm not a bartender, I'm an actor. But I serve drinks like a bartender and I work in a bar like a bartender, and you're asking questions like a cop or a reporter. I don't know nothing." He took the money I had laid down for the drink and walked to the cash register.

I turned at the sound of a group of people laughing as they walked through the door. They passed me on their way to the tables in the back.

The door opened again and two women came in, looked around, and took the last empty stools at the bar. I spent some time looking at them. They were easy to look at. As I regarded them, a universal question, one which has kept me awake nights and been debated by men throughout the ages, once again pushed its way into my mind: Which is sexier on a pretty woman, a short skirt or tight jeans? The blonde was wearing a black mini, the redhead a pair of faded jeans that looked like they had been painted on by a close friend.

Just as I began to consider ways of asking the two of them to help me find the answer to that burning question, my attention was pulled to the drunk at the end of the bar. He stood up and began to walk toward me. His stride was slow and steady, not the classic drinker's stagger. Either he wasn't as drunk as I had thought, or else he spent so much time under the influence that he had managed to master the strange things gravity does to you when you've been drinking.

He wedged himself into the space next to my stool. I turned my back on him and pretended to watch the television at the other end of the bar. The person on the stool behind me caught a ninety-proof whiff of him and quickly left. I couldn't blame him. I considered doing the same. It didn't look like I was going to learn anything at Jimmy Ray's.

Watching the reflected images in the bar's mirror, I saw

the drunk take the vacated stool and lean toward me in an angle that defied everything I had learned in high school physics class. "Your name's Arnold something, right?"

Great, he knew my name.

"I bet you're wondering how I knew your name, huh?" he said in a voice that was part croak and all whine.

I turned to face him, but I didn't say anything. I didn't really want to encourage a conversation.

Apparently he didn't need encouragement; he kept talking like we were old friends. "I saw your picture in the paper," he croaked enthusiastically. "You're involved in that big party killing, right? Hey, Bill." He waved at the bartender, who headed back in our direction. "Another round for me and my friend Arnie, here."

"Arnold's my last name," I said. "Pat Arnold." Hell, he was buying me a drink, he should know my name.

"Lew Steiger." He finished his drink and carefully set the glass down on the bar, deliberately placing it exactly in the wet ring it had made before he picked it up.

The bartender brought the drinks, another New Amsterdam for me, a boilermaker for my new drinking buddy, and then went over to chat up the redhead. Apparently he had answered the timeless question and decided jeans beat out a miniskirt.

Lew picked up a cocktail napkin and used it to dab at his lips. Then he folded it twice and set it down on the bar. "I been reading about that murder. I figure you didn't do it."

"Thanks. I'd appreciate your telling that to the police."

Lew chose to ignore my remark. He apparently knew what he was going to say, and the alcohol he'd consumed didn't leave room for new thoughts anywhere in his brain.

"Ever since I retired as stage doorman over at the Winter Garden Theater, I've had lots of time, so I read all the papers, cover to cover, every day. I especially like reading the big crime stuff. But of course this one held special interest for me."

"Oh," I said, not really interested, but trying to be pleasant. After all, he had bought me a beer. "Because it involved performers?"

He looked at me like I was the one who was two sheets to the wind. "I been following it because of Bob buying me a couple of drinks last Wednesday. I remember commenting on it to Bill here." He called to the bartender who was filling a drink order for one of the waitresses. Bill nodded at us, finished pouring some thick green stuff from a blender into two glasses, added little umbrellas, handed them to the waitress, and then came over.

"Another round?" he asked, although I still had almost half my beer left.

Again Lew chose to ignore the question and instead focused on his own thought. "Say, Bill, remember a couple of nights ago when that guy Bob was drinking with me?"

"Can't say I remember it, Lew."

"Sure you do. We talked about it the next day, when his picture was in the paper. I pointed it out to you. You told me to mind my own business."

"I don't remember nothing," Bill the bartender said and walked away.

Lew turned his red-rimmed, brown eyes on me. "He was sitting over there, at the end of the bar, dressed like a techie—like they used to dress at the theatre; that's how we got to talking. Did I tell you I used to be the stage doorman at the Winter Garden?"

"You mentioned it."

"Anyway he looked like a techie; that's a person who does technical stuff for a theatre, like lighting or set work or—"

I cut him off. "I know."

"You in the business?"

144

"I'm a juggler."

"No kidding? What do you do to earn a living?"

He sounded like my father and I told him so. That started him talking about *his* father. The conversation definitely wasn't going in the direction I wanted.

I noticed Lew had finished his drink so I got Bill's attention and told him to bring another round. I really didn't want to drink this much, but I felt I was on to something if only I could swing Lew's attention back to Bob Johnson.

"Do you remember what Bob was wearing that night?" I asked.

"I told you," Lew squeaked out between gulps of his drink. "Like a techie."

"Overalls?"

"Nahh, blue work clothes. With his name, Bob, embroidered on his chest. That was something I always loved about techies, they always wore those shirts with their names embroidered above the pocket. I'll tell you, Arnie, I wasn't always so good with names and it helped a lot to be able to read it off someone's shirt."

"I bet." I felt I had hit pay dirt. He knew what Bob was wearing that night. I'd seen all the papers too. Only the *Post* had used Bob's picture, and it had been a head shot. It didn't show his clothes. For Lew Steiger to know what Bob was wearing, he must have seen him that night.

"There was one guy that worked at the theatre," Lew continued, unaware of the excitement he had sparked in me, "who had a different name embroidered on each of his shirts, just to confuse me. Smart-ass punk."

"Lew, Lew, my good friend Lew." He looked at me. "Do you remember what time he came in?"

"Who?"

"Bob Johnson." I practically screamed. I was trying hard not to lose control.

"Nope, sorry."

All my excitement fluttered away like doves pulled from a magician's sleeve. The adrenaline left my system and the beers took over. I felt a pressing need to go to the bathroom, to relieve myself and to retreat into the comfort and security of white-tiled surroundings. If Lew couldn't remember *when* Bob had come to the bar, it didn't matter that he had been there at all. He could have come *after* the murder.

"Excuse me," I mumbled and got off the bar stool.

"Funny," Lew said, still following his own tumbled thoughts, "him being attracted to that girl."

"Who?" I asked, not really caring.

"Your friend, Bob Johnson."

I returned to my seat. The bathroom wasn't going anywhere. "What girl? What do you mean?"

"I thought about it because of your heading to the john just now. But don't let me stop you."

"No, Lew, really, I can wait. What about the girl?" The adrenaline was pumping again.

"Well, like I just said, I had gone to the head and when I came back your friend was talking up some girl. But she wasn't the kind of girl I figured he would be going after."

"What do you mean?"

"Well." He lowered his voice to a croaky whisper, looked around to make sure no one else was listening, and then leaned his head in conspiratorially. "She had the biggest bazonkers I'd ever seen." He sat back, nodded his head, and gave me a look like he had just uttered an important truth.

I waited for a few moments, hoping he would explain the significance of the woman's chest. He didn't, so I finally asked, "So?"

"So?" He snorted. "So Bob's a leg man. Why, just after he came in here we was watching that 'Entertainment Tonight' show, you know, where the woman crosses her legs at the end."

"Mary Hart?"

"Whoever. Anyway Bob was all gah-gah for her. Said how he loved legs like that. So you see why I was surprised later that him being a leg man, he should be hitting on a woman with big bazooms."

"That's very interesting, Lew. . . ." I stopped short. Suddenly I realized, it *was* interesting. "Lew, you're sure it was 'Entertainment Tonight'?"

"Sure. A guy doesn't forget those legs. Know what I mean?"

I was back to pay dirt. "Entertainment Tonight" is on at 7:30 every night. It runs for half an hour. If Bob watched the end of the show with Lew, he had to be there, at the bar, before 8:00. The police said Gary's murder occurred between 8:15 and 8:30. Lew had just provided Bob Johnson with an alibi for the time of the murder. I could hand D. L. Blacker an airtight defense for one of his clients. Now if only someone would return the favor and come up with a defense for me. . . . I bought Lew another round, wrote down his address and phone number so I could give them to Blacker, and excused myself. I paid a quick trip to the bathroom and then headed to the pay phone.

Blacker wasn't in. I got his answering machine and left a long-winded message about how I had dug around and established an alibi for Bob. I put in a few choice comments about how much time he was spending with the Saudi princess and what Arabs were known to do to people who diddled their royalty. Then I hung up, put in another quarter, and called Bob Johnson's number. It was busy.

I was too excited to just go home and wait. I decided to take a subway to Bob's apartment and tell him the good news in person. I also figured it would be a good time to talk about the job he had mentioned the night before. He was bound to be in a good mood when he heard my news. I told Lew he'd be hearing from me, left the bar, and walked to the subway. It was just getting dark and the sky had that special look it sometimes gets in the half-dozen heartbeats that separate day and night, even in New York. I stood at the entrance to the subway and marveled at the colors of the clouds, then I took a deep breath of the city and headed down into the ground.

Chapter

FOURTEEN

*T*he address Bob had written on the scrap of paper was in Brooklyn Heights, a *better* neighborhood of Brooklyn. I don't really know New York outside of Manhattan, so I wasted almost an hour trying to find his street. Some of the streetlights weren't working, making it tough to read addresses, so it took even longer to locate the right building. When I did, it was a four-story brownstone on a block filled with four-story brownstones. I walked up the stoop and, looking at the names on the bells in the foyer, saw that the building had only four apartments, one to a floor. I pushed the button beneath Bob's name, but got no response. I tried again, still nothing. "Great," I mumbled, "I came all the way to Brooklyn, and he's not home."

As I stood there, weighing my options, a short, plump woman with long, kinky brown hair came skipping down the stairs. She stopped when she saw me, looked me over and smiled.

"Hi," she said, coming down the last few steps and opening the security door. She was young, probably just out of college, and dressed in jogging shoes, ankle socks, and a short T-shirt dress that showed off legs that would have been better left hidden. "Looking for someone?"

"Bob Johnson. His phone's been busy, but I just pushed his buzzer and he didn't answer."

"Oh," she said, smiling in a way that caused her eyes to squint and her nose to crinkle, "the intercom is always on the fritz. We keep telling the landlord, but he never does anything."

"I know what you mean," I said and smiled back. "My bathroom faucet is New York's leading source of toxic waste. My landlord has been promising to look into it since I moved into the place."

"You're cute." She giggled. "Listen, I just passed Bob's apartment on the way down. His door was kind of open and his stereo was on. You want to just go on up?" She held the door open in a way that required me to rub against her to get through.

"Thanks," I said as my chin passed over her head.

"Anytime," she said, trying too hard to let me know she meant it. "Say, if you're going to be around for a little while, my roommate and I are having a party tonight. We live on three, right above Bob. Why don't you stop by? I was just on my way out to get beer and chips, but I'll be back soon."

"Sure, sounds like fun, I'll try to make it," I said, knowing it didn't and that I wouldn't.

"Great!" She smiled the squinty, crinkly smile again. "By the way, my name's Cindi; spelled with an i instead of a y." She offered a small clammy hand. I took it.

"Pat," I said. "Spelled just like it sounds."

She squeezed my hand with both of hers, winked at me, said, "See you later, Pat," and went skipping out the door.

I took the stairs to the second floor, two at a time. If possible, I didn't want to be around when Cindi with an i instead of a y got back. Maybe I could convince Bob to go out for a burger or something while we talked.

As I reached the second-floor landing I could hear music blaring from the open door. The song ended and a disc jockey came on. Bob was listening to a radio station. I knocked on the door, but another song had started and the music drowned out my knock. Pushing open the door, I called Bob's name. He didn't answer.

The only illumination in the room came from the hall behind me and from the dancing lights and dials on Bob's stereo system. It was quite an impressive wall of state-of-the-art equipment: a separate tuner and amplifier, twelve-band-per-channel graphic equalizer, programmable compact disc player, one of those dubbing cassette decks that lets you make high-speed copies of your friends' cassettes, a stereo VHS videotape deck, a digital audio tape deck, what looked like a direct-drive turntable, four Altec Lansing speakers, a huge subwoofer, and a large-screen projection TV.

I found the wall switch, flicked it on, and the room lit up. Across the room I saw the phone. It was off the hook. I began to get a very bad feeling in the pit of my stomach. I went over to the stereo and turned it off. Then I called Bob's name again. Still no answer. I walked slowly and delicately across the living room, past the kitchen, toward a closed door at the far end. I opened it and peered into a room steeped in darkness. I could make out the shadowy shape of a bed and other furniture you would expect to find in a bedroom. As my eyes slowly became adjusted to the dark, I scanned the room, not sure of what I was looking for. Even in the gloom I could see that Bob wasn't there.

I crossed over to the bed and turned on a lamp. Then I saw it. It had been invisible in the low light. Blood.

A trail of blood, starting at the foot of the bed and leading toward a door at the other end of the room. The bad feeling came rushing up from my stomach, but I swallowed it back down again and forced my feet to walk toward that awful door. I opened it slowly, knowing even before I turned on the light what I would find.

It was worse than I could have imagined. On the floor of his bathroom lay a tangle of ripped flesh and shredded clothing that had once been Bob Johnson. Blood was everywhere. He had been stabbed over and over again, and his blood now covered the room. My knees gave way and I landed in a crimson pool. A sound like the ocean filled my ears. Through the crashing waves I thought I heard someone calling Bob's name, then calling mine. I looked over my shoulder and saw Cindi skipping into the bedroom. I tried to get up, to stop her from seeing, but I was too late. Her hands flew up in front of her in a needless attempt to keep me away; or perhaps to just blot out the image of what she saw. She started to scream, and then she turned and ran from the apartment.

I followed her from the bedroom and reached the living room just as she ran out the door. I had to force myself to think. What should I do? First, I closed the front door. I had enough problems without Cindi coming back. Then I went over to the phone. It was still off the hook. I hung it up, looked at it for a moment, and then put it to my ear and called Blacker. He picked it up on the second ring.

"Hello, Blacker here."

"Uh, D. L., this is Pat."

"Hi, Pat. I just walked through the door with a dozen fresh Dunkin' Donuts, if you feel like stopping by. How'd the job go?"

"Fine, uh, I've got a problem here."

He must have heard the tension in my voice, because his became more urgent. "What's wrong? Where are you?"

"I'm at Bob Johnson's apartment. He's dead."

I heard him take in a long steady breath, let it out slowly, and then the creak of what must have been him sitting back in his office chair. "Tell me about it," he said gravely. "Start at the beginning."

I did. It didn't take long; there wasn't much to tell. I figured my finding an alibi for Bob didn't matter much anymore.

When I got to the end of my short tale, telling him about Cindi running from the apartment, he did exactly what I had hoped. He told me what to do.

"When we hang up, I want you to call the police right away. That girl may have already called them, and if you don't, they'll want to know why. When they arrive, tell them that your lawyer is on the way, and then don't say anything more until I get there, okay?"

"Sure, okay, fine."

"Good, I'll be there soon as I can." And he hung up.

I dialed 911. A woman answered, asked me to wait, and clicked off. I was trying to report a murder and the emergency operator had put me on hold. After a wait that felt like hours, but was probably just minutes, someone came back on the line, a man this time. He asked how he could help me, and I told him I wanted to report a murder. That got his attention. He seemed primarily interested in getting information about *me*. I told him my name, but said that for the rest he'd have to come to the scene of the crime. He didn't like that much. I didn't care. I gave him Bob's address and then hung up and waited.

Time passes slowly when you're alone with a dead body in the next room. I couldn't stop thinking about it. About Bob's crumpled, mutilated body; about the blood that seemed to be everywhere in the bathroom. The bathroom. I was clubbed senseless in Donna's bathroom and then discovered the dead body of Bob Johnson in his. I knew that I would never again be able to enter a bathroom with the anticipation of security and comfort that had been formed in my youth. Forever after I would hesitate before pushing open the door, unsure of what might await me. The scene in *that* bathroom, just a few steps away, would never fade from my mind.

Any further thoughts or self-pity were interrupted by the far-off call of a single siren, cutting through the night. I settled back into the overstuffed cushions of the sofa and listened. The siren's wail pulled up in front of the building, faded to a moan, and finally disappeared, absorbed into the brownstone buildings lining that little section of the fourth largest city in America. In the silence my ears, straining to hear the approach of Brooklyn's finest, picked up the staccato tapping of syncopated footsteps racing down the stairs. Cindi was going to meet the police. I continued to listen and was rewarded with the sounds of the security door being opened, some mumbled conversation, and then heavy footsteps hurrying up the stairs.

After everything I had been through, I thought that nothing could rattle me any more than I had already been rattled. I was wrong. Two policemen came bursting through the open door with their guns drawn. They dropped into the classic shooter's pose you always see television cops take: legs apart, guns held with both arms straight in front of them. But this wasn't TV, this was real, and they were pointing those guns at me.

I slowly raised my hands and gave them the best smile I could get my lips to form. They kept their guns aimed at my stomach and began to inch forward. From behind them I heard the sound of another set of feet racing up the stairs. I silently prayed that it was someone in authority who would tell them not to shoot me. I was half right.

D. L. Blacker raced into the room, but stopped short, clutching his briefcase, when he saw the pointed guns. "Don't shoot him!" he shouted. I noticed he was careful not to get between the police guns and me.

One of the cops transferred his attention to Blacker. "Who are you?" he barked.

"My name's D. L. Blacker. I'm this man's attorney. He discovered the body and then called me after he phoned the police."

"Woman downstairs said *she* called the police."

"That's right," Cindi said from the hallway, "I did." Cindi's eyes peered from the side of the open doorway. She kept her body safely hidden. Apparently she wasn't taking any chances with a dangerous character like me in the apartment.

"I assure you," Blacker said, slipping into that lawyer's voice I had previously admired, one-third evangelical preacher, one-third father figure, and one-third snake-oil salesman, "my client is completely innocent. The fact that he waited here for you to arrive shows his good faith. Now, how about putting down your guns?"

"No!" Cindi screamed, bounding into the apartment, her arm extended, her finger pointing at me. "He's a murderer. I saw him kill Bob. It was awful." She started to cry and hiccup at the same time.

One of the cops, the one who had been talking with Blacker, told her to go upstairs and wait in her apartment. She plodded out, her gray furry house slippers shuffling across the floor as she walked away. Blacker told me to sit, and then sat down beside me on the sofa as the sound of Cindi's sniffles faded away. I noticed that he was careful not to sit too close to me. I understood, since the blood on my clothes was not yet dry. One of the policemen came over to us.

"Where's the body?" he asked.

I started to stand up, but he placed a hand on my chest and pushed me back down, saying, "Just tell me."

I did.

"Jack," he said to his partner, "keep an eye on them. I'm going to go have a look."

"Sure, Ted, go on." Jack kept his eye on us. In fact, he had barely moved since he first aimed his gun at me. A dedicated cop, this Jack.

Ted went to take his look. While he was gone the sound of sirens in the street below heralded the arrival of still more city employees whose sworn goal was to serve and protect. As they trooped up the stairs and into the apartment, I had the feeling that it was going to be a long night. The look Police Officer Ted gave me as he came back from examining all that was left of Bob Johnson convinced me I was right. I couldn't blame him, I remembered the scene in the bathroom.

Things happened quickly. A police inspector, so fat that his jackets could have been propped up and used as temporary shelters for the homeless, came in, was briefed by Ted and Jack, looked in the bathroom, sneered at me, refused to acknowledge Blacker's existence, and went up to talk to Cindi. I heard one of the cops call him Inspector Burke.

While he was gone a steady stream of people came into the apartment and were quickly ushered through to the bathroom: photographers, fingerprint men, and a little balding guy with thick glasses, carrying a black doctor's bag, all paraded past.

Just three nights before I had waited nervously as the police investigated Gary Johnson's murder. Now I waited, with a calm resignation that came from my new familiarity with the routine, as they investigated the killing of his brother.

Three nights ago Blacker had told me to eat; I ignored him and was sorry. As I sat with Blacker on the sofa in Bob's living room, I remembered that advice and pulled out my sack of bagels. The four hours on the street for Artie the bagel baron seemed like they had taken place in another lifetime rather than just a few hours before. I offered the bagels to Blacker, who took a cinnamon raisin before returning the bag to me. I pulled one out without looking and bit into a very fragrant garlic bagel. Perfect, I thought, for my upcoming session with the rotund Inspector Burke.

The cop named Jack had continued to watch me, so I offered the bag to him. He smiled a little, took a pumpernickel bagel, and resumed his protective stance. Somehow he didn't seem so threatening with his mouth munching away.

Blacker and I talked quietly. He asked how the job had gone, whether Artie had paid me, and, getting the hint, I pulled out the wad of money Artie had given me and peeled off Blacker's commission. Jack made a snide comment about lawyers as Blacker tucked the cash into his wallet.

Inspector Burke finally reappeared, gave me a look that made his earlier sneer seem like a soul kiss, and grabbed the half-eaten bagel from Jack's hand. He took a bite that cleanly removed most of what was left of the bagel, returned the remaining silver to Jack, and went through into the scene of the crime.

As I sat there I was becoming uncomfortably aware of a physical problem that was not going to go away on its own accord. The beers I threw back at Jimmy Ray's had finished working their way through my system and now wanted out. It wouldn't have been much of a problem, except Bob's apartment seemed to have only one bathroom and I didn't think anyone was going to let me use it just then. I whispered my problem to Blacker. He chuckled and turned to Jack.

"Pat here has to go to the bathroom. What should he do?"

This was too big a problem for Jack. He went over to a plainclothes detective who was in a corner talking to Officer Ted. Apparently it was too big for him too, because he looked at me, snickered a little, and walked back toward the bathroom. Maybe, I thought, he was going to see if my using the toilet would get in the way of the investigation.

After a wait of several minutes that felt like hours to my now-distended bladder, the plainclothes cop came back. He talked to Ted, who walked across to us and said something to Jack, who had resumed his position slightly to the left of our sofa. Then Ted turned to me.

"Let's go," he said.

I stood up. "Where?" I asked, not really caring, so long as it had something with plumbing that flushed.

"The inspector says I should take you upstairs and ask the ladies up there if you can use their bathroom."

And so, up we went. Ted knocked on the third-floor apartment, and the door was opened by a girl who wasn't Cindi but seemed to have all of her unattractive physical qualities. Ted explained the situation, and she solemnly consented and directed me to their bathroom, which was located off the living room. As I closed the door, Cindi came into the living room to ask who had knocked, caught sight of me, and let out with a shriek that could have curdled milk. Finally, I thought, I had come up with a way to avoid casual entanglements with new women who have expressed passing interest: Convince them that I'm an ax murderer.

As I washed my hands I heard Ted talking, through the door. I missed part of what he said, but as I turned off the water and dried my hands on a massive pink towel with little baby blue flowers on three corners and a big letter C on the fourth, I heard him say, "The doc estimates Johnson's been dead for at least five hours, so if you're sure about when you let him into the building, he couldn't have done it." I assumed I was the "him" Ted was talking about.

A singsong voice that was instantly recognizable as Cindi's said she was sure about the time, and then invited Ted to her party. I figured I would return the favor he had done in bringing me to a bathroom, so I opened the door and stepped into the room in time to keep him from having to accept Cindi's invitation.

Since no one had told *me* I was innocent, I did my best to look just as guilty coming out of the bathroom as I had when I went in. "Shouldn't we be going?" I asked.

"Right," Ted said and started for the door.

"Oh, Officer." Cindi was staring at a bad plastic reproduction of a schoolhouse clock that hung on her wall, next to a poster proclaiming that Today Is the First Day of the Rest of Your Life. I found myself thinking that for Bob Johnson, today had been the *last* day of the rest of his life.

As Cindi peered at the clock, her body stiffened and her face slowly twisted in tense thought, suggesting that all her energy was being used to make some massive mental exertion. "If it's been five hours," she said, "and it's seven o'clock now, that would mean he was killed around two o'clock, right?"

Officer Ted didn't say anything. He just looked back and forth between Cindi and me. He didn't seem happy. Maybe I wasn't supposed to know this stuff.

"Now," Cindi continued, too busy thinking to notice Ted's discomfort, "I heard someone get buzzed through the security door at around one thirty, and Bob started playing his stereo a few minutes after that. At first he played it kind of quietly, but then he turned it up and left it loud till later, just before when I went into his apartment and. . . ." She stopped talking and looked at me. I looked at Ted and then back at Cindi. "I guess," she mumbled, "*Bob* didn't turn his stereo up loud. Someone else did, huh?"

I nodded. "I think that's right."

"But who?"

I didn't have an answer to that question, and I told her so.

Ted told her the police would get to the bottom of it. She didn't seem to believe him, and I know I didn't.

Blacker had said *he* was going to find the murderer, but I was starting to lose faith in him too. Gary was Blacker's client. He was killed. Bob had been a client too. Maybe I was getting paranoid, but I found myself regretting my decision to retain Blacker in this thing, and wondering if he would be able to find the murderer before one more name was added to the list of his clients who turned up dead.

Chapter

FIFTEEN

*H*aving overheard Officer Ted's conversation with Cindi, I knew that the police thought me innocent of Bob's murder. It took a lot of the pressure off when his boss finally got around to questioning me. Inspector Burke tried to convince me that I had come to the apartment earlier, killed Bob, left, and then returned to the scene of the crime. But I knew I hadn't, and he didn't really believe that I had, either. Still, he didn't want to let me go.

"I could hold you as a material witness, Arnold," he said. "I'm sure you know more than you're telling."

Blacker had been relatively quiet through the questioning; advising, when Burke started, that I tell the truth, and then quietly interrupting at one point to ask that a question be clarified. Now he spoke up. "Inspector, *I'm* sure I don't have to remind *you* that under New York law a material witness order can be obtained only if an indictment has been filed, a grand jury proceeding has been commenced, or a felony complaint has been filed with a local criminal court.

Have any of these occurred?" There were times I loved that guy.

Burke looked at D. L. Blacker like he was a piece of fried chicken, and then said, "Get out of here. We'll be in touch."

As Blacker and I reached the street, it was just past midnight; the wind was blowing and a light rain was beginning to fall. Not enough to make puddles, not enough to rattle people's windows, just enough to make it impossible to find a taxi in New York City. By the time we reached the subway station, the rain was falling harder. Blacker didn't seem to mind; why should he—he had worn a raincoat. All I had on were a shirt and jeans, stained brown with clotted blood that no amount of rain would ever wash away.

Our train arrived and we sat down in an almost empty subway car, surprisingly free of graffiti. Blacker immediately pulled a yellow legal pad from his briefcase and began making notes, flipping from page to page, checking things at various places throughout the pad.

My mother once said that I had enough curiosity for a carload of cats. Sometimes, like when I was very tired, that curiosity caused me to ask questions about things that I didn't even know I was curious. "Mr. Blacker, D. L.," I found myself asking, "I couldn't help noticing that you spend a lot of time jotting things down. Just what is it you've been writing on those yellow pads?"

Blacker stopped writing, looked at me, smiled, and took a deep breath.

"In law school," he began, and I sat back, prepared for another one of his long stories-as-explanation, "I knew several people with truly remarkable memories, much better than mine will ever be. You have a great memory, Pat, but some of these people were almost frightening. One woman in my study group was like a walking casebook. She could

162

rattle off page after page of some obscure legal decision she had read weeks before."

"Sounds like a fun date," I muttered.

Blacker looked out the window of the subway car and his lips twisted into a lopsided smile. "She was. Law wasn't the only subject in which she was well read."

Before I could ask him if he meant what I *thought* he meant, he picked up the yellow pad that was laying in his lap.

"This," he said, "is how I learned to compensate for my unexceptional memory. A professor of mine used to tell us to write down everything, trust nothing to memory. 'Law school,' he would say, 'isn't going to teach you everything about the law. Even if all the law could be taught in three years, the law is always changing so what you learned in school would be outdated a few years after you graduate. What law school does best,' he told us, 'is teach you to think like a lawyer; to look at everything with a detached, analytical eye, recognize the problems inherent in any situation that presents itself to you, and then know where to look for the answers to those problems. If you kept good notes,' he would say, 'you'll probably find the answer to any question on your yellow pad.' That's why I've been taking notes on everyone and everything connected with the murders."

"So," I asked, a trace of sarcasm slipping into my voice, "you think you can look through those notes and come up with the killer?"

"Yes," Blacker said, "that's what I intend to do."

"But this isn't a lawsuit or a contract, D. L., this is someone who's killing people."

"When the D.A. gets ready to prosecute a defendant, he puts together a pile of evidence, sifts through it, and tries to build a case that, when presented to a jury, will convince them of the defendant's guilt. While doing that, if he finds an obvious flaw in his case, a hole in his argument, he'll try to find something with which to fill in that hole. He knows

he's got to build an airtight case, because of what the defendant's lawyer is going to do."

"What do you mean?"

"When a good defense lawyer prepares for a case, he
starts by looking over all the evidence that the prosecuting
attorney is going to use against his client. He does that
specifically to search for the weaknesses in the prosecution's
case. Then, in front of the jury, he points out those holes,
using them to create a reasonable doubt in the minds of the
jurors. And that's all he needs do to get a verdict of not
guilty for his client."

"But why does the prosecutor let the defense attorney
know what evidence he's going to use?"

"Under the rules of criminal procedure, the defendant
always has the right to know everything the prosecution has
against him. The way it works is that the defense attorney
makes what's called a *demand* on the prosecutor, who then
has to turn over all the evidence he's collected and the names
of all the witnesses he might have testify at the trial. After
he's told the defense everything he's got, the prosecutor can
decide *not* to call someone as a witness, or *not* to introduce
some piece of physical evidence. That's okay, but the D.A.
can't use anything at the trial that he didn't tell the defense
about."

I noticed the yellow pad sitting in his lap and was reminded of my initial question. "All of this is interesting I'm
sure, but what does it have to do with what you've been
writing on those pads?"

He held up the pad with one hand and patted it with his
other. "If you look at all these notes as being like a pile of
evidence collected by the D.A., you can use them to create
a case against just about anyone connected with this thing;
you, me, everyone else who was at that party. So what I
have to do is go through these notes first as though I'm the
prosecutor, building a case against each person. I'll find the

holes, trying to plug them, and see against whom I can build the strongest cases. Then I'll go over those individual cases as though I'm the defense attorney for each person, looking for weaknesses, things that would create a reasonable doubt as to my client's guilt."

"Like what?"

"Like the facts that Artie the bagel baron could testify that you were in front of his Manhattan store from noon until four and"—he flipped through his legal pad until he found what he was looking for, and then continued—"and this Lew Steiger can testify that you were at Jimmy Ray's from four thirty to six or so. The medical examiner will establish that Bob was killed during those hours. That clears you in Bob's murder, and since it's fair to assume the two killings were done by the same person, it creates a reasonable doubt as to your guilt in Gary's murder."

"Sounds good to me. Who else?"

"Well, I'll really need to go through the notes to be sure, but I figure I'm innocent."

We both smiled, and he continued. "You've said that Gary was alive after I left him in the dressing room, and I went from the room to the stage, where a party full of people watched me perform until Donna discovered the body."

I nodded.

He continued. "I can clear Andy because he was in the D.J. booth when Gary was killed; everyone at the party heard him doing that rap thing from the time you left the dressing room and a living-and-breathing Gary, until Donna went in and found him dead. And, though we haven't conclusively established that his girlfriend Debby left before the party began, she doesn't seem to have a real motive for either murder."

"It seems to me that the defense lawyer in you will always be able to come up with holes in the case against everyone."

"Everyone," he said, "except one person. Every new piece

of information plugs an old hole. There will come a time when I have a case against *one* person that satisfies the prosecutor and frustrates the defense lawyer in me, and then I'll have our killer."

The train screeched to a halt at the Ninety-sixth Street station and he slid the yellow pad back into his briefcase.

"Care for a nightcap?" he asked, getting up and leading the way out of the subway car and onto the platform. "I have another bottle of that tequila."

"No, thanks. I don't think I'm ready for a repeat of the other night; I know my stomach isn't. Anyway, I'm pretty beat." We walked side by side toward the exit. Neither of us spoke as we climbed the stairs to the street and started walking downtown.

We stopped at the corner of Broadway and Ninety-fifth Street. "See you tomorrow," he said, although we had made no plans to meet.

Perhaps I should have questioned this simple statement on his part that seemed to take so much for granted. Maybe I would be busy tomorrow; maybe I would just spend the whole day in bed. But at the time I didn't think of any of this. Too much had happened in the last four days. I had allowed my life to be too closely entwined with his to question this most simple of statements. Of course I would be seeing him the next day, so I just said, "Right, tomorrow," and headed home.

Ten minutes after I walked into my apartment I was asleep. Fifteen minutes after I fell asleep I was awake again, groping for a telephone that, despite a string of my best muttered obscenities, refused to stop ringing. I blindly groped my way to the phone. Not that my apartment was pitch-black at night. Perhaps due to some obscure scientific principle like Newtonian physics or Einstein's conservation of energy, my apartment always seemed to be too dark during the day and too bright at night. Anyway, when awakened in the middle of the night, I quickly found that the best policy was to keep my eyes tightly shut. In that way the sight of all my worldly possessions strewn about my one-room apartment wouldn't shock me more awake than I already was.

I put the phone to my ear and mumbled something appropriate.

A voice that even in my half-comatose state was instantly recognizable as belonging to D. L. Blacker asked, "Pat?"

I admitted it was and opened my eyes. Something in the way he said my name convinced me I wasn't going back to sleep.

Chapter
SIXTEEN

"Can you come over right away?" Blacker asked. The underlying tension in his voice made it something more than a polite request.

"Sure, certainly," I stammered, "right away."

I was out of bed before I had hung up the phone, and out the door before my shirt was buttoned. I threw on my jacket as I reached the street, barely noticing that the rain had started again. By the time I reached Blacker's building it was really coming down and I was soaked. Roberto recognized me and made some sympathetic comment about the need to stay warm and dry, to avoid the flu. I sneezed my agreement, jerking my head and throwing water from my hair like a hunting dog shaking itself dry after a quick swim in a mountain stream. Roberto muttered something in Spanish and waved me toward D. L. Blacker's door.

Blacker answered my knock as though he had been waiting by the door.

"What happened?" I asked. But he said nothing, just gestured me in and shut the door. I peeled off my jacket and handed it to Blacker, who hung it in a bathroom to dry.

Then he led me to his kitchen and made us a pot of tea. While he worked I kept trying to get him to tell me what it was that had led to this nocturnal invitation, but he didn't, or wouldn't, say. As he handed me a cup, I asked again.

He poured tea into my cup and said, "Try the tea."

I sipped it and smiled. "Earl Grey?" I asked.

He just nodded.

It meant a great deal to me that he had taken the time to get my favorite tea amid the confusion of the last few days. If, however, the urge to serve tea was what had motivated his phone call, I had seriously misread the edge in his voice. "Thanks," I said, "for the tea. Now, why did you call?"

"You're welcome, come on."

D. L. Blacker led the way from the kitchen to his office. On his desk was a telephone answering machine. We sat and slowly Blacker began to speak.

"Usually, as soon as I walk in the door, I listen to my phone messages. As a lawyer I feel I have a responsibility to my clients, and as a performer I know that if I don't return a call promptly, I might lose a great job."

I grunted my agreement. On more than one occasion I'd returned a call too late and lost a booking to another entertainer. I doubted, however, that a lost performance was what had bothered him enough to wake me up and call me over on that dark and rainy night.

"When you called me tonight from Bob's apartment, I had just gotten home; I hadn't listened to my messages yet. Then, when we hung up, I just grabbed my coat and my briefcase and went running out. I didn't listen to my answering machine before I left. So, I didn't get to listen to today's messages until just a few minutes ago."

He stopped and we sat in silence. I sipped my tea. We both stared at the machine on his desk.

"And?" I finally asked.

"And, there was a message on it. A message from Bob."

169

An invisible, gloved hand grasped me a few inches below my navel and squeezed. I struggled to take a breath. My hand shook and a little of the tea spilled from the cup onto my jeans. I put the cup down on the desk and then slumped back into the chair.

Blacker slowly nodded as though he knew what I was feeling.

"Can I hear it?" I managed to gasp out.

D. L. Blacker nodded again, wearily raised his hand, and pushed a button on the machine.

"D. L., this is Bob, Bob Johnson. If you're there, could you pick up the phone?" Hearing the recorded voice brought back to me the image of Bob as I had seen him last, torn and bloody on his bathroom floor. I squirmed in my seat as the unseen hand that held my groin turned icy cold and squeezed a little harder. "Shit. Okay," the voice continued, "listen, I've been going over a bunch of Gary's stuff that I picked up yesterday, and I think I know who killed him. The asshole's coming over here, any minute now. I had hoped you could come too, but since you're not home, maybe I'll call Pat Arnold. I don't think I have anything to worry about, but it'd be nice to have a backup. Just to be safe I'm going to try to make a copy of this thing and mail it to you. I guess I could leave it on your answering machine—I know that when you heard it you'd agree with me—but I don't know if there's time to do that *and* make a copy before my guest arrives. Give me a call when you get home, okay? Thanks."

The machine beeped twice to signal the end of the message.

I started to speak, but Blacker stopped me with a wave of his hand and a mumbled "There's more."

The machine continued to play. "D. L., Bob again. I copied it. Arnold wasn't home, and it occurred to me that I should tell you who it was that killed Gary. You know, just

170

in case." Bob laughed nervously, but the laugh was cut short by the sound of a doorbell ringing in the background. "Shit, hang on a second. This could be it. You'll have the whole thing on tape." We heard the phone being set down, footsteps, and then assorted vague sounds for a few seconds before the machine beeped twice, signaling the end of the message. Blacker reached out and turned off the answering machine.

"What happened?" I gulped out.

"The machine is voice activated. Bob stopped talking into it and it turned itself off. That was probably the killer at the door, and Bob figured their whole meeting was being taped on my answering machine. Damn."

I remembered the off-the-hook phone at Bob Johnson's apartment. "Yeah," I said.

We stared at each other. My mouth felt bone-dry, so I picked up my cup and took a sip of the tea. It had gone cold.

"He tried to call me, to ask for help," I murmured.

"He called us both," Blacker said. "But we weren't home."

I wasn't home because I'd been off passing out leaflets, dressed as a clown on a street corner in midtown. Suddenly my line of work seemed very wrong. For the first time in my life I found myself agreeing with my father's often expressed judgment that I should "grow up." I felt severely depressed.

"So," I said, in a desperate attempt to get my mind on a more positive track. "He found something that allowed him to figure out who killed his brother, and he invited the guy over for a confrontation. Then he called you, and, hopefully, made a Xerox of whatever he found and mailed it to you before his killer arrived. What do you think he found, a contract, a letter?"

I don't know if Blacker even heard me. He had pulled

out one of his pads and was once again writing and flipping pages. As I watched, he stopped, put the pad on his desk, and began absentmindedly twirling his pencil between the fingers of his left hand. He gazed at a spot several feet over my head. "Why," he said, and slammed the pencil down on the desk, "did he call the killer and invite him over *before* he was sure someone else could be there? That's just stupid and Bob wasn't that dumb."

"I guess," I offered, "he figured either you or I would be around."

Blacker looked at me but didn't respond to what I had said. "And another thing: Where was he going to copy the thing? Bob lived on a quiet residential block; no copy center nearby." He went back to flipping through his legal pad. "Where was he going to photocopy the damn thing?"

"Does it really matter?"

"Now everything matters."

"I could go to his neighborhood," I offered. "Try to find out."

Blacker considered my offer for a moment and then, without saying anything to me, pulled several other yellow pads from a drawer, all of them filled with his distinctive scribblings. He scattered them across his massive desk and began furiously to pull one after another to him—reading from some, jotting down additional notes in others, and occasionally mumbling to himself.

After several minutes of this I asked, "Okay if I get some more tea?"

He nodded his head and waved his hand, but he didn't look up from the sheaf of papers before him. I took my cup and went to the kitchen.

Perhaps because bathrooms had lost much of their attraction for me, and I needed something to take over the importance that they had held in my life for so long, I couldn't help but feel better as I entered D. L. Blacker's kitchen. Viewing the room through the eyes of a former bathroom lover, it had a lot going for it. Like a good bathroom, its walls were covered with ceramic tile. It had smooth, clean surfaces and a porcelain sink. Unlike the less-than-desirable bathrooms I had been in lately, it had no shower stall in which a mugger could hide, and no dead body spilling pools of blood over the checkerboard pattern of the black and white linoleum tiles on the floor below. I had never paid much attention to kitchens before. Never being much of a cook, they had only been a place where someone else prepared food. But at that moment I felt like I had found a new refuge from the cares of the world. With that new-found security came an all-consuming tiredness.

The door to what had been my room just a few nights before stood open, invitingly. I went over and looked inside at the bedroom that, even in the dead of night, seemed safe and warm. I stepped in and sat down on the edge of the bed. It felt great. I lay back, put my head on the pillows, and closed my eyes. I intended to just rest for a moment, "Blacker," I said to myself, "might need me for something." I yawned, stretched, and kicked off my shoes. "If he needs me," I answered, "he can find me. The apartment's not *that* big." Satisfied, I fell asleep.

I awoke with a feeling of déjà vu—the comfortable bed, the sun streaming in through the window, the smell of coffee brewing in the next room. I rolled off the bed and dragged myself through the door into the kitchen.

D. L. Blacker was standing at a counter, scrambling eggs. He smiled when he saw me. Other than that, he looked like hell. He was still dressed in the clothes he had been wearing the night before. His hair was unkempt and dark circles rested behind his glasses, beneath both of his red-rimmed eyes. It was clear that he hadn't been to sleep. A twinge of guilt at my own few hours of slumber nibbled at the back of my mind, but the warmth of his smile quickly put me at ease. He handed me a cup of coffee and his smile broadened into a grin.

I may not be the most perceptive guy in the world, but even I couldn't help but feel that something had happened while I was asleep. "Something you want to tell me?" I asked.

Blacker nodded his head. Then he sat at the kitchen table and took a sip of his coffee. I walked over and stood across from him. His sense of the theatrical—making me wait so as to build the tension, until he finally revealed all—was starting to piss me off.

Finally, he looked up at me and spoke. "I know who did it."

Chapter

SEVENTEEN

I dropped into the chair across from D. L. Blacker. "Who?" I managed to gasp out. "Who killed them? How. . . . What? . . ."

He took another sip of his coffee and smiled at me again. "It's just like I told you last night. The answer was right there in my notes. It just took me a little while to find it." He stood and went to his stove. "Eggs scrambled, okay for you?" he asked.

"Sure, anything."

He poured the eggs into a fry pan. I watched impatiently as he stirred them around.

"It took me almost all night to figure out what Bob found that helped him decide who murdered Gary. Once I had that, everything became clear. The killer was really quite ingenious."

He slid the eggs into two plates, pulled English muffins from the toaster oven, and set it all down on the table. He began to eat. I continued to stare at him.

"So," I asked again, trying not to let my frustration and

anger at his dragging it out creep into my voice. "Who did it?"

"I'd rather not say just yet. I have one question I want to ask Donna first. I'm pretty sure I know what the answer will be, but if I'm wrong, anything I said right now could be construed as slander." He went back to eating his eggs.

"Wait a second. You're not going to tell me because you're afraid of slandering a person who has brutally murdered two innocent people?"

He looked at the untouched eggs and English muffin on my plate. "Are you going to eat that?"

"No!" I practically exploded.

He reached over, took my plate, and set it down in front of himself. "I didn't realize how hungry I was," he said, as he began to eat the eggs that had been mine. When he finished he wiped his lips with his napkin and looked at me.

"Listen, Pat, why don't you go home, clean up, and come back here around eleven o'clock, okay? By then I'll have talked to Donna and also have finished up some other business I need to do." He glanced at his watch. "I have a client coming over around ten thirty, but that shouldn't take long. I know you want information, but I promise not to tell anyone anything until you get back here, how's that?"

I looked at the digital clock on his stove. It read 7:10. I couldn't believe he was going to do business as usual for nearly four hours while the killer was out there walking the streets.

"Why don't you just wait and see if the letter or contract or whatever comes in the mail?" I said through anger-clenched teeth. "Bob said he was going to try and mail it to you. Hell, what with New York mail it should be here in a week or so."

My sarcasm was wasted. He either didn't notice, or chose

176

not to. D. L. Blacker took the dishes to the sink and gestured for me to follow him from the room. We walked down the hall, to the front door, and he helped me into my jacket. It was still damp.

"I'll need your help," he said as he opened the door for me. "Others may be in danger. See you at eleven?"

I nodded and left the apartment. As the door closed behind me, I found my anger rapidly fading and in its place a sense of fear began to rise. Fear that D. L. Blacker might have made the same foolish mistake as Bob. Fear that when I returned at eleven o'clock I might find not the answer to this whole grizzly puzzle, but rather one more victim added to the list of those who had been killed by the person whom we so desperately sought.

I'm not really sure what I did during those next three hours and forty-five minutes. I must have been driving on automatic pilot. By the time I got back to Blacker's door, at eleven o'clock on the button, I was wearing clean clothes, so I must have gone home and changed. I also noticed that I had showered and shaved. I wasn't hungry, so I must have eaten, though I couldn't remember what or where. I did vaguely remember having picked up the phone on several occasions, intending to check with Blacker and make sure he was all right, but I always hung up before the call went through. All in all, it was not an easy three hours and forty-five minutes.

D. L. Blacker let me into his apartment and said, "Hi, Pat. Glad you could make it. I'm just finishing up with a client in my office."

I followed him to the office. Andy Costello and his girlfriend, Debby Brill, were seated in the client's chairs. Andy was studying a letter and Debby was leaning over toward him, trying to read it at the same time. I took the seat by the computer and D. L. Blacker went back to his place behind the desk.

"Andy," Blacker said. "You don't mind if Pat sits in, do you? It seems to me that we're almost done here."

Andy looked up at me, nodded, said, "No problem," and went back to reading the letter. Debby gave me a big smile and a wink. It probably wasn't possible, but she looked even thinner than when I had last seen her, a few days before. She was living proof that the person who said "You can't be too rich or too thin" was at least half wrong.

As I sat there waiting, I couldn't help but imagine the two of them in bed together. It was not a pretty image. Andy was a nice guy and a real talented disc jockey, but not much in the looks department. Considering how bony Debby was, I found myself picturing Andy's body covered with bruises from banging against Debby while making love. Also, Debby was a strong girl; I had seen her lugging around Andy's speaker cabinets. She was clearly capable of inflicting some serious injury in those moments of unbridled passion. An old girlfriend of mine once referred to lovemaking as "bumping uglies." In the case of Andy Costello and Debby Brill, this seemed especially appropriate.

"So, D. L.," Andy said, looking up from what he had been reading. "Let's go over this one more time, just so I'm sure I understand the terms of this retainer letter."

"Good," Blacker said. "Basically it says that I can now cash the five thousand dollar check you gave me a few days ago. That money will serve as a nonreturnable advance for certain legal work I'll be doing for you. Of course nonreturnable means that if you change your mind and want to fire me, or for some reason you don't need my services, I get to keep all the money anyway."

"I still don't like that part," Andy grumbled, "but, okay."

"Good," Blacker continued with a smile. "Let's see, where was I? You're only retaining me to negotiate your deal with WZBQ radio. Not to represent you in any other way, and because I'm serving as your lawyer, not your agent, I'll not be entitled to an ongoing commission. That is to say, the legal fee is all you'll be paying me."

"Seems to me," chirped in Debby, "it's plenty."

"I've no complaints," Andy said as he signed the letter and slid it across the desk to the waiting hands of D. L. Blacker. "An agent would get ten percent of everything I made at the radio station. That would be more than twice your fee in the first year alone."

"Well," Debby jumped in, "now that that's settled, we have a little announcement. Should I tell them, Andy, or do you want to?"

Andy just smiled at his girlfriend, so she barreled on.

"Andy and I are getting married. Isn't that great?"

That seemed to me to be one of those rhetorical questions best left unanswered.

"We'd talked about doing it before," Andy said, smiling at his girlfriend. "Debby really wanted to, but I always told her that I couldn't even consider getting married until I was making more money. Enough to, you know, support her in the style to which she deserved to be accustomed. Anyway, now it looks like I'll be making more money, lots more money, so we're going to do it."

"Stop it, Andy," Debby cut in, "they don't want to hear all the details." She got to her feet and pulled Andy up with her. "Come on, we'd better be going."

Blacker placed the letter into a file on his desk and then stood up too. As he rose, my attention was drawn to the door where, out of the corner of my eye, I saw someone else coming into the office. I turned to see who it was and stopped breathing. It was Donna Johnson.

"Hi," she said to everyone. "Hello, Pat," she said to me, and I forced myself to start breathing again.

"Donna," I heard myself saying. "Hi, what are you doing here?"

She glided over to me and I stood to meet her.

"D. L. called this morning and asked me to come over," she said in a voice that, I allowed myself to believe, suggested she was happy that I was there too.

"With everything that's happened over the last few days," Blacker said, "I thought Donna might be a little happier and *safer* staying in my guest room for a few days."

"Safer?" Andy asked. The tone of his voice said volumes more than the one word. He didn't really believe that Donna was in any danger. In fact, he seemed to be suggesting Blacker wanted Donna there for something a whole lot more intimate than her protection.

Debby smiled an enigmatic smile, but said nothing.

Blacker let the whole thing pass. "Andy, why don't we get together in a day or two. I'll have had time to go over the contract by then, and we can talk about what I should try to get for you."

Debby didn't think this was such a great idea, and she said so. "Look, D. L., you've got to move on this fast. Can't you read it over today and then Andy can stop by tonight to talk about it? That way you can call the station tomorrow."

Blacker gave Debby a sour look. I understood. He wanted to spend the day working on the murders, not reading through a contract, but, with a sigh, he agreed to her suggestion.

"Great," Debby said, "around nine o'clock?"

"Fine, nine o'clock tonight," the lawyer agreed. "And, Debby, you'll come too?" I had to marvel at Blacker's ability to keep sarcasm from his voice.

"Wouldn't miss it," Debby said.

"Sure, no problem," Andy said, stretching out the words

and allowing them to resonate as only as person with his voice could. "Debby can visit with Donna, while you and I work."

I doubted that was the arrangement Debby desired. I was sure it wasn't what Donna would want.

I looked at Donna. She smiled at Debby and said, "That would be great."

I could think of several ways to spend the evening that would be great; visiting with Debby Brill wasn't one of them. In fact, I thought, there was no one in the world that could get me to agree to spend an evening in cozy conversation with Andy's girlfriend.

"Maybe," Donna said, looking at me with a mischievous smile, "Pat would like to join us."

"I'd love to," I said, admitting to myself that there was in fact *one* person for whom I would agree to spend a few hours with Debby.

Blacker led Andy and Debby from the room. I started after them, but Donna placed her hand on my arm and I stopped.

"Do you think, maybe, you'd like to stay for a little while now?" She seemed suddenly shy and unsure of herself, as though she was afraid I might turn her down. Could she really doubt that I would want to stay with her? I'd never been very good at hiding my feelings, and with Donna, I figured I'd been about as subtle as a Mack truck. Heck, by then I thought it must have been clear to just about everyone that I would have been happy to drink her bath water. I didn't say all this, what I did say was "Yes, sure, I'd be happy to."

"Unless you have something to do, someplace you have to go?"

"No, of course not."

"Thank you." I thought she was through talking, but then she looked away, and in a very quiet voice said, "The last couple of days, since Gary ... died, have been ... hard. Everyone is so uncomfortable around me; so worried they'll say or do the wrong thing. Everyone except you, Pat. I wanted to tell you that I don't believe what the police have been saying. *I* know you didn't have anything to do with Gary's death, or Bob's. You're a very special person, Pat— sensitive, warm, understanding. Thank you for being here for me. Your ... friendship ... means a lot to me. From the first time we met, I was drawn to you. Do you believe in reincarnation?"

I didn't answer. I probably nodded. Hell, I would have agreed with her no matter what she asked.

"Maybe," she continued, "we knew each other in a recent past life. Maybe we were lovers, maybe. . . ."

She looked up into my eyes, and then neither of us said anything for what felt like a very long time. I slowly became aware of my own breathing and of the fact that we were standing close enough for me to smell her. She smelled great. Pleasant as it was, I thought maybe I shouldn't be standing quite so close to her, but the computer table was pressing into the backs of my thighs, Donna was right in front of me, and, to move by her, we would have had to touch. I felt myself beginning to shiver at the thought of touching her. It was just like being back at those damn junior-high sock hops; wanting to slow-dance with the girls but afraid they'd laugh at me because of my shakes.

"Are you cold?" Donna asked.

"No, why?"

"Your teeth are chattering."

D. L. Blacker came back into the office, saving me from having to come up with some half-assed lie to explain my behavior. Donna stepped away from me and sat down in one of the client's chairs as Blacker went to his desk and began stuffing file folders into a very expensive looking briefcase.

182

"Pat," he said to me as he looked through one of his yellow legal pads and then slid it into the briefcase, "you could do me a big favor."

"Sure," I said.

"I have to go out for a while. Could you stay here with Donna?"

Before I could answer he turned to her and asked, "If you don't mind?"

"I think that would be very nice," she said.

"Pat?"

"I was planning on it."

He gave me a funny look and then grinned when he saw that both Donna and I were smiling.

"How long will you be gone?" I asked.

"A couple of hours. I'm going to stop at the bank and deposit Andy's check. Then I'm going to the D.A.'s office to talk with Jim Wyman, and if he can use his assistant district attorney's pull to get me in, I want to go and have another look at Bob's apartment."

"You think the Brooklyn police may have missed something?"

D. L. Blacker smiled an enigmatic smile. "Maybe," he said, and started out the door. I followed him.

Before he left the apartment I stopped him and asked, "Do you really think Donna might be in some kind of danger?"

He stopped and some of the energy drained from him. He suddenly looked like what he was: a middle-aged man who had not slept for much too long. "Pat, I just don't know. And I don't want to take the chance. Stick close to her, please." He took a deep breath and some of the humor returned to his eyes. "I have a feeling that's one assignment that shouldn't bother you too much. Later on you can let me know if it was painful duty."

Before I could think up an appropriate response, he was gone.

I stepped back into the apartment and double-locked the door. From somewhere behind me, I heard Donna call my name.

Chapter

EIGHTEEN

The shivering started almost immediately. My teeth began to chatter, covering up the sound of Donna humming some tuneless melody from the kitchen. As I walked toward her my involuntary tremors worked like a personal Geiger counter; the closer I came to her, the more I shook. I clenched my teeth and tried to convince myself that I was being stupid. Her husband had died just a few days before. Things like that didn't usually inspire a woman to engage in the kind of activities that were prefaced by my getting the shakes. I convinced my mind but my body didn't seem to get the message. By the time I reached the kitchen even my knees were unsteady. I leaned against the doorframe, clamped my mouth shut, and smiled.

Donna was pouring tea from a pot into two tall blue mugs. "I thought you might like some tea," she said as she brought me one of the mugs. "I hope you like it. It's Earl Grey. It's my favorite."

"Mine too," I managed to rasp out through clenched teeth. I took a long drink of the hot tea, but when I tried to put the mug down on the counter my hand shook and Donna looked at me with alarm.

"Oh, Pat, you still have that chill. Are you all right? You're not catching a cold, are you?" She placed a small cool hand on my forehead and looked up into my eyes. There must have been an electric generator hidden in that hand, because her touch sent a jolt racing to every nerve ending in my body. My shivering increased a hundredfold.

"You poor dear. You're flushed."

She took the mug from me and then, grasping my hand in her own, led me to the guest room and sat me down on the edge of the bed. Then she left me for a moment and pulled down the window shade. The feel of the room immediately changed. The light, now having to fight its way through the brown material of the shade, cast the room in a warm sepia tone, giving everything the feel of an old and familiar photograph. Without a word Donna went to the closet and reached up to get something from a high shelf. The act of stretching caused her blouse to pull out of her jeans and for a brief moment, which burned across my eyes, through my mind, and down my spine, I saw a band of perfect flesh.

She pulled a comforter from the shelf and brought it to me. "Lie back," she said and gave my chest a little push.

When I was horizontal she spread the comforter over me and sat down on the edge of the bed. As I became aware of her thigh pressing into my waist, the shakes started up again.

"You poor dear," she whispered and gathered me into her arms.

I should have stopped her. She was like a fairy princess sheltering a little bird she thought to be in pain. I should have told her that the only pain the little bird felt was of longing for her; but I didn't. I put my arms around her and I kissed her. Not a big kiss. Not the kiss I wanted to give her. But a kiss nonetheless. She didn't kiss back, but she didn't push me away either.

When the kiss ended I didn't know if I should run away, or hang onto her because I was sure that she would bolt. Instead she pulled me close to her and I held her a little tighter. I barely breathed, waiting for her reaction to my overture. It wasn't what I expected. She started to cry— not big wracking sobs, in fact there was no noise at all. The only way I knew she was crying was that my shoulder was getting wet.

I pulled away from her and, without saying a word, asked her, "Why?" She took my head in her hands, pulled me to her, and kissed me, first gently, but then her lips parted and her tongue, strong and urging, found its way into my mouth and the gentleness was abandoned in a rush of feelings that left all thoughts of propriety behind. Her hands went from my head to my shirt and began tearing at the buttons. I became dimly aware that the comforter was bundled up between us, so I grabbed it and threw it aside. Without breaking our kiss, she removed my shirt and I pulled off her blouse. I realized she wasn't wearing a bra, she didn't need one. Her breasts belonged in a museum. Kissing them brought me closer to perfection than I'd ever been. Had I not been so wrapped up in what we were doing, I might have pulled my head back to admire first one and then the other. They were full, firm, and tipped with perfect pink nipples that hardened, swelled, and seemed to protest my leaving them as she brought my face back up to hers and molded her body into mine. I felt the nipples, like twin medals pressing into my chest, refusing to be forgotten. We kissed again. Another long, hot, wet, open-mouthed kiss that felt like we were exchanging souls. In the middle of the kiss we peeled off our pants. She wasn't wearing panties either.

Somewhere between removing and discarding our pants

the kiss broke for air. I gulped in a few cubic yards of oxygen through my mouth and then thought of a more pleasant use for it. I started at a spot behind her right ear and began working my way down her body, using my tongue to trace every curve and soft spot I found along the way. She lay back on the bed and a succession of sighs, gasps, and soft moans that came from her lips told me I was doing something right. My fingers moved lightly down her body, following the trail that had been blazed by my mouth, feeling, exploring, discovering those spots on her that my tongue had found to be the most sensitive. My lips didn't want to leave her breasts when my hands arrived, but they knew that they had more discoveries to make.

A girl I once knew back in Texas, who did more than anyone else to teach me the difference between making love and having sex, told me something interesting about women's breasts. "Pat," she once said to me, after what I had thought to be a particularly good session on the mattress in the back of my Ford Econoline Van. "There's more to a tit than the nipple. What you do to my nipples is nice, but spend some time on the rest of my breast. It'll make it better for me, and if it's better for me, then I'll want to make it better for you." Ever since then I've tried to follow her advice and slow down when I'm making love to a woman's breasts.

My tongue had worked its way first around one of Donna's breasts and then the other, taking its time, tracing the entire outline of each breast. Then I slowly moved to the left nipple and began sucking it in and out of my mouth quickly, over and over again. When my mouth moved to her right nipple I used my finger to draw little wet circles around the breast I had just left. Finally, as my mouth continued its downward path, I grasped both of her breasts in my hands and gently squeezed the nipples between my thumbs and index fingers. "Oh God," she cried, and started to move her hips, pushing them up and down against me. The movement didn't deter me as my mouth traveled below her waist and began to tease and kiss between her thighs. Her first orgasm came quickly. She cried out my name, tensed, and then relaxed. I started to pull away from her, to give her time to afterglow, but she didn't want that. She pulled my head back up to hers, wrapped her arms around me, and then, in a quick motion, rolled me over so that I was on my back and she was on top of me.

She bent over and kissed me—a long, slow, sensual kiss. The kind of kiss that focuses your entire awareness on that small area between your nose and your chin. Somewhere in the middle of it she began grinding her hips slowly against mine in a rhythm that my body responded to without conscious thought. The kiss and the rhythmic motion of our hips grew in intensity until I felt we would both burst. In a way, she did. A second orgasm shook her body. The scream of pleasure that formed at the back of her throat was blocked by my mouth, still locked against hers. As her shudders subsided, she pulled her lips from mine and moved them to my chest, sucking on *my* nipples and growling at them as though they were responsible for the situation in which we found ourselves. Throughout this her body kept moving as if, with her second climax, she had lost any control she may have had left. I closed my eyes and she seemed to be all over me, everywhere on my body at once, kissing me, licking me, stroking me, grinding against me. Then the movements stopped, she lifted herself up, off my body, and in one fast plunge she slid me all the way into her. My eyes flew open and the air left my lungs in a sharp gasp. She was incredible!

The next few minutes were filled with blurred motion and sounds but crystal-clear sensations. Several times I was on the verge of climaxing and she would stop just long enough for me to regain control. It was as though she could see inside me. She knew just what to do, when to stop, and when to start us all over again. After an eternity on the edge, which didn't last nearly long enough, she had a third orgasm. Her climax caused contractions that brought me over the top and seemed to squeeze me over and over again, until there was nothing left inside of me. We both fell asleep with smiles on our faces.

I awoke first. By now I was getting used to waking up in that room and so I wasn't disoriented by my surroundings. I was, however, a little concerned that I couldn't feel my left arm, until I noticed that it was under Donna. I may have been awake, but my arm, and Donna, was still asleep. I was reminded of an old joke, told to me by my college roommate.

"Hey, Pat," he once said to me. "That girl I saw you with last night was coyote ugly."

"What," I asked him, "is coyote ugly?"

"Coyote ugly is where you wake up in the morning with your arm under a girl with whom you've spent the night. You look over at her and she's so ugly that you chew your arm off rather than take the chance of waking her. *That's* coyote ugly."

Looking at Donna, asleep on my arm, I realized that the joke could be used another way: coyote beautiful. Where the girl asleep on your arm looks so beautiful, so at peace, that you would gnaw off your arm rather than disturb her sleep. I thought about it for a moment and came up with a more sensible alternative: I lay back down and did my best not to wake her.

Time passed, maybe an hour, maybe less. As my arm began to silently scream at me, each minute seemed to stretch out longer and longer. And if the dull throbbing pain in my arm weren't enough, the thought of Blacker's possible return at any moment made it impossible to really appreciate the situation.

The past hour, lying naked beside Donna, had given me time to think, however. And thinking had given me a new reason not to want to wake her. She was likely to be a little uncomfortable around me, maybe embarrassed. Hell, I was. All the reasons I had thought of before, as to why we wouldn't do what we had just done, were even better reasons for her to feel uncomfortable around me now that we had in fact done it.

So, I figured, the best thing would be for me to slip out of bed, get dressed, and leave her sleeping. Then, when D. L. Blacker returned, I could honestly tell him that Donna was sleeping. Blacker would wake her and his presence would help us to avoid any embarrassing scenes. Also, if she was angry with me—if she blamed me for what happened—Blacker's presence would keep her from yelling at me. I hoped. On the other hand, if she woke up with happy memories and warm fuzzy thoughts about me, she could decide and let me know that she wanted to be alone with me again.

That was my plan. Simple in the planning; more difficult, I feared, in the execution. In fact, getting my arm out from under her proved easier than I had thought. She was lying on her back, her head on my left arm. I gave her a gentle shove, and she rolled over on her side, away from me. As she rolled, I pulled my arm free. So far, so good.

She was to the left of me and a wall was to my right, so I inched myself down to the foot of the bed and crawled off onto the floor. As I stood up, she sighed and rolled back toward what had been my side of the bed. I froze, but she didn't wake up and so, slowly, I started picking up my clothes. Or rather, I should say, I started looking for them. The room was becoming dark and, what with one thing and another, we hadn't taken the time to neatly fold our clothes and place them at the foot of the bed. I found a shirt, but it was hers. Next I located a pair of pants, also hers. I folded them and put them on the end of the bed. When she awoke, her clothes would be waiting for her. By groping on my hands and knees, I finally located my pants, shirt, socks, and shoes. My underpants were still missing. I cursed under my breath. Things were not going smoothly. It was now almost night out, and the room was practically pitch-black. I realized that I was never going to find my shorts without help, so I opened the door to the kitchen slightly. A crack of light came through, painting a yellow-white band up the sculptured line of Donna's calf . . . and across the corner of my shorts. Donna was lying on my underpants. A small piece of material peeked from between her thighs. I began to reach for it, but discretion beat out the better part of modesty. I decided that if Donna had spent much of the day not wearing underwear, I could spend the next few hours without wearing mine. So, I slipped on what clothes I had, slid out of the room, and closed the door behind me. I stood in Blacker's kitchen and smiled. Pamela Lockheed, when she read my palm, had told me I would end up in bed, making love with a beautiful woman. She had been right. Maybe she really was psychic.

I decided to take a tour of Blacker's apartment. So far I had been in the kitchen, office, guest bedroom, and living room. On several of my visits, while passing through the foyer on my way between these few rooms, I had been attracted by a hallway going back, seemingly forever. I thought I might as well take advantage of the opportunity and see what lurked at the end of it.

I found a light switch and turned it on. The hall, when filled with light, didn't seem quite so long or half as enticing. I suppose I should have taken that as a sign to abandon my quest, but I never was too good with signs. I walked down the hall. On the left, behind etched-glass French doors, was a formal dining room. A cherry-wood table, polished to a mirrorlike sheen, dominated the room. It was surrounded by eight matching, delicately carved chairs.

A few steps farther down the hall, on the right, a door was ajar. I pushed it open and stepped into what was probably intended by the builders to be a den or small bedroom. D. L. Blacker had turned it into his playroom. As my eyes grew accustomed to the murky light of the room, I felt myself grinning in wonder. The room was packed with what could only be described as adult toys: a collection of magic illusions including an ornately painted mismade lady and a full-size guillotine; two arcade pinball machines; and, filling up one entire wall, shelves crowded with books on magic, circus, vaudeville, burlesque, and the like, and boxes of carefully labeled magic props and paraphernalia. I felt like a kid in a candy store.

I went to the shelves and took down a book I recognized: *Clowns* by John H. Towsen. I had read the book during my studies at clown college. I opened it and found that this copy was personally inscribed by the author: "To D. L., many thanks for all your help. Next time I need legal work, you must wear the red nose to court! John Towsen." I closed the book and put it back. The room deserved more time, but I wanted to see the rest of the apartment.

I slipped out of the room, set the door back to the angle it had been at when I arrived, walked a few more steps down the hallway, and opened a door on the right. It was a closet. I closed the door. Five more steps brought me to the open door of a bathroom on the left. As I looked into the bathroom a quiet sound, somewhere behind me, made me jump. I looked around quickly, saw nothing, and managed a nervous laugh at my own skittishness. My recent experiences in bathrooms had made me edgy. The noise, I figured, must be Donna getting up, or perhaps D. L. Blacker returning. I didn't want either of them to know that I had been snooping, so I turned to head back toward the living room. I took one step before I heard it again. This time, the sound sent a surge of adrenaline pumping through my body. It sounded like someone scratching and bumping against a wall, as though trying to get out. The plot to Edgar Allen Poe's *Cask of Amontillado* flashed through my brain as I pictured someone hideously sealed behind a wall in Blacker's grand old apartment building. I stopped moving, stopped breathing; I just stood there, straining to hear the sound again. And then, I did. It was coming from behind a closed door, at the end of the hall.

"Hello?" I whispered in a throaty croak that sounded like a roar to me, but which couldn't have carried to the door, let alone through it to who or whatever was making the noise on the other side. "Are you all right?"

I got no answer, but the scratching stopped. I took a few more steps toward the door, leaned my head to within a few inches of its surface, and tried again. "Hello. Is there anyone in there?"

This time my entreaty met with success, of a sort. I heard a scrambling behind the door and then a crash of breaking glass. Had the burglar, with whom I came in such painful contact at Donna's, decided to come snooping around the apartment of D. L. Blacker? I threw open the door and lunged inside, ready to attack whomever I found.

A large, long-haired, black cat came flying at me. Before I could react, it darted between my legs and raced off, down the hall toward the living room and Blacker's office.

I straightened up and looked around. I was in Blacker's bedroom. A lamp, its ceramic base shattered beyond repair, lay on the floor beside the bed. Other than that, the room was perfect. The furniture was all antique, mahogany and walnut. A large armoire with ornate carvings was against one wall, a king-size bed with matching headboard against another. By one side of the bed stood a small open writing desk. Blacker must have used the desk for a night table, as a clock radio and book sat upon it. Until a few moments ago it had also held a lamp. The cat's influence showed in more than just the shattered lamp. A large oriental carpet in subtle reds, golds, and browns covered the floor. One area of the otherwise perfect rug was stringy and worn, showing the effect of repeated sessions with cat claws. In a small bathroom at the far end of the room I found a litter box and two bowls, one filled with water, the other with dry cat food. Printed on both, in large capital letters, was the name SPIKE. As I headed back toward the broken lamp I had to smile; Spike seemed an odd name for a cat owned by D. L. Blacker.

I started picking up pieces of the lamp when I realized that I had a problem. If I cleaned up after the cat, Blacker would know that I had been in his bedroom. I was reasonably sure his request that I look after Donna hadn't included an offer to nose around his personal space. Even if he wouldn't mind, I knew I didn't want him to think me a snoop, so I carefully replaced all the pieces of the lamp, left the room, and closed the door, secure in the feeling that I had covered my tracks and my secret was safe. This confidence lasted until I turned around to head back down the hall and saw Blacker's cat, Spike. He was staring up at me from the middle of the hall where he had settled down to groom himself. Or rather to groom *her*self. The act of grooming revealed a part of the cat's anatomy that made determination of her sex self-evident. I started to laugh. I had smiled when I saw that Blacker named his cat Spike. I couldn't help but laugh when I saw that the cat to whom Blacker had given that tough name was a girl. My laughter must have spooked the cat, because she whirled around and, claws and padded feet slipping on the polished wooden floor, scampered away. Her speed, once she got moving, seemed absolutely amazing in light of her bulk. Staring at her retreating backside, I realized that she wasn't a large cat so much as a fat cat. As I watched, she went sliding around a corner. For a brief moment it seemed as though her belly wasn't going to make the turn with her. She had managed to start that impressive bulk moving forward, but inertia didn't seem to want to let her change its direction.

I raced after the cat. I had to catch her and get her back in Blacker's bedroom before he returned. Spike had turned into the living room, but when I stood in the archway to that impressive room, she was nowhere to be seen. I got down on my hands and knees and began looking under the furniture, making appropriate cat sounds.

"Here, Spike. Here, girl. Boodgie, boodgie, boo," I crooned as I crawled along, my nose inches from the floor. I mentally applauded my ability to draw on all the words in the English language and come up with such an original phrase. If I were a cat I knew I would respond to such an interesting monologue. Apparently Spike agreed; her nose peeked from behind a large potted plant. I slowly crawled over to her.

"Good Spike," I told her as I slid forward on all fours. "That's a boo boo boodgy boo boo." She must have liked those B words because she started moving toward me too.

I thought I had her. Clearly, I had captured her interest. She was staring at me, sniffing at me, almost within reach. But then the sound of a key in the front door caused her ears to twitch and she looked away. When we heard the door open, Spike ran for the safety of the hall, and I knew I had lost. All I could do was get to my feet and go to greet the return of D. L. Blacker.

Blacker wasn't alone. With him was Assistant District Attorney James Wyman. The two of them looked like an ad for Harvard Business School. They were both dressed in the kind of suits that you don't get off the rack, with power ties carefully knotted on handmade shirts. I figured they were wearing more money than I made in a good month. The quality of their clothes made me feel distressingly under-dressed for whatever activities Blacker had in store. Hell, I wasn't even wearing briefs under my jeans.

Blacker hung up their coats and was closing the closet door when he noticed me.

"Evening, Pat," he said. "Everything okay?"

I nodded.

"You remember Jim Wyman, don't you?"

I said I did and shook the assistant D.A.'s hand. We all moved into Blacker's office. Out of the corner of my eye I saw a streak of black fur disappear into the kitchen. Blacker, talking to Wyman, had his back to the door. This pleased me as I still harbored some impossible dream that I could get the cat back to the bedroom without Blacker being any the wiser. So long as Blacker didn't see Spike, there was still a chance.

I comforted myself with this thought until Donna walked in the room and I watched my chance fly out the window. She was carrying Spike in her arms, cradled across her chest. The cat's front paws were draped over her shoulder and its head was rubbing against her left ear. Donna used her free hand to scratch it between its ears, and it responded with a rhythmic purring that was almost loud enough to rattle the windows.

"D. L.," said Donna, over the cacophony being generated by the mass of whiskers, fat, and fur she cradled in her arms, "look what I found in the kitchen. I didn't know you had a cat."

Blacker eyed the cat in a way that he might, on another day, in another place, look at something disagreeable he found stuck to the bottom of his shoe, and said, "Donna, meet Spike; Spike, Donna."

Donna said, "Hi, Spike," and gave the cat a little kiss. Spike answered by purring even louder.

"I don't know," said Blacker, "how she got out. I usually keep her closed up in the back, in my bedroom."

"She?" asked Donna, thankfully changing the subject and saving me from having to fall on my knees and beg Blacker's forgiveness for violating his trust and prying into his personal bedchamber. "Spike is a she? Why would you name a female cat Spike?"

Donna seemed genuinely surprised. I have to admit, since discovering Spike's true sex, I was a little curious myself. The cat seemed unconcerned. Apparently Spike was secure in her sexuality, she already knew the answer, or else she just didn't care.

"The cat," Blacker said, "is one of the dangling threads still left from my marriage." He turned to me. "You haven't known me that long, Pat, but several years ago I was married for a short period of time. Anyway"—he turned back to Donna and the cat—"when she first brought the cat home, I looked at this very pretty, effeminate feline and decided that it would have to have a real butch name to keep it from developing a complex."

I couldn't tell if Blacker was kidding, but I did notice that Jim Wyman was fighting to hold back a grin.

"When the marriage broke up we fought over custody of the cat, and she won."

"*She* won?" I asked. "But *you* have the cat."

"That's right," said Blacker, with the trace of a sigh. "I still have the cat."

As if to emphasize his last statement, Blacker took a step toward Donna and reached out as if to pet Spike. The cat, sensing his approach, turned its head toward him and let out a very unladylike yowl. Then she leapt from Donna's shoulder and raced from the room. I felt a little better. Apparently I wasn't the only one Spike didn't like. Maybe, like so many women I'd met since moving to New York, she just didn't like men.

"Spike seems to really like you," Blacker said to Donna. "How would you like a cat?"

"Thanks, D. L., but, I don't think I'm ready to commit to another living creature just now." She was looking at D. L. Blacker, but I knew she was talking to me. I felt my heart turn into a lump of wet cardboard and pass up into my throat, where it was wrung out and hung up to dry. Donna turned her crystal-clear blue eyes toward me to see if the message had sunk in. It had. I'm sure my washed-out green eyes told her so.

My slide into a first-class depression was interrupted by a jarring ring from one of the phones on Blacker's desk. He sat down and picked up the receiver. After listening for a few seconds, he said, "Thank you, Roberto, send her back," and hung up the phone. Then he swiveled in his chair, looked up at me, and asked, "Pat, could you get the door?"

"Sure," I said, glad for an excuse to get away from Donna for a little while. As I left the office and started down the hall I found myself thinking that if I never saw another woman again for the rest of my life it would be just fine.

It wasn't fated to be quite that long a wait. The bell rang just as I reached the door. I opened it and found myself staring at the almost-perfect smile of Pamela Lockheed.

It's a good thing I got a chance to see the smile as I opened the door. It didn't last long.

"What are you doing here?" she hissed.

Now there was a loaded question. Should I tell her I had come over that morning to confer with Blacker on the multiple murders, been asked to stay and protect Donna's life because Blacker feared the murderer may have targeted her as his next victim, spent the afternoon in bed with Donna, making love like two crazed weasels, then snooped all over Blacker's apartment, ultimately scaring his cat, causing it to break a lamp in the bedroom and scamper uncontrollably throughout the apartment?

I chose an easier response. "What," I asked her, "are *you* doing here?"

"D. L. invited me over for dinner," she said. "I thought . . . that is . . ." She looked down and I looked with her. Her coat was open and underneath she was wearing an evening dress that covered a bare minimum, leaving just enough to the imagination or, in my case, to recent memory. The part of my mind that wasn't reliving the time I had passed with Pamela during our fifteen minutes of foreplay on her couch was remembering something she had said about Blacker. How she would welcome the chance to brew his morning coffee. It looked like she had brought along everything she'd need to do just that, except the beans.

She caught me staring and pulled her coat closed.

I didn't know quite what to say, so I didn't say anything. I just opened the door the rest of the way, stepped aside, and let her walk in past me. Then I closed the door, took a deep breath, and followed.

Pamela reached the office several steps ahead of me. By the time I got there Blacker was helping her off with her coat, and Donna was saying something complimentary about her dress. It was a great dress.

I had to hand it to Pamela, she was showing a lot of class. The scene in Blacker's office clearly was not what she expected, but she settled into one of the client chairs, took a cigarette out of her bag, and waited while Wyman located a book of matches to light it for her. Then she sat back and blew a slow stream of smoke toward the ceiling.

"D. L.," she asked, in an icy-cold, carefully controlled voice, "what is going on here? I was under the impression this was going to be a more intimate party."

"Sorry, Pam," Blacker started, but didn't get a chance to finish. The intercom phone on his desk rang again and

Blacker used the interruption to turn his attention from the beautiful fortune teller.

As Blacker told the doorman to send back the new visitor, I amused myself by thinking that if Pamela was really such a great psychic, she shouldn't have been surprised to see us all there.

"Pat," Blacker asked, "could you get the door again?"

"Sure," I said, glad for any excuse to escape the chill that was sweeping through the room, emanating in frigid waves from Pamela's deep green eyes.

I walked quickly down the hall to the front door. On the way I saw a flash of black fur that was Spike, disappearing into the kitchen.

There was a syncopated knock on the door just before I got to it. this time I decided I didn't want any surprises, so I looked through the little peephole, conveniently located at eye level in the middle of the door. I understand that they put fish-eye lenses in those security peepholes so you'll be able to see more of what's in front of your doors. Sometimes, however, there are people in front of the door who don't benefit by being seen more of. I found myself staring at two people for whom seeing less would have been much better: Andy Costello and his girlfriend, Debby Brill. Those two didn't look so good normally. Distorted by the fish-eye lens they looked positively grotesque. I let them in anyway.

I remembered Andy had an appointment to talk with Blacker about his contract, so I wasn't surprised. He was. The smile he had carefully arranged on his face before the door opened melted off, leaving a questioning scowl.

"Pat, what are you doing here?"

Pamela had just asked me the same question. Either these people were going to have to get new writers, or else I was going to start feeling like I didn't belong.

Debby saved me from having to come up with a witty response by saying, "Don't you remember, Andy? Donna asked him to keep her and me company while you're doing your business with D. L. tonight."

Andy nodded, and said he remembered.

With all of that finally cleared up I beckoned them in and said, "Welcome to the party."

Debby let out with a little squeal of excitement, danced past me into the apartment's foyer, and said, "Party? I didn't know there was going to be a party. Is it an engagement party for us? I'm so glad we dressed up."

She was wearing a ruffled white blouse and—thank God, I didn't have to look at her legs—a long skirt. Andy wore black slacks, a sport coat, and a shirt that was unbuttoned to show off two gold chains and a not-very-impressive chest. I wondered what their plans were for the rest of the evening.

"I just love parties," Debby prattled on. "Where's Donna, where's the bar?"

All Andy asked as he walked by me was "Where's Blacker?"

I told both of them "in the office," and then closed the door and stood there for a while, watching their backs as they walked down the hall and turned into Blacker's room.

Spike had apparently been waiting for them to leave. She stuck her head out of the kitchen, looked at me, and when she didn't say anything, I asked her, "What's Blacker up to?" She didn't respond, except to curl up in the doorway, flick her tail a few times, and continue to watch me with a suspicious eye. Since she apparently wasn't going to help, I figured there was only one person left who could answer my question.

I started for the office when a fresh rapping on the front door caused Spike to scramble back into the kitchen and me to turn back to the door. A quick look through the peephole showed me something I'd hoped never to see again—the dour countenance of Lieutenant Jesse Longreen.

Showing that his patience hadn't improved any more

than his face, Longreen waited all of five seconds before he raised his fist once more to hammer on the door. In order to save his knuckles I waited until just before he would have connected with the door, then I pulled it open. It gave me the effect I had hoped for. The lieutenant, caught off balance, fell through the doorway. It did nothing to improve *his* temperament, but it cheered *me* up. I noticed that Sergeant Koslow, who followed him into the apartment, seemed to enjoy it too.

"Arnold," Longreen said as he regained his balance. "I figured you'd be here."

Now there was a switch, so far everyone else had questioned my presence.

"Is this a social call, Lieutenant?"

He wasn't amused. "Come on," he said, and pulled me toward the office.

Over my shoulder, as I was dragged down the hall, I asked Koslow, "Could you close the door? We don't want just anyone wandering in."

Koslow smiled, pushed the door shut, and followed us to Blacker's office.

When we got to the office everyone seemed to be talking at once. Debby and Donna were sitting in the two client's chairs, chatting away and looking like a before and after picture for beauty makeovers by Elizabeth Arden. Pamela Lockheed and Assistant D.A. Wyman were leaning against Blacker's desk smoking cigarettes. Pamela was going on about something, waving her cigarette in the air to illustrate whatever point she was trying to make, and Wyman was looking like he had nothing else in the world he would rather be doing than watch and listen to her. At the same time, Andy and D. L. Blacker were standing behind the desk conferring about some papers Blacker was holding.

The cacophony of sounds and sights caught Longreen by surprise. He loosened his grip on my arm, and I was able to slide away and get over to Blacker.

When the lawyer shifted his bespectacled eyes from Andy to me, I said, "More company, D. L.," and gestured toward Longreen and Koslow.

D. L. Blacker looked at the policemen, checked his watch, and said, "Right on time. Glad you could make it, Lieutenant. We're almost ready to begin."

This raised a new outburst of protest from around the room. Longreen howled because he wanted to begin immediately, and because he didn't know what was going on anyway. Andy complained that Blacker wasn't giving his full attention to the radio station contract. Pamela complained that Blacker wasn't giving his full attention to her.

Blacker ignored all the protests. Over the din he asked me, "Pat, could you get a couple of extra chairs from the dining room? It's right down the hall, on your left."

I stopped myself from saying that I knew the dining room. Instead, I just said, "Sure," and headed out of the room.

Longreen stopped me as I passed, grabbing the same spot on my arm he had been squeezing moments before.

"Where do you think you're going?" he snarled.

"To get chairs."

"Koslow," Longreen said, without taking his eyes from mine. "Go with him."

"Thanks," I said, intentionally misinterpreting his motives. "I could use the help."

Sergeant Koslow followed me out of the office and down the hall to the dining room. We each grabbed two chairs and carried them back to the office. Luckily, the room was big enough to accommodate the extra furniture. Koslow and I put them down and the sergeant asked Blacker where he wanted the chairs placed.

Blacker didn't respond, but rather counted people and

chairs and then said, "Pat, if you'd get one more, I think we'll have enough seats for everyone."

"Never mind," Lieutenant Longreen snarled, "the sergeant will stand. Get on with it."

We arranged the chairs close together, in a semicircle behind the client's chairs. With all the extra chairs the office was crowded, but not uncomfortable.

Everyone but Koslow found someplace to sit. Donna and Debby were still in the client's chairs, Donna on the left, Debby on the right. Blacker settled into the mammoth chair behind his desk. In the dining room chairs, facing Blacker from left to right sat Wyman, Longreen, Pamela, and Andy. I sidled over to the chair by the computer and eased myself into place. Sergeant Koslow followed me toward the far corner of the office and then stuck his hands into his pockets and leaned against the oak bookcase on the right wall between the file cabinets and the computer. From there he could see the faces of everyone in the room. I felt like the stage was set; now it was up to Blacker to raise the curtain.

Chapter
N I N E T E E N

"*P*at, Sergeant, Andy, Debby, Pamela, Lieutenant, Donna, Jim," Blacker said as he slowly moved his head from left to right, looked at each of us, and then moved his gaze on to the next. "Thank you all for coming. I apologize for the subterfuge in getting some of you here tonight, but I felt the end would justify the means. And I do mean the end. Tonight, I think, we will be able to resolve this whole unfortunate affair."

"Look, Blacker," Longreen interrupted, "enough is enough. I don't know *how* you got the rest of these people here, and to be honest with you, I don't care why. All I care about is that *I* came because Wyman told me you had something for me on the Johnson murders. So give it to me and I can go. It's been a long day and my wife's holding dinner."

"Speaking," Pamela crooned, "of dinner, D. L. Was your dinner invitation, how did you just put it . . . a subterfuge? I'm getting awfully hungry."

I looked at her, smiled, and thought, I'll bet. I noticed Wyman was watching her and smiling too.

D. L. Blacker gave Pamela an apologetic look, and then turned back to Longreen. "Like you, Lieutenant, I figured the murders of Gary and Bob Johnson were related. I also thought the person Pat and Donna surprised in her apartment the other night was connected to the murders. Now there were plenty of things that could tie the two murders together: Bob and Gary were brothers, they ran a business together, there were any number of possible connections between the two of them. But what, I kept asking myself, was the connection with the burglar in Donna's apartment? What was he looking for?"

"*He?*" Debby asked. "You said 'he.' Does that mean you think the killer was a man?"

"Good question," Blacker said to her. "For now, let's just say I'm using the male pronoun as a convenience."

"Look, Blacker," Longreen cut in, "I don't want to hear your whole summation to the jury, just cut to the chase. What have you got for me?"

"I appreciate your mixed metaphors and your patience, Lieutenant, but I must ask you to wait just a little longer."

Longreen began to growl his opinion of Blacker's request. But before the growl could turn into understandable words, Blacker continued.

"That the burglar turned the apartment upside down told me he *was* looking for something. That he grabbed Donna's purse on the way out suggested to me that whatever he was looking for could have fit in the purse, and that he hadn't already found it *in* the apartment."

"What," asked Donna, in a breathy whisper, "was he looking for?"

"I had an idea about that early on. When Gary was killed I took a quick look through his briefcase."

"You what?" Longreen exploded. "You tampered with evidence at the scene of a crime? I'll nail you for that,

Blacker. I don't care who you know." He glared at Blacker, who ignored his invectives, and then at Assistant D. A. Wyman, who squeamishly looked away.

Blacker continued as though there had been no interruption. "When I looked in the briefcase, I could tell that someone else had already gone through it. As Donna can tell you, Gary was a very methodical, organized man. He kept everything in its place."

Donna, transfixed by what Blacker was saying, nodded her agreement.

"The papers in that briefcase were in total disarray. At the time I couldn't tell if anything was missing. Later, when the burglar broke into Donna's apartment, I figured that he hadn't found what he was looking for in Gary's briefcase and so had gone looking for it at Gary's apartment. This still seemed right when I got the phone messages from Bob, saying he had found something which made it clear to him who had killed his brother. I figured he must have turned up the elusive object the killer was searching for."

Longreen jerked forward in his chair. "What phone messages? Why didn't you tell me about this before?"

Before Blacker could respond, the intercom phone on his desk buzzed, signaling yet another visitor's arrival.

Blacker picked up the phone, listened, said, "Thanks, Roberto, send him back," and carefully placed it back on the cradle. Then he turned to me. "Pat, could you . . ."

I was up and said, "Sure," before he finished his sentence. Unfortunately, Longreen had stood up too.

"Sit down, Arnold," the lieutenant barked. "Koslow, get the door."

I looked to Blacker. I noticed that Koslow did too. But Blacker just shrugged. So I sat and Sergeant Koslow went to answer the door.

"Lieutenant," Blacker said with a self-satisfied smile, after Koslow left the room. "I think, in a moment, I'll be able to answer your questions, *all* your questions. So please, sit, relax."

Lieutenant Longreen sat, but he didn't relax. Looking at him, sitting on the front edge of his chair, wedged between Pamela Lockheed and Assistant District Attorney Jim Wyman, I suspected that it had been so long since Jesse Longreen last relaxed, he had probably forgotten how.

Although everyone was full of questions, no one spoke. We all just sat still and waited for Sergeant Koslow to return with Blacker's late and, I hoped, last guest.

To break the tension in the room I stood up, reached over to the bookshelf, and took the silver ball with which I had played a few days before. I looked to Blacker who, with a slight nod of his head, told me that whatever I wanted to do was alright with him.

Facing toward the lawyer, I tossed the ball up in the air a few times, knowing it would get everyone's attention. Then I let it fall, caught it on my foot, and tossed it from there all the way up to my head, where I balanced it on my forehead, between my eyes. I held that position for a few seconds, but with the ball between my eyes all I could see was the ceiling, and I couldn't help wondering if my impromptu performance was being appreciated by the people in the room. Keeping the ball centered on my head, I turned slowly until I was facing Donna directly. Then I jerked my head to the left, allowing the ball to roll onto my right ear. Now I could see the people in the room. They were all watching me. All of them, that is, except Donna. She was looking at her hands, clasped in her lap. I wondered what she was feeling: Was it regret over what we had done just a few hours before, or perhaps embarrassment at what I was doing then? A sudden thought caused a surge of adrenaline to pump into my system, and I almost dropped the ball from its precarious perch on my ear. Blacker said he knew who had killed the Johnson brothers. Clearly he had brought all those people together to expose the murderer. What if the emotion Donna was feeling was guilt or fear of discovery? Could Donna have been involved in her husband's and Bob's murders? Did she kill them herself, or perhaps have someone do it for her? Blacker had asked me to protect Donna, but what if what he really wanted was for me to protect others *from* Donna?

When Debby asked, Blacker had refused to rule out a woman as the killer. Was that because the killer *was* a woman? A woman with whom I had spent the afternoon?

As these thoughts flung themselves around in my brain, I became painfully aware of my audience watching, waiting for me to continue my impromptu performance. Like a goldfish swimming in a tiny bowl, I realized that there was nowhere I could hide from view. Luckily, I was just the opening act. In a moment Sergeant Koslow would return with the late guest. Then everyone would once again direct their attention back to the night's star, D. L. Blacker.

As I stood there, staring back at the crowd, the silver ball balanced on my right ear, the means to my end of removing myself from the spotlight appeared at the entrance to the office. Sergeant Koslow had returned from answering the door.

There are moments in time that become frozen in memory. Kodak would like you to believe that those special occasions require a camera. Not true. All they require is some visual image that comes as such a surprise that you will never be able to forget it. A camera could never hope to capture all the thoughts and feelings that accompany those truly special once-in-a-lifetime moments. The moment that Sergeant Koslow reentered Blacker's office was one of those moments for me. It may, in fact, be the page-one picture in my personal image photo album of the mind. In front of me, staring at me, sat a group of people with whom my life had, in just a few calamitous days, become inextricably entangled. We all hoped for something. The police and the assistant D.A. wanted information. All the rest of us wished for an escape from the nightmare that these murders had brought crashing down into our lives. And one person desired an escape of a different kind. One person in that room hoped his crimes weren't going to be tracked back to him . . . or to *her*, I reluctantly found myself thinking as I looked once more at Donna. All the people in that office hoped Blacker would satisfy their personal desires. He had given them reason to hope that he would do just that, as soon as Koslow returned from answering the front door. I had temporarily distracted them. Their attention was on me, not the door to the office, so they didn't see what I saw. Even if they had, it probably wouldn't have been as momentous a moment for any of them as it was for me. Perhaps it was the burst of adrenaline, pumping through me as it always does when I'm performing, that helped to focus that moment for me. Whatever the cause, I will always remember the vision of Sergeant Koslow standing in the doorway to the room, behind all those people. Koslow walking into the office not with another visitor, but rather with a large box marked *Sony*. At that moment I knew what Blacker knew. I knew who had killed Gary and Bob Johnson, I knew how, and I knew why.

The ball slipped from my ear and crashed to the floor.

Longreen was the first to realize that I was staring at something. He jerked his head around to see what it was and then grunted at the sergeant to enter. As the others turned to watch, Koslow wove his way through the chairs and brought the box to Blacker's desk.

The lawyer took the carton, set it down, opened it, and pulled out a very expensive portable stereo. It looked kind of like the things kids balance on their shoulders, walking down the street; that is, kids who have a lot of money. The boom box was clearly something special. Living in New York I'd seen hundreds of those things, but I'd never seen one quite like the unit Blacker was then holding.

"Can we get on with this now?" Longreen asked with mock civility. "Or, now that you have your boom box, are you going to bring in a couple of street kids to break dance for us? By the way, Arnold, you dropped your ball."

I picked up the silver sphere, put it back on the shelf, and sat when Blacker inclined his head toward my chair. The lawyer then acknowledged Longreen's attempt at humor with a smile and pulled a cassette tape from the center drawer of his desk.

"I think we can continue. As I was saying, I got two phone messages from Bob Johnson. They were left on my answering machine. I didn't hear them until several hours after he was dead. This is the tape from my machine." Blacker popped the cassette into one of the orifices on the portable stereo and pushed the play button.

Once again, the recorded sound of Bob Johnson's voice filled the room; this time with greater volume and fidelity, but the words were the same. "D. L., this is Bob, Bob Johnson. If you're there, could you pick up the phone? Shit. Okay, listen, I've been going over a bunch of Gary's stuff that I picked up yesterday, and I think I know who killed him. The asshole's coming over here, any minute now. I had hoped you could come too, but since you're not home, maybe I'll call Pat Arnold. I don't think I have anything to worry about, but it'd be nice to have a backup. Just to be safe I'm going to try to make a copy of this thing and mail it to you. I guess I could leave it on your answering machine—I know that when you heard it you'd agree with me—but I don't know if there's time to do that *and* make a copy before my guest arrives. Give me a call when you get home, okay? Thanks." Blacker turned off the tape player and looked at the group. So did I. They were all looking at me.

Knowing who the murderer was, I had been more interested in watching that person's reaction to the tape than in listening to it again. As a result I didn't know why they were all staring at me.

Longreen wasn't going to make it any easier for me. "Well?" he asked.

"Well, what?" I had no idea what he was talking about.

"Did he call you?"

"Lieutenant," Blacker jumped in, "you're focusing on the wrong part of that message. If Pat had heard from Bob, he certainly would have told the police before now."

"Yeah, sure," the lieutenant snapped. "Like you told us about this tape. But anyway, Blacker, you said *two* messages. Where's the second?"

Blacker pushed the play button again, and Bob's voice returned. "D. L., Bob again. I copied it. Arnold wasn't home, and it occurred to me that I should tell you who it was that killed Gary. You know, just in case." Everyone in the room stared, as if hypnotized, at the machine on Blacker's desk as Bob's nervous laugh and then his doorbell sounded. "Shit, hang on a second. This could be it. You'll have the whole thing on tape." Blacker put his finger on the stop button, but didn't push it until the machine beeped twice, signaling the end of the message. Then he spoke.

"That would have been the murderer at the door, but the answering machine clicked off."

Longreen let out a series of snorts. It was, I had come to realize, what he produced on those rare occasions when something amused him. When he finished, he looked at Blacker and said, "Joke was on Bob Johnson. He probably figured your machine was recording the whole thing. Probably even shouted out the bastard's name two or three times to make sure it was clear on your tape. Poor son of a bitch must have died thinking he had given you the name of his own killer. Ah well, life sucks." He took a deep breath and let it out. "Okay, Blacker, you say I'm focusing on the wrong thing. We police are kind of dense, not like you lawyers; tell me what I *should* be focusing on."

Blacker smiled at the policeman. "I told you before, Lieutenant, the focus of this whole case must be the *thing* that Bob found, that he copied."

"Yeah," Longreen said, but he didn't sound like he was convinced. "What about it?"

"Bob said that it tipped him off as to who killed his brother."

Longreen may not have been keeping up with Blacker, but Wyman was. The assistant D.A. leaned forward in his chair, a look of concentration on his face, and said in a carefully controlled voice, "He also said that he was going to try to copy it and mail it to you before his guest arrived. Then he said that he *had* copied it. That's what this get-together is all about, isn't it, D. L.? It came in today's mail."

Blacker shook his head and said, "No."

Before either of the lawyers could continue, Lieutenant Longreen was on his feet again, leaning over the lawyer's desk and reaching for the portable stereo. "Enough's enough," he said as he popped the phone-machine tape from the player and slid it into his pocket. "If you don't have this mysterious *thing*, I'm taking the tape and getting out of here. It doesn't take a law degree to see what happened. The killer, whoever he is, after he hacked up Bob Johnson, took whatever the *thing* is and if Johnson *did* have time to make a copy, he took the copy too. By now they're probably so much shredded or burned-up paper. Come on, Koslow." The two policemen headed out of the office.

"Lieutenant," Blacker said, his low voice stopping Longreen at the door. "You seem to have twice misunderstood me. First, I never said that this mysterious thing that Bob

214

found was a paper, and second, I didn't say that I don't have it, only that it didn't come in the mail. If you'll stay a few moments longer, I believe you'll be able to leave with a murderer."

For once, Longreen didn't have a reply, not even a growl. He just looked at Blacker with a mixture of curiosity and distrust, and returned to his seat. Sergeant Koslow followed his superior's lead and went back to his spot, leaning against the bookcase, beside me.

"Thank you, Lieutenant," Blacker said. "I think the best way to go about this would be if you'd just let me say what I have to say, and then if you have any questions, ask them when I'm through. Okay?"

The lawyer didn't wait for a reply.

"I approached this whole thing from a different direction than you did, Lieutenant. From the start, you seemed to favor both Pat here and Bob Johnson as prime suspects in Gary's murder. There was certainly reason to suspect both of them, but they were both my clients, and they had both paid me retainers to prove them innocent. I quickly recognized that the only way to do that was to find some other person who was guilty.

"You had your suspects, but I was still looking for mine. Even before I got Bob's message, I believed that there was something, some object, that was the focus of this whole terrible mess. After all, someone had broken into Donna's apartment and torn the place apart, looking for something. And as you know, the burglar grabbed her purse on the way out, so I figured it had to be something that could have fit in that purse.

"Like you, when I heard Bob's message on my answering machine, I assumed that the key to this whole thing was a paper of some kind, a contract or letter perhaps. After all, the papers in Gary's briefcase had been gone through, and Bob said he wanted to mail me a *copy*. This held me up for a while until I tried another track. What if, I asked myself, the elusive thing that Bob found wasn't the same *thing* the killer had been looking for in Gary's briefcase?"

"I don't understand," Donna said in a voice so quiet it was almost not spoken.

"Welcome to the club," Longreen muttered, and sat farther back in his chair.

"I'm presenting this poorly. My ego wanted to show you my whole thought process, everything I worked through to solve this. But maybe it would be better if I just tell you who the killer is, and then explain how I discovered it."

"That would be nice," Longreen said, not really believing Blacker could do it. "Why don't you tell us who the killer is?"

Blacker spoke in a slow, cool voice. "Andy Costello killed both Bob and Gary Johnson."

There was a moment of silence and then Andy shouted, "Are you nuts?"

I said, "No, he's right." But no one heard me because Gary's girlfriend, Debby, was shrieking some unintelligible string of invectives at Blacker.

When things quieted down a little, Blacker continued. "As I said, there were actually two things Andy wanted to get back. The first was tied into his motive, the second to *how* he was able to kill Gary when everyone thought he was in his disc jockey booth."

"Do we have to sit here and listen to all this?" Debby shrieked.

Andy ignored his girlfriend, focusing instead on the man he had, until moments before, thought was going to represent him in the biggest deal of his career.

"I've heard of sleazy lawyers before but, Blacker, you take the cake. I paid you five thousand dollars to be my lawyer, and then just this morning you made me sign a letter saying you could keep it even if I don't use you to negotiate my contract. And now what's this supposed to be, a way to guarantee that I *won't* use you? Go screw yourself. Tomorrow morning I'm stopping payment on the check, *and* finding another lawyer, *and* I'm going to have that other lawyer sue your ass."

"If you're not in jail tomorrow, you can certainly *try* all those things. Except for stopping payment on the check. I went to your bank today and cashed it." Blacker wasn't smiling, but I could tell that he was enjoying himself. "But I think you're going to be in jail tomorrow, and for a long time after tomorrow."

Andy seemed to regain his control. He sat back in his chair, crossed his arms, and the tension left his voice. "You talked about some *thing* that the killer was looking for. If I'm this killer, what's the thing, show it to me?"

"It's a good point, D. L.," said Assistant District Attorney Wyman. "If Costello *is* guilty, I'm going to need more than your accusation to get a conviction for murder."

"I can't believe this conversation," Pamela said, crushing an empty package of cigarettes and dropping it into a large marble ashtray that was balanced on the arm of her chair. "Anyone here got a cigarette?"

The assistant D.A. absentmindedly slipped a cigarette case from his inside jacket pocket, flicked it open, reached across Lieutenant Longreen, and offered it to her, as he listened to Blacker's assurance that he had more than just a simple accusation with which to convince a jury of Andy's guilt.

"Let's go back to the beginning," said D. L. Blacker. "The MegaBank party. Before the party Andy and Gary had an argument. We all know that. Apparently, Andy had received an offer from a radio station that would have been a great career move. But he was under contract to Gary's company, and Gary wasn't going to let him take the radio job. Gary

217

had me review the contract that night, because he wanted to make sure there weren't any loopholes. There weren't. I know, because I drafted it. Gary had the legal right to keep Andy from working for anyone else. If Andy took the job, Gary could have gotten a T.R.O. to stop him from working."

"T.R.O.?" Debby asked.

"Temporary restraining order," Wyman shot back without taking his eyes from Andy.

Andy didn't notice, he just continued to glare at Blacker. "Lots of people fought with Gary that night, why pick on me?"

"Like I said before, because of one of those *things*." Blacker turned his chair slightly so that he was facing Wyman. "You remember, Jim, I said I took a quick look through Gary's briefcase."

"Uh huh," the assistant D.A. said, not really wanting to remember that his old law school friend had admitted to tampering with evidence at the scene of a murder.

"And that I said it looked like someone else had already been through the papers in the case."

"Uh huh."

"Andy's contract wasn't in the briefcase. Gary showed it to me before the party, but after he was killed, it wasn't in his case."

"Uh, D. L.," broke in Wyman, "I hate to stop you when you're on a roll, but this is not the kind of evidence on which murder convictions can be based. Gary might have just put the contract in his pocket or something."

"You can check that. The police must still have Gary's personal effects. Right, Lieutenant?"

"Yeah." Longreen grunted. "We still got 'em. You know, Blacker, I'm surprised when you were riffling through his briefcase you didn't go through his pockets too."

Blacker let that go by. He and I both knew that he *had*

gone through Gary's pockets. Apparently that was one secret he chose not to share.

"So," Andy boomed out, "you're saying that when he told me before the party that he wouldn't let me take the radio gig, I decided to kill him to get back my contract? Aren't you forgetting that over a hundred people, including Donna, Pam, Pat, and even you, have told the police that I was in the D.J. booth when Gary was killed?"

"He's right, D. L.," Donna said softly. "He was doing that rap song. We all heard him."

D. L. Blacker leaned back in his chair and smiled. "That's right, we all heard him. And that brings us to the second *thing*. Something so small that it could fit in Donna's purse, and yet so important that Bob Johnson was killed for it. Something that allowed us all to hear Andy doing a rap song at the same time he was brutally murdering Gary Johnson."

"A cassette tape," Donna whispered.

I nodded, and Blacker said, "Yes, a cassette tape."

"This is crazy!" Andy said, tension making his voice a frantic rasp.

"It took me awhile," Blacker went on, "but I finally figured it all out. You came to that party *intending* to kill Gary. You knew you were going to be working inside a closed booth, so you recorded a rap that would sound like something you were doing live at the party. Then, when you saw through the booth's one-way glass that Gary was alone in the dressing room, you put on the rap tape, slid out of the booth, down the hall, and into the dressing room. It was gutsy. Someone could have come to the room while you were in there with Gary. Perhaps you stuck your head out the door and made sure no one was coming, right before you killed him. By the way, you couldn't have known the machete was going to be there. How did you *plan* to do it?"

"This whole thing is nuts," Andy protested. "I didn't kill anyone. You're making the whole thing up."

"Anyway," Blacker continued, "you got back to the booth without being seen, and then just played your music and waited for the body to be discovered. After a while, the police came and began questioning people. You figured you had nothing to worry about, until Pat came back after being questioned by Lieutenant Longreen."

Longreen, hearing his name, jumped into the conversation with a typically snappy question. "What do you mean?"

"When Andy asked Pat what had happened, Pat told him. . . . Just a second." Blacker pulled one of his legal pads from a drawer and flipped through it, until he found what he wanted. Then he read to Andy from the pad. "Pat told you that you'd be called into the room too, and then, and this is important, all your stuff would be searched before they let you go home."

The man was amazing. Days before, when he had pressed me to tell him everything I could remember about the night of Gary's murder, I had recounted that conversation with Andy. He had carefully written it down in one of those legal pads. Now he was demonstrating what he told me he had learned in law school: that putting down all the *information* in a pad meant that later he could find the *answer* in a pad.

"Hearing that the police might be searching through your stuff must have thrown you into a panic. If they found and played the cassette of your rap, it would raise the possibility that you hadn't been in the booth when Gary was killed, and your alibi would be shot to hell. Worse, people would wonder why you had prepared the tape. Only one conclusion could be drawn—you did it so you could kill Gary.

"You couldn't erase the tape because the professional cassette decks in your D.J. booth only play tapes, they don't record over them. So you knew you had to get rid of it, and Donna provided you with the perfect place to hide it. You saw her changing cassettes in her Walkman, and you borrowed those tapes because, as you said . . . and I quote." Blacker paused to once again check his yellow pad. " 'What this party needs is some music. Say, Donna, how about letting me put one of your jazz tapes on over the sound system?' " The lawyer looked up from the pad. "When Pat first told me you said that, I wondered why you asked to borrow a tape from Donna. After all, you had brought boxes of recorded music to the party. I finally realized you didn't borrow the tapes because you wanted to take one of *her* tapes; you borrowed them in order to *hide* one of your own. You put your rap tape into Donna's bag, along with the rest of her tapes. She carried it out of the party for you."

I looked at Donna. She was staring at Andy, a look of shocked awareness on her face, as she learned how she had been tricked into carrying the instrument of her husband's murder.

"Are you through?" Andy asked, his powerful voice filled with threats and anger.

"Almost." Blacker leaned back in his chair. "Your idea worked insofar as it got the tape out of the building, but then you were faced with another problem, getting the tape back. You knew you wouldn't really be safe until you had destroyed that tape."

"So," Donna said to Andy, her soft voice interrupting Blacker and drawing everyone's attention from the lawyer to her. "It was *you* that broke into my apartment and hit poor Pat on the head."

"I didn't," Andy protested. "I never. . . ."

"You did," I said. "It was you."

But no one heard me, because at the same time Andy's girlfriend screeched, "Isn't this libelous or something?" Even with two lawyers there, she got no answer to her question.

Blacker continued. "You *did* break into Donna's apart-

ment and search for the tape. You might remember, Lieutenant, that the burglar didn't take anything, but he did tear
the stereo apart and cassettes were thrown all over the
place."

"Yeah," Longreen said, staring at Andy Costello's profile.
But then a thought, entering the apparent virgin territory
of Longreen's mind, caused him to jerk his attention back
to the lawyer and ask, "How did *you* know that?"

"Pat told me. Anyway"—Blacker turned his gaze back
to Andy—"when you didn't find the tape among those in
Donna's apartment, you figured she was still carrying it with
her, so you waited for her return. When you heard her
talking to someone, outside the door, you rushed to hide in
the bathroom. You hadn't counted on her bringing anyone
home with her, but you had already demonstrated that you
could think fast in an emergency. I don't know if you had
a plan at that point or not, did you?"

When Andy didn't respond, the lawyer continued. "Anyway, you knew you had to get Donna's bag; so when Pat
came into the bathroom you slugged him with your flashlight
and ran from the apartment, grabbing Donna's purse on the
way out."

"Look, Blacker," Longreen rumbled, his voice sounding
like an old gramophone slowly getting up to speed, "I'm
not saying I believe all this and I'm not saying I don't, but
if all this *is* true, why would Costello here kill *Bob* Johnson
when he had already gotten the tape back? And if *he* had
the cassette, what is it Bob Johnson was going to copy and
send to you?"

Everyone looked to D. L. Blacker for the answers to these
questions. I already had figured out the answers, so I looked
at all the people looking at Blacker. Most of them watched
the lawyer with tense interest. Debby stared at him with
barely controlled rage. Andy sat all the way back in his chair
with his feet on the ground, his hands gripping the chair's

arms, and regarded the lawyer with an unreadable expression on his face.

Blacker answered Lieutenant Longreen's questions with a smile. "Andy didn't get the tape. It wasn't in Donna's bag. Earlier that day she had given it to Bob."

Longreen held up his hand to stop Blacker and turned to Donna. "Mrs. Johnson, is this true?"

Donna looked from the police lieutenant to Blacker and then back to Longreen. "Well, I gave him a tape. I don't know what was on it."

"What do you mean?" Wyman snapped out, apparently forgetting that he wasn't interrogating an unfriendly witness. Then he caught himself and said, "Sorry."

Donna said, "That's okay," and turned back to Longreen. "You see, Lieutenant, the morning after my husband died, I found a cassette in my bag with a Johnson Entertainment sticker on it. Johnson Entertainment was Gary's and Bob's company."

"I know that," Longreen said. "Go on."

"Well." Donna paused to take a deep breath and let it out. "Bob stopped over during the day and I gave him a bunch of Gary's papers and stuff relating to their business. I guess that included the tape."

Wyman jumped in again. "So, you didn't listen to the tape and you *guess* you gave it to Bob?"

"I never even thought about it until this morning when D. L. asked me if I had given a cassette to Bob that day."

Andy bolted forward in his chair. "Lieutenant, this is just too much. Can't you see this guy is trying to frame me? It's obvious he *told* Donna what to say."

Donna's protest went unheard as Andy got angrier and louder. "I suppose now he's going to say I somehow *knew* Bob got the tape, so I went over and killed him too!"

"No," Blacker replied softly, his voice a welcome contrast to Andy's belligerent shouts. "I think you called Bob and asked to meet with him to discuss your contract with Johnson Entertainment. But before you got there he listened to the cassette, figured out what had happened, and tried to call Pat and me for help. I think when you arrived at his apartment he played the tape for you, and yes, I think you killed him too."

"You think," Andy said as he settled back in his chair. "That's really all it comes down to, isn't it? What you *think*. You don't have any *proof*, do you? On that message you just played, Bob said he was going to mail you a copy. You *think* it was of a tape. Did you get it? Play it for us. Without a copy of that cassette this whole thing is just a fantasy of yours, Blacker. So go ahead, play the tape."

"Bob had a very sophisticated stereo system in his apartment," Blacker said, ignoring for the moment Andy's challenge. "It included a high-speed, dual-cassette, dubbing deck. I think he used it to make a copy of the rap tape."

"Again, you *think*! Admit it, Blacker, you don't have squat." Andy was once again leaning forward in his chair, trying to push at Blacker with the force of his voice. "Debby was right, this whole thing has been libel, or defamation or something. I'm going to sue you for everything you've got."

Blacker just kept talking. "After you killed Bob, you must have found the cassette copy and taken it, along with the original."

"You've got an answer for everything, don't you, asshole? But without any proof you're also going to have some big regrets for leaning on the wrong person. You think you're something special? You're shit! You're worse than shit."

"What you didn't realize, Andy, was that Bob made more than one copy."

A sudden silence that said more than any words could have filled the space between D. L. Blacker and Andy Costello.

Chapter

TWENTY

*A*fter waiting to be sure Andy had nothing more to say, D. L. Blacker continued. "As I said, Bob had a great stereo system, including a cassette deck that allowed him to make copies. When, thanks to Jim Wyman pulling a few strings, I was allowed back into Bob's apartment this morning, I found the deck set up to make copies, but no tapes in it. Of course there wouldn't have been, since you took the original and the one copy with you. But, perhaps because he knew you were coming over, Bob took an extra precaution when he copied that tape.

"Bob's stereo was state of the art. He had, in his system, something that just recently became available in this country, something you probably had never seen before, a D.A.T. recorder."

"D.A.T., what's that?" Wyman asked.

"Digital Audio Tape," Blacker said, without taking his eyes from Andy. "It's a new technology that allows for perfect recording, without any background hiss or loss of sound quality from the original. The decks aren't very common. Not many people have ever seen them; even fewer own one."

Longreen lost his patience. "So, Johnson made an extra copy of the rap tape on this digital thing?"

Blacker nodded, his eyes never leaving Andy. "That's right." The lawyer opened a drawer, pulled something out that looked almost like a tape cassette, only smaller, and held it up in front of him. "And here it is."

Blacker slid it into an opening in the complicated boom box that sat on his desk. He said, "I had to call in a favor to get a portable unit that could play these things on such short notice." Then he pushed a button and the sound of Andy's amplified voice spewed from the small stereo's speakers and filled the room.

"We got a great group here tonight. You MegaBank people are party animals. And the party's going to continue all night long. A beautiful lady just came up to me and asked if I could play a rap song and dedicate it to the accounting department. Well, I can do better than that. I'm going to do my *own* rap song for you."

By the time the rap actually started on the tape, all the people in Blacker's office were staring at Andy, even his girlfriend, Debby.

Andy, perhaps responding to all those eyes, slowly stood.

At the same time, Sergeant Koslow, who had been nonchalantly leaning against the bookshelf, straightened himself up.

Blacker lowered the volume, but kept it playing, the heavy beat of the music adding to the tension in the room.

Andy put his hands into the pockets of his jacket and turned slowly, looking into everyone's face. When he looked at me I gave him a little grin, to show that there were no hard feelings over his hitting me on the head, but he didn't return it. As he looked around, he began to move slowly to the side of his chair, toward the office door.

Longreen jumped up and said, "Hold it right there, Costello." But he was a little too late.

At the same moment, Andy pulled a small gun from his pocket and aimed it at a spot in the middle of the lieutenant's chest.

Pamela, who was sitting between Andy's gun and Lieutenant Longreen, gasped.

Debby shrieked, "Oh my God!"

Andy said, "Shut up," to her, and gestured with his gun toward Blacker's desk. "Lieutenant, if you'll move over there where I can see you until I leave?"

Longreen moved.

"So." Pamela gulped some air and said, "Everything D. L. said was right?"

"Shut up, just shut up," Andy shouted, moving his gun from one person to another. No one spoke and Andy just stood there, waving his gun.

I became painfully aware of the rap music, still coming from the boom box on Blacker's desk. My heart seemed to be beating in time to the tape.

Andy looked like he was having trouble deciding what to do. Finally he pointed his gun at the tape player and said, "Turn that thing off."

Blacker did.

"Give me the tape."

Blacker pulled out the tape and gave it to Longreen, who carefully handed it to Andy. The disc jockey stuffed it into his back pocket and used his gun to wave Longreen back to the desk. Then he said, "I'm leaving, and I don't want any of you to follow me, okay?"

We all agreed that that was just fine with us. But I noticed that Sergeant Koslow had shuffled a few feet forward and was now almost within reach of Andy. I found myself thinking that I was sitting in a bad spot. If Andy noticed what the sergeant was doing, and shot him, the bullet might pass through Koslow and hit me.

Andy wasn't interested in Sergeant Koslow. He raised his

gun, cocked it, and pointed it at Blacker. "I should kill you," he said, and then slowly backed out of the room.

And fell over.

In less than a heartbeat Koslow was on him, yanking the gun from his hand. Then he pushed Andy facedown on the floor, pulled his wrists behind his back, and slapped handcuffs on him.

It was over.

Maybe there is something to the ancient belief that black cats are really witches, capable of mind reading, transformations, and teleportations. Or maybe the tension of the moment just kept me from noticing. Whatever the cause, I didn't see Blacker's cat, Spike, until Andy fell over her.

Apparently Spike was sitting in the doorway when Andy tried to back out of the office.

As scientists tell us, when an unstoppable force meets an immovable object, something spectacular has to happen. Andy had made it clear when he started to leave that he wasn't stopping for anything. And when Spike, one of the largest, fattest cats I'd ever seen, plopped down in the doorway, she had become as close to an immovable object as any scientist could envision.

So, when Andy backed out of the office and into Spike, both of them went flying. It was pretty spectacular. Andy fell on the floor and was immediately set upon by Sergeant Koslow. Spike, who had looked more surprised than hurt, took off down the hall to hide.

An hour later Blacker, Lieutenant Longreen, and I sat in the living room, sipping coffee and eating day-old doughnuts. Sergeant Koslow had taken Andy downtown, to book him. Andy's girlfriend, Debby, had run off in tears. Donna had gone home, turning down my offer to go with her. And Assistant D.A. James Wyman, having invited Pamela Lockheed to dinner, had left with the beautiful psychic on his arm and a smile on his lips. Watching them leave, I wondered if Pamela would be showing her appreciation for the meal by inviting Wyman to stay for breakfast. I hoped he liked fresh orange juice.

"Well, Lieutenant," Blacker said with a slight smile, as he put his cup down on a coaster and reached for a doughnut from the box on the coffee table, "anything else I can do for you?"

"Look, Blacker," the policeman said, "you managed to figure this whole thing out and beat us to it. I can appreciate that. But what the police do isn't a game. Instead of pulling this grandstand stunt tonight, you should have come to me with what you had. In all the excitement, you may not have noticed, but Costello didn't confess to the murders. All we have now that we didn't have before is that rap tape, a lot of your guesses, and Costello's antisocial reaction to you. That may not be enough for Wyman to get a murder conviction. It's not like we can tie Costello's gun in to either of the killings. Hell, at least he *had* a gun; maybe we can get him on possession of an unlicensed handgun or something."

Mention of the gun opened a little door in my brain, and the light that poured through made me choke on a mouthful of slightly stale Bavarian cream doughnut.

"Lieutenant," I said when I had finished coughing and had burned my tongue with a gulp of too-hot coffee, and once again could speak. "If the gun might have been used for a murder, how would you find out?"

Longreen looked at me funny. "We'd have ballistics run a check. If they have a bullet that killed someone, and a gun, they can establish if the bullet came from the gun. Why?"

"On the day after Gary was killed, I called and left a message on Andy's answering machine. I meant it as a joke. I said I had a copy of his greatest hits tape, and that I carried it with me all the time. I told him to give me a call, that I wanted to discuss it with him."

"So?" Longreen asked.

"I disguised my voice. I told him I was Sergeant Sheski."

"Oh my God," Longreen rasped out.

"That night," Blacker quietly said, "Sheski was shot to death."

"I meant it as a joke," I mumbled, but Longreen didn't hear me. He was on his way out of the room. A few moments later we heard the front door slam.

D. L. Blacker and I sat there for a long time without speaking. Everything had been said. Everything had been done.

Chapter

TWENTY-ONE

A few months have passed since that night in D. L. Blacker's apartment when Spike tripped up Andy Costello.

As I sit here, remembering everything Andy did, and using Blacker's computer to put it all down in a readable form that, I hope, some publisher will want to publish and lots of people will want to read, the events of the few months since then pale in comparison.

Lieutenant Longreen checked with ballistics, and Andy's gun *did* fire the bullets that killed Sergeant Sheski. That, together with what Blacker had given them on the two Johnson murders, was enough to convince Andy's lawyer to agree to a plea bargain that should keep Andy off the streets for a long, long time.

I told Donna that I really loved her. She told me she really *liked* me, but needed some time to get her head together. As the sole remaining stockholder of Johnson Entertainment, she had become the beneficiary of both Gary's and Bob's business life insurance policies, in addition to being the beneficiary of Gary's personal policy, all to the tune of two million dollars. With that kind of money she could afford to take all the time in the world—and she did. She went on an extended around-the-world tour. Yesterday I got a postcard from Spain. It looked nice.

I did a little traveling myself. I moved out of my ratty studio apartment and into Blacker's guest room, next to the kitchen. When he offered me the room I told him I couldn't afford any more in rent than I had been paying for my one-room hovel. He told me that would be fine so long as I also helped him with projects from time to time. I agreed, moved in, and quickly learned what he meant. I've become butler, typist, secretary, and general handyman to D. L. Blacker. I've also done some digging for him on some of his cases, and last week he suggested that I consider getting a private investigator's license so I could carry a gun. Not exactly the life I envisioned when I moved to New York from Texas.

But I can't complain. The room is great, he's letting me use his computer to write this book, and there's always food in the refrigerator.

Blacker also sets me up with juggling work from time to time. A birthday party here, a corporate industrial show there, it all adds up. Of course he takes his percentage off the top, but I can't complain. He even got me the audition that led to my being in a Terry Town Restaurant commercial. Maybe you've seen it. I'm the dancing chicken juggling eggs and singing about the Terry Town biscuit breakfast. I'm still getting residuals from that spot. But I think I told you that already.